CURLY SMOKE

Also by Susan Holtzer

Something to Kill For

CURLY SMOKE

SUSAN HOLTZER

ST. MARTIN'S PRESS ✹ NEW YORK

CURLY SMOKE. Copyright © 1995 by Susan Holtzer. All rights reserved. Printed in the United States of America. No part of this book may be used or reproduced in any manner whatsoever without written permission except in the case of brief quotations embodied in critical articles or reviews. For information, address St. Martin's Press, 175 Fifth Avenue, New York, N.Y. 10010.

"Sanctuary" by Dorothy Parker, Introduction by Brendan Gill, copyright 1931, renewed © 1959 by Dorothy Parker, from THE PORTABLE DOROTHY PARKER by Dorothy Parker, introduction by Brendan Gill. Used by permission of Viking Penguin, a division of Penguin Books USA Inc.

Library of Congress Cataloging-in-Publication Data

Holtzer, Susan.
    Curly smoke: an Anneke Haagen mystery / Susan Holtzer.
        p.   cm.
    "A Thomas Dunne book."
    ISBN 0-312-13458-4
    1. Women detectives—Michigan—Fiction.   I. Title.
PS3558.O4374C87   1995   95-30625
813'.54—dc20   CIP

First edition: October 1995

10 9 8 7 6 5 4 3 2 1

To Alan, because otherwise . . . well, he knows.

Every writer has a "without whom" list—people who provide us with the information and expertise that make us look like we know what we're writing about. Mine includes, first, Mason Jones, who taught me everything Anneke and I know about computers; then, Loren Rhoads, for favors above and beyond, plus a lot of things that can't be put into words; and finally, a special thanks to Charles Walgreen IV, of Walgreen Drugs, who answered a frantic SOS from an unknown writer with extraordinary graciousness.

Sanctuary

My land is bare of chattering folk;
   The clouds are low along the ridges,
And sweet's the air with curly smoke
   From all my burning bridges.
—Dorothy Parker

CURLY SMOKE

ONE

• • • • • •

In the nightmare the smoke was even thicker, the air even more suffocating. Flames fell around her in small, bright droplets, and where they touched the ground, glittering ice flowers bloomed. The terror and the beauty of it held her transfixed, in nightmare paralysis, unable to flee the deadly radiance, unable even to scream. . . .

She came awake gasping and disoriented, struggling in panic against the grasp of twisted, sweat-sodden bedding. She leapt to her feet and grabbed the big fire extinguisher next to the bed. Fumbled for the flashlight on the night table. Lurched across the room to where coat and fleece-lined boots lay ready to hand.

"Oh shit," Anneke said aloud to the empty room.

Nightmare. She took a deep, shuddering breath and looked at the fire extinguisher—industrial-size—clutched in her shaking hands. Just a nightmare. She put the ungainly thing down, shoving it away from her in embarrassed self-contempt. Nothing like being prepared for last week's disaster.

Shivering, she groped for the borrowed bathrobe and huddled into it. She aimed the flashlight beam at the borrowed clock, hoping it was nearly morning but unsurprised to see its digital face reading 2:17 A.M. Nightmare time. Sighing, she reached for the bedside lamp, fumbling with the unaccustomed switch.

Only then did she see the lights.

They flickered almost subliminally at the window, where the heavy drapes didn't quite meet at the center. The regular, pulsing on-off rhythm of red that signaled, everywhere, the presence of emergency vehicles: the stigmata of fire engines.

Terror rose in her throat like bile. With a strangled sob she hurled herself from the bedroom, racing for the front door, coat and boots forgotten. She rammed her shin against something—coffee table?—lost her bearings in the darkness of the unfamiliar room, and wasted precious seconds before she located the pale rectangle of light that indicated the door's leaded glass panel. Through the glass the pulsating red light was just visible, off to the side of the cottage. She stumbled toward the door, toward the light.

Off to the side. She stopped with her hand on the doorknob and pressed her face against the icy glass, twisting her head to see at an angle through the frost-covered panes. There, two houses to her left—not a fire engine, but the yellow and white of an EMS ambulance.

"Oh shit," she said again. And this time she laughed aloud, shakily but with genuine humor as she cataloged her bare feet, inadequate bathrobe, and empty hands. So much for preparedness. She'd done the same damn thing tonight that she'd done four nights ago, when the fire had been real—abandoned everything and simply fled.

And because of that, she told herself firmly, I'm here and alive, my instincts validated. So what if I'm living in a rented two-room cottage and wearing borrowed clothes? *Things* could be replaced —yes, even houses.

She wasn't ready yet to think about her house, now reduced to a pile of charred rubble. Instead, she peered through the door at the dark semicircle that was Mackinac Court. Aside from her new landlords next door, she knew none of the other residents of the small enclave. She had no idea who inhabited the house before which the ambulance stood. There was a police car, too, she noted for the first time—standard procedure for a 911 emergency call. She peered more closely, wondering if the patrolman was anyone she knew.

For a while, though, the courtyard remained empty. Then a small procession moved into her field of vision. First a dark, bundled figure in the uniform cap of an Ann Arbor police patrolman, but so heavily muffled against the cold December air that even its sex was indeterminate; then two equally bundled shapes carrying a long, narrow burden between them. The policeman opened the back of the ambulance and the paramedics disappeared inside with the stretcher. As they passed briefly under the light from the streetlamp, Anneke saw that the blanket on the stretcher had been drawn all the way up, completely covering the shape underneath.

She shivered and backed away from the door. Her bare feet felt nearly numb, and she registered for the first time the icy blast pouring in from the crack under the door. She should ask her new landlord to add weatherstripping, she thought, knowing it would be weeks before she got around to anything that inconsequential.

The sight of a body being removed from a house should, she supposed, prompt profound musings on love and death and the meaning of life. But she was all mused out. With a sigh, she padded into the kitchen, extracted a bottle of brandy, and poured herself a stiff shot to take back to bed.

The bed, a standard double, seemed small and cramped after her own queen-size bed. I'm never going to be able to share a bed this size with Karl, she realized suddenly; she recalled from something she'd read once that a standard American double bed was just twice the width of a baby's crib. Laughter bubbled inside her at the mental image of Karl Genesko, former Pittsburgh Steelers linebacker and now Ann Arbor police lieutenant, squeezing his six-foot-five, 250 pounds into a crib.

She swiveled the knob of the radio, searching past music stations for news or talk shows, something to occupy her thoughts. If Karl were here, she thought, instead of jaunting in California with the Michigan football team, it wouldn't be so bad. Which is precisely why, she reminded herself acidly, you refused his offer to come back.

"You are all right?" His voice over the long-distance wire Monday evening had been concerned. "You're not hurt?"

"I'm fine," she assured him. "No bumps, no bruises. I just thought I'd better let you know what happened. I'll be staying at Joyce's for a couple of days, until I find something permanent."

"I can't get a flight out anymore today," he said, "but I'll catch the early plane tomorrow morning. With the time difference, I should be there by midafternoon."

"Don't you dare," she said at once, both touched and disturbed by his instant response. "You've been looking forward to this Rose Bowl since September. And besides, you promised to make all those recruiting appearances. And anyway," she lied, "I'd probably be too busy to see you. I'll just be running around all week."

"Are you sure?"

"Positive." She tried to pour conviction into her voice.

"All right then." He could have been more insistent, she thought unreasonably. "I'll be home Sunday as planned. In the meantime, of course, you can use my place if you like."

"Thank you, but I'm better off at Joyce's for the time being. Her clothes fit me better than yours."

"That's certainly true." He laughed sympathetically at her feeble jest, and although they spoke for a few minutes longer, he made no further offer to return.

Does he have to believe everything I say? Anneke asked herself, feeling irrationally resentful as she sipped brandy and waited for sleep. Well, yes; one of the things she loved about him, she acknowledged, was his refusal to play mind games. He would always take her at her word, even when he knew she was lying.

Besides, she really hadn't wanted him to cut short his trip to race home and hold her hand. She needed to work this out by herself, exorcise her own demons. She set down the brandy glass and arranged herself for sleep after a reassuring glance at the fire extinguisher.

TWO

• • • • • •

Mackinac Court in pale December daylight had a tentative look, as if it were not sure whether to come into full focus. The sun was a watery orange disk riding low in the southern sky, partially screened by tangles of naked tree branches, adding no perceptible warmth to the frigid air.

Anneke wheeled her chocolate brown Alfa-Romeo into the court's communal parking area and levered herself carefully out of the driver's seat, trying not to destabilize the young mountain of packages surrounding her. She'd wakened energized, finally, after four days of emotional narcolepsy, and when Hudson's opened at ten o'clock she'd gone through the store like a tornado, heedless of cost.

She hadn't even bothered to check in with her office. She knew Ken Scheede, her office manager, could cope; besides, during Christmas break Ann Arbor came to a near standstill, even those elements that had no direct University of Michigan connection. Refusing to feel guilty (which meant, she admitted to herself, that she felt exactly that), she stood next to the Alfa for a moment, puffing out patterns of frosty breath and savoring the bitterly cold air on her face.

It had been an odd winter all around—if there was such a thing as a "normal" Michigan winter. A seemingly endless succession of Alberta clippers had kept the temperature hovering near zero for weeks, yet there had been little snow. Only a light frosting of rime dusted lawns and shrubbery.

The cold, of course, had compounded the effects of the fire. Anneke tried not to think about the ruins of her house, buried under a fantastic edifice of ice where the water from the fire hoses had frozen, it seemed, almost in midair.

It didn't do to think about the house. Instead, she concentrated on Mackinac Court, taking in her new home for the first time. She'd seen the cottage, rented it, and moved in, all in one evening, paying little attention to its surroundings. But now, looking at the court with some interest, she recognized it as a true oddity.

It had been carved out of the center of a block that was now an agglomeration of commercial and University buildings, but towering oaks and looming hedgerows made the residences inside wholly invisible from Division Street. Standing in the parking area, Anneke saw a ragged semicircle of five houses and two tiny cottages, in a mismatched assortment of periods and architectural styles.

Two of the houses were massive Victorian structures, one at the edge of the entry, the other taking pride of place at the center of the semicircle. The other three full-sized houses had clearly come later—what Anneke referred to mentally as elderly McKinleys. A pair of them, on either side of the small parking area, took up the north arm of the court. The third was on the other side of the court, with two tiny cottages squeezed in beside it.

The two Victorians—mansions now, to contemporary eyes— still dominated, but they had a harassed look, like Great Danes surrounded by yapping terriers. Anneke, pleased by the image, plucked several parcels from her car at random and headed across the court toward her cottage.

As she fished for her key, she heard the clangor of Burton Tower, just a few blocks away—first the full four sections of the Westminster chimes, then twelve long, sonorous strokes, and finally the boisterous cascade of sound that signaled an infrequent carillon concert.

And then, as if on cue, the empty courtyard was abruptly populated, as the glossy red front door of the adjacent house burst open and small bodies seemed to come boiling out.

The smallest of them reached her first, tumbling down the wooden steps and skidding on the icy turf in his haste. He reached to just above Anneke's waist, and she guessed his age somewhat doubtfully at five or six. Close behind him was another boy, two or three years older, and finally, bringing up the rear with a certain self-consciousness, a pair of girls at the edge of their teen years.

"You're the new lady, aren't you? We wanted to come say hello, but Mommy said not to bother you till you came outside, so we've been waiting to see you—and now you're here, so we can come say hello." He paused for a prodigiously deep breath. "Do you like your cottage? Are you going to stay for a long time? Did your house really burn down?"

"Cashin!" One of the girls nudged the child sharply, and he subsided, looking sheepish. "I'm sorry, Miss Haagen," she said. "He gets carried away sometimes."

"That's all right." Anneke smiled at the girl. "He was just being enthusiastic."

"We did want to welcome you to Mackinac Court." The other girl, serene in a pink down-filled parka and fur-trimmed boots, moved forward gracefully, as if to distance herself from the younger children. "I'm Victoria Roper, and this is Marcella Smith, and that's Cashin Smith, and that's Ross Barlow." She indicated each child with a small, leather-gloved hand.

"All right, you lot, leave Miss Haagen alone. She's got enough problems without havin' a batch of kids around." Barbara Smith, Anneke's new landlord, descended the porch steps behind the children and made shooing motions with her hands. She was tall and angular-looking in an olive green parka and brown pants tucked into short, no-nonsense winter boots. "Are you moved in okay?" she asked Anneke. "It's a pretty good place for an Ann

Arbor rental, if I do say so myself, but of course it's hard to keep a place looking nice when there's tenants, you wouldn't believe what some of them get up to when it's someone else's property. I know you didn't have much to bring with you, so if you need anything, just come next door to me, I'm the only one who's usually around all the time anyway."

"Thank you." Anneke wedged the words in as Barbara paused for breath. Obviously this was Cashin's mother. "I think I'm starting to pull myself together. And I've spent the morning buying out the stores." She indicated her packages.

"So I see." Barbara's sharp eyes, under her tightly curled hair, took in Anneke's full-length red shearling coat and high fawn-colored suede boots. The coat had been an insane extravagance, far too elegant for the hypercasual Ann Arbor culture, but just now Anneke didn't give a damn. As soon as she'd tried it on, she knew she had to have it.

She was aware that she looked overdressed, especially with the big gold earrings that had been a last-minute purchase. But then, she admitted, she usually did. She had realized, when she'd reached the age of forty, that she was simply one of those women who looked either dowdy or elegant, no middle ground.

Besides, Karl would appreciate the coat.

"It's going to take me forever just to carry everything inside." Anneke laughed, refusing to be apologetic. "And some of it weighs the earth—I never realized how heavy sheets and pillow-cases are."

"Can I help?" The newcomer appeared out of nowhere so abruptly that Anneke started visibly. "Sorry." He grinned and extended his gloved hand. "Cleve Marshall. I live next door." He motioned with his chin toward the second cottage, an apparent twin to Anneke's.

"I'm Anneke Haagen." She turned toward him, juggling packages to accept his handshake. He was medium height, with a narrow, rather British face and razor-cut, straw-colored hair. Almost, but not quite, too young to be interesting—say, early thirties, with a good deal of intelligence underlying his bland expression.

Still, he lacked the force of Karl's personality, she thought, and then laughed at herself—had she really reached the point of comparing every man she met with Karl Genesko?

"Have you lived here long?" she asked politely, making sure her voice held no hint of personal interest. The last thing she wanted was an emotional complication with someone living next door.

"Just since September. I'm here on sabbatical."

"Oh? What are you in?"

"History. UC Berkeley." Cleve responded to the academic's usage of the word *in*. "And you?"

"Not faculty. Computer consulting."

"With the U?" His face held a combination of surprise and reevaluation, the mixture as usual.

"Independent," Anneke answered automatically. She had long ago decided that *freelance* was too casual, the phrase "my own company" too pretentious. "Some academic work, some government, some business."

"Sounds interesting." He didn't sound interested; humanities types, Anneke knew from frequent experience, often made a point of disdain for "electronic gadgetry."

"Barbara, I wanted to catch you anyway." Cleve lowered his voice. "When is the funeral?"

"There's not gonna be a funeral," she replied. "Rosa always said she didn't want one, she'd arranged ahead of time to be cremated. And anyway, they figured it'd be too hard on Ross." Barbara glanced meaningfully out into the courtyard, where the children were involved in some complicated activity. The older of the two boys was standing slightly aside, with the group but not of it. His small face looked pinched and withdrawn.

"Damn it, they're wrong," Cleve said angrily. "Ross adored his grandmother—he was named after her, for God's sake. He needs a chance to mourn her properly."

"He needs to forget about it." Barbara's thin lips tightened. "He'd only get all upset, dwellin' on it."

"But you can't pretend it didn't happen," Cleve argued. "My

God, she only died last night, and you're behaving like she never existed."

"Was that what the ambulance was all about?" Anneke asked, suddenly remembering.

"Yeah," Barbara answered. "She lived over there"—she jerked her head toward the big Victorian house at the edge of the court—"with her son Harvey and his boy Ross. Harvey found her when he got home last night. She'd been sittin' up watching television when she went."

"Where was Ross?" Cleve asked sharply.

"Upstairs asleep. He slept right through it all, don't worry."

"What did she die of?" Cleve pursued. "Do they know yet?"

"Hell, she died of being seventy-eight years old, I guess," Barbara responded irritably.

"But she was a perfectly healthy woman," Cleve insisted.

"Oh, let it be, Cleve," Barbara snapped. "She's gone and that's the end of it, and I'll never know what you saw in her anyway, an old woman like that, and a nasty one too, for a fact."

"Your definition of *nasty*, of course, is anyone who stands in your way," he said poisonously. "Good ol' T.G. probably broke out the champagne when the ambulance drove away."

"If you think I'm gonna say I'm sorry she's gone, you're mistaken," Barbara retorted, unmoved by his anger. "Anyway, I can't stand around talkin' all day, I'm not one of those spoiled college types who gets to sit around for a month and do nothing just 'cause it's Christmas break."

"What on earth was that all about?" Anneke asked as Barbara stalked away.

"Just that, with Rosa dead, there's nothing standing in the way of the project," Cleve said bitterly. But before Anneke could ask him what project he meant, an errant football caught him neatly on the shin, followed by a tumble of breathless children.

"Hey, do I look like a goalpost?" He laughed.

"Sorry, Professor Marshall," Marcella gasped.

"*De nada.*" He patted her head, all signs of anger smoothed away. "How about you folks helping me unload Ms. Haagen's car? She seems to have succumbed to terminal white-sale fever."

"I can help!" Cashin shouted, racing toward the Alfa. "My daddy says I'm real strong!"

"We'll all help," Marcella said, following him.

"Be careful of the car!" Anneke called out anxiously. Thank God the cherished Alfa had been parked at the curb the night of the fire. She'd bought it, as a kind of defiance, after her husband left town with his twenty-three-year-old graduate assistant, fully aware of what a cliché the purchase was. But even as she told herself that "it's only a car," she acknowledged that sometimes things have symbolic importance even when the symbol is a cliché—and that sometimes a thing becomes a cliché because of its underlying truth. Besides, she reasoned, at this point it was about the only personal possession she had left.

"Be careful, gang," Cleve echoed her. "You get the door"—he grinned at Anneke—"and I'll deploy the troops, okay?"

"Ready when you are," she capitulated.

By the time she deposited her own parcels on the table and shed her coat, the others arrived in procession, Cleve bringing up the rear with two bags of groceries.

"You know what?" Cashin said, depositing his burdens on the floor and eyeing the grocery bags. "We haven't had any cookies all day!"

"Well," Anneke said amid general laughter, "I just bought two big boxes, and they'll only make me fat if I eat them myself."

"All riiiight!" Cashin crowed. "Cookies!"

"Are you sure we're not bothering you, Ms. Haagen?" Marcella asked anxiously.

"Not a bit," she replied, discovering somewhat to her surprise that it was true. The cottage felt better with people in it—more like a home. "I'll even make some hot chocolate."

While she heated milk in the microwave and arranged Pepperidge Farm cookies on a plate, she looked around the cottage, really seeing it for the first time. It was charming in its way, she admitted reluctantly, with a bright, airy quality despite its small size. In the kitchenette, a double casement window over the sink flooded the area with light; other casement windows next to the door opened toward the courtyard. On the north and south walls, under the beamed ceiling, light filtered through clerestory windows and brightened the surprisingly spacious main room. There were expanses of soft matte-finished wood that Anneke tentatively identified as birch, warming without overpowering.

Most of the furniture was inoffensive but uninspired, leaning to brown tweed and white Formica. But along the south wall, a built-in banquette surrounded by cantilevered bookshelves, also of birch, seemed to spring almost organically from the paneling. And for a wonder there was a comfortably spacious Formica-topped desk, with enough room for a computer and its associated peripherals. There was even an actual, full-size file cabinet.

In the bedroom, she knew, the architect had skimped on space. The double bed, which nearly filled the room, was set on a semidiagonal in one corner, flanked by a triangular night table of the same wood used throughout the cottage. There was also a small Formica-topped dresser. The far wall was all doors—one to the small bathroom, another to the closet. In this room, too, there were clerestory windows, along with the single casement over the night table.

"Do you always shop in job lots?" Cleve asked, taking a cookie from the plate and arranging himself on the floor.

"Only when I'm reduced to borrowing underwear," she retorted. Then, in response to his quizzical look: "My house burned to the ground Sunday night."

"My God." His eyes widened. "Totaled?"

"Completely. I got out with nothing but a bathrobe and slippers." She felt her throat close at the memory of the heat and flames, the terror-filled struggle with the recalcitrant bedroom window, the hysterical flight across the frozen lawn to the house next door.

"Can they salvage anything?" Cleve asked.

"They don't know yet." She spread her hands, pushing back memory. "The insurance company is sending someone in, but right now it's all under a couple of tons of ice."

"Well, at least you're insured," he said consolingly. "And you've found a decent place to live, too. Considering the Ann Arbor rental market, you were lucky to find this place."

"I suppose so," Anneke said grudgingly. For the last four days people had been telling her how lucky she was—to be alive, to be insured, to have found a new place. She thought if she heard the word one more time she would definitely scream. "It'll do for a while at least." She was still unwilling to concede the cottage's virtues. As if I'm being disloyal to the memory of my dead house, she jeered at herself.

THREE

* * * * *

"Miss Haagen?" Ross Barlow, his voice hesitant, stood before her but at a little distance, as if afraid to approach too closely.

"Yes, Ross?" Anneke recalled herself from futile regrets, trying to put encouragement into her voice. This child, she remembered, had just lost someone he loved.

"Is that a real computer?" He pointed to the small gray laptop sitting open on the desk. "Is it hard to learn?"

"Yes, and no." Anneke took his questions seriously, aware somehow that asking them had taken an effort of will on the boy's part. "Would you like to try it out?"

"Oh boy, could we?" Cashin interrupted excitedly. "Do you have Doom?"

"No, I don't." Anneke shook her head. Doom, like John Madden and his football game, were among the hundreds of discs melted into a large plastic puddle under the ice mountain that had been her house. "Besides," she added firmly, seeing Ross begin to edge away, "Ross was the one who asked first. Come on," she said to him, "let's see what I do have."

Not much, she knew; most of her vast ten-year collection of software was destroyed, including irreplaceable early games like the original Adventure, a first edition of Zork, even the very first Ultima.

Her home desktop machine, of course, was also gone. Luckily, her laptop had been at the office—mostly because it was already more than a year old and virtually obsolete. She'd been about to replace it, since at only 33 megahertz, and with an 80-meg hard drive, it was barely usable except as a terminal linked to her office Compaq.

The only game she'd loaded onto the small hard drive was an old DOS version of SimEarth. She sat Ross down and riffled through the pitifully small selection of discs she'd brought from her office, looking for something to interest a child. Then she stopped as a thought struck her.

"When you asked if it was hard to learn," she asked him, "did you mean just to use it, for games and things, or did you mean programming?"

"Programming . . . I think. Making it do what you want it to. Do you think I could learn to do that?" He sat with his hands folded in his lap, forbearing even to touch the keyboard, but he looked at the computer with such hunger that Anneke found herself caught. She remembered that feeling.

"Let's find out," she said briskly, hitting the power switch and waiting for the blinking cursor to appear. "The first thing to understand," she told Ross, "is that a computer is like a rather stupid dog. It does what you tell it to do, but it does *exactly* what you tell it to do."

"So you have to be careful what you tell it." Ross nodded. Good, Anneke thought, the child has intelligence. Now, start him on a simple PRINT program. . . .

"Good Lord, what time is it?" She looked up guiltily, to see that the other children were gone, while Cleve still sat on the floor, grinning up at her.

"Around two o'clock," he said.

"My God, do you know how much I still have to do today?" she groaned, flurrying.

"I'm sorry, Ms. Haagen." Ross jerked his hands from the keyboard and jumped to his feet, looking stricken. "I didn't mean to cause trouble, honest." The expression of pinched anxiety, missing for the last hour, was back on his face.

"Trouble? Nonsense," Anneke responded quickly. "That was the best time I've had all week." And it was true, she realized; for one hour at least, she'd managed to forget the fire, her work, her personal problems, everything that had screwed up her orderly life. In fact, she seemed to have shed several layers of self-pity as well.

"I want you back here tomorrow, okay?" she said to Ross.

"Do you mean it?" he asked, almost holding his breath.

"Absolutely. You're too good to let get away." That too was true. Ross was one of the naturals, one of those rare ones who connected instantly, for whom the electronic mind inside the gray box was perfectly in tune with his own. "Okay?" she said again.

"Okay!" He leapt across the room for his coat, looking for the first time like a real child. Laughing, she stood and followed him to the door, stretching out stiff muscles.

"I'll get out of your hair too," Cleve said, rising from the floor in one smooth motion. "By the way," he added quietly, "are you aware that you're a natural teacher?"

"No I'm not." She shook her head. "I can only teach the bright ones; I don't have any patience with the others. I can't understand how anyone can't understand, if you follow me."

"Yeah, I know exactly what you mean." He shrugged into his coat and opened the door to let Ross scamper outside. "By the way," he said with his hand on the knob, "if you need anything, I'm right next door."

"Thanks," she said, hoping he was merely being neighborly.

"For that matter, everyone here will help out if you need something," he added casually. "In a tiny enclave like this, neighbors have to be supportive of each other, regardless of personal feelings." She wondered what sort of emotional tangle that last phrase implied, hoping she could avoid being drawn into it. "It's a nice little neighborhood," Cleve said, waving an arm to encompass the courtyard.

Her gaze followed his gesture across the court to the pair of post–World War I houses. Neither of them was particularly well cared for; the one at the corner of the drive, in particular, was a dirty white with streaked windows, sagging porch steps that looked positively hazardous, and a tangle of bicycles blocking the door. It might have once been handsome, too, Anneke thought; it boasted a small turret on one corner and an attractively asymmetric roofline.

The other house, slightly smaller, at least had clean windows, and the front walk was neatly shoveled. It was not exactly dilapidated, but it had a weatherbeaten appearance.

"Who lives there?" she asked.

"Prof Carfax." Cleve made a word of the title. "Zoology, emeritus. He used to be the world's foremost authority on waterfowl— still is, as a matter of fact. He and his wife bought that house when they were first married."

"And they still live there? How nice."

"Unfortunately, no. His wife died almost ten years ago. Now he lives there alone, although there's always a steady stream of graduate students. He plays a mean guitar, by the way; believe it or not, he collects protest songs of the sixties."

"What about the other house?"

"Student slum," Cleve replied. "Owned by the Jayelle Corporation. The corporation wants it to deteriorate for the tax loss and the students want cheap rent; works out fine for everyone but the neighbors."

"The usual Ann Arbor real estate shell game." Idly, she watched as a tall, thin figure appeared on the porch and descended the steps, pausing to allow a white Buick to enter the court and wheel past. The figure proceeded toward the break in the hedge, heading for the street beyond.

And then leaped back, shockingly, avoiding by bare inches the large black Lincoln that barreled into the drive and swerved wildly into the parking area, ramming to a halt with a screech of brakes.

"My God, that's James Kenneally." Anneke let out the breath she'd been holding.

"You know him?" Cleve shot her an odd look.

"He's a grad student in architecture. In fact, he's the one who told me about this cottage." She craned for a better look; James sprawled unmoving on the icy ground, where he had fallen in his scrambling escape from the car. "Is he all right?" she asked anxiously. "And who the hell was that lunatic?"

"T.G. Smith—Barbara's husband. I'd better get out there." He plunged outside, and Anneke grabbed her coat from its hook by the door and followed him. James was getting up, she saw with relief, slowing her steps; and there came the driver of the Buick, a small woman in a long drift of pale fur. Behind her, sauntering along with his hands in his pockets, came the driver of the Lincoln, a wiry-looking man in a brown topcoat.

At his approach, and without the slightest warning, James launched himself forward.

It would have been a clean tackle had Cleve been one step slower—or faster. As it was, Cleve's unwary progress and James's enraged leap coincided perfectly in time and space.

The two of them collapsed to the ground in a tangle of limbs. The man in the topcoat roared with laughter. James leapt finally to his feet, with Cleve clinging to his arm remonstrating. James tried to pull away and his free arm, pinwheeling madly, struck Cleve a glancing blow on the forehead. Cleve released his hold and sat down, hard, on the frozen turf as the fur-coated woman jumped forward and interposed herself between the maddened James and his grinning target.

By the time Anneke reached the improbable scene, the two primary antagonists were jawing at each other over the woman's head.

". . . about the level of combat I'd expect from a petunia." T.G.

Smith snickered, leering at the red-and-white GAY LIB button on James's jacket.

"Oh, right. Whereas big macho types like you have to do it with machines, don't you?"

"And what do *you* do with machines, Tinker Bell?"

"James, stop it!" The blond woman stumbled backward as James flailed in her grasp, struggling to get at the other man.

"How can you defend him?" James turned on her. "He's the one who's going to tear your house down around you!" He swung his glare from the woman's face to the big Victorian house in the center of the court.

"Well, a fistfight isn't going to help anything," the woman said. She was quite remarkably beautiful, Anneke realized, with fine, pale skin slightly flushed from cold and exertion, and astonishing hazel eyes so deeply colored they were almost copper. Only her mouth, perhaps, held a trace of mature hardness. "The project's going ahead now," she said to James, "whether we like it or not."

"Yeah. Now that Rosa's out of the way, you mean." James's flushed face swung toward T.G. again. "That was almost too lucky, y'know?" he growled. "Harvey's a lot easier to bully than that tough old lady, isn't he?"

"Harvey knows a good deal when he sees one," T.G. drawled. "With the money he'll get for that old pile, he can pay off that bitch of an ex-wife and still be rolling."

"Money." James's voice held loathing. "That's all you sharks care about, isn't it? You gobble up everything in your path and create concrete monstrosities in their place."

"You types don't create *anything*, do you?" T.G. leered again, then pointedly turned his back, bringing Anneke into his line of sight for the first time. "Hullo. Who's the new girl in town?"

"Anneke, this is T.G. Smith." Cleve, who had risen from the ground but stayed out of the altercation, now moved forward hastily to make introductions. His barely suppressed grin, Anneke guessed, was in response to her own expression of loathing directed at T.G. "And this is Brenda Roper." He indicated the blond woman. "Anneke is renting the other cottage," he told them.

"I'm glad to meet you." Brenda's smile seemed genuine, although her eyes flicked appraisingly over Anneke's red shearling coat.

"So you're our new tenant." T.G. reached for Anneke's hand, but she took a step backward, unwilling to shake his hand yet not wanting to make a scene. "I can see Barb got lucky." He chuckled, apparently unoffended. "Too bad it's only for six months, but even for a looker like you, the project's gotta come first."

"What is this project, anyway?" Anneke firmly quelled her impulse to use the toe of her boot on some vulnerable part of his anatomy.

"Division Square." T.G. waved his hand expansively.

"Division Square?" The name rang a bell only dimly in Anneke's memory.

"Yeah, you must of heard of it. Sixteen-story building, offices, retail space, the whole package. Right here where you're standing."

"That's the 'project'?" Anneke asked in real horror. "You mean *this* is where Division Square is going?"

"That's right." T.G. puffed out his thin chest proudly, mistaking her reaction for admiration. "TGS Enterprises is puttin' together the whole package."

"Don't count your permits yet," James muttered savagely. "You may have won a round with the Zoning Board of Appeals, but there's still the Historic Review board, and after that the courts, and after *that* the next City Council election. We're not going to give up, I'm warning you."

"You got no idea how worried I am." T.G. chuckled. "Once all the houses are demolished, who's gonna vote to leave a vacant lot? And once I have all the options, these houses *are comin' down*." There was a ruthlessness in his voice that transformed him suddenly from a slightly buffoonish bigot into something else, a viciousness that made Anneke shiver. "Unless you think you're gonna stop me by waving your magic wand, fairy godmother?"

"T.G., that's enough," Brenda said sharply, saving Anneke from violently terminating her lease.

"Now, Brenda, you don't really wanna go on living in that drafty old pile. You just relax, lean back, and count your profits."

"You're not really giving up, are you?" James asked Brenda when T.G. had strutted away across the courtyard.

"What else can I do?" She spread her hands in their pale, fur-lined kid gloves. "Now that he's got the Barlow option he controls every other house in the court. If I hold out he's threatened to build around me." She patted James's hand. "Thank you for wanting to help. I've got to go; I've got half a hundred things to do before tomorrow night. You will come to our New Year's Eve party?" She turned to Anneke.

"New Year's Eve party?"

"Yes. We have one every year. It's a big event. This year Edward Pryor is going to be there." Her smile managed to be both charming and smug as she named an English professor whose latest book had unaccountably reached best-seller status. "Please do come; everyone in the court is always welcome."

"I'll try," Anneke equivocated; the last thing she needed was a noisy, crowded, drunken party.

"Please do if you can. It's a Mackinac Court tradition, and this will be the last time. See you all tomorrow night." With a final brilliant smile, she headed back toward her car.

"She's quite something, our Brenda, isn't she?" Cleve remarked as they walked back across the courtyard. His voice was neutral; Anneke couldn't tell which way to take the ambiguous comment.

"She's beautiful," Anneke replied finally, watching Brenda pull parcels from the Buick.

"She's a d'Aumont, of course, which she'll tell you at the drop of a pedigree."

"One of *the* d'Aumonts?"

"The very same—direct descendant of one of the First Families of Ann Arbor. And then her great-grandfather was Mackinac State Bank, of course, which is where the money came from."

"I've heard her name around town, but I've never known her," Anneke commented. "What does she do?"

"Good works, mostly. She's on half the committees in town—museums, historic preservation, beautification. She's pretty good at it, too, as a matter of fact. Not a brilliant mind, but surprisingly efficient."

"Still, with all that money, and her connections, it's a shame she can't save her home."

"Oh, she'll find somewhere else to live." It was James who spoke, coming up behind them as they paused at Anneke's door. "But that's the original d'Aumont mansion. Built in 1872. Survived more than a hundred years of human stupidity, and now this."

"You sound like you think houses are more important than the people who live in them," Cleve commented curiously.

"They are." James sounded surprised that the question would even arise. "The good ones, anyway. Look at that." He waved a long arm erratically in the direction of Brenda's house, and Cleve instinctively ducked. "Built practically by hand, every brick and beam set individually. Real hands-on architecture." He glowered in the direction of the mansion for a moment, swung his gaze around to Anneke's cottage, and then without warning plunged past her through the door and on inside.

"Would you like to come in for a moment, James?" Anneke said sardonically to the empty air.

"What's that all about?" Cleve grinned.

"Your guess is as good as mine." She shook her head in perplexity.

"Had to talk to you anyway," James said obscurely as soon as they entered. "Can't get the CAD program to work with the new plotter." His pale blue eyes passed over them unheedingly, coming to rest on the wall beyond. It seemed to fascinate him; after a moment he wandered across the room and stood, nose almost touching the wall. He examined the paneling briefly, then dropped faceup to the floor and wiggled his body under the banquette.

"Lose something?" Cleve asked in amusement when Kenneally reappeared.

"No. Never been in here before." He pulled a small notebook out of his pocket, wrote furiously in it for a moment, then disappeared into the bedroom. Anneke and Cleve burst out laughing.

"Is he always like that?" Cleve asked.

"Pretty much." Anneke grinned. "He doesn't actually know he's being rude. He just lives in his own world. He's also brilliant —architecture, ecosystems, all facets of human environment. I think he knows everything about human life except people."

"How long have you known him?"

"A year or so. He's working at LifeSites while he finishes his Ph.D. I met him there when I did a CAD installation for them. Computer-aided design program," she explained in response to his blank look.

"Did that night table come with the cottage?" James demanded, coming out of the bedroom.

"I've no idea," Anneke answered. "You'd have to ask Barbara."

"*She's* not going to tell me anything," James said darkly. He turned away and stared toward the door, writing something more in the notebook. Anneke peered over his shoulder at the page, which was covered with tiny print composed entirely of small, square, beautifully formed capitals.

"Is your cottage the same as this?" he asked Cleve suddenly.

"As far as I can see."

"Identical? Same furniture? Night table and banquette, too?"

"Mostly the same. The banquette's identical, certainly; I haven't seen the night table in this one."

"Come look." He grabbed Cleve's arm and hauled him into the bedroom, giving him time only to cast Anneke a look composed of equal parts exasperation and amusement. She had a moment of panicky embarrassment before she recalled that the fire extinguisher, her idiot security blanket, was out of sight under the bed.

"It's the same as mine, as near as I can tell," Cleve agreed when they returned to the living room. He rolled his eyes and held out both hands, palm upward, in an exaggerated pantomime of bewilderment. Anneke shook her head and grinned. James, ignoring them both, strode into the kitchen, where he stood in the middle of the floor, head back at an impossible angle, studying the ceiling. No, not the ceiling, Anneke realized, the light fixture. She hadn't noticed it before, and looking at it now, she wondered at his interest—two squares of wood at right angles, with circular cutouts to surround a simple white globe.

But when he returned abruptly to the living room, all he said was: "What about the plotter?"

"I'll get someone over there tomorrow morning."

"Can't you fix it today?" He sounded plaintive.

"No I cannot," she answered firmly. "But you can dump your work to disc tonight, and I'll send you someone first thing in the morning to show you and the rest of the department how to reformat for any plotter you've got."

"Well, I've gotta go to Chicago tonight anyway." He looked at his watch. "I think there's a train around five. But you better go yourself," he insisted. "I think there's something wrong with that plotter."

"James, do I tell you how to design buildings?"

"I don't design buildings. I design ecosystems."

"James, go home." Anneke sputtered with laughter, and Cleve joined her. James looked blank.

"Okay. See you." He nodded once, picked up his notebook, and stuffed it back into his pocket. Then he strode to the door and was gone, as abruptly as he had come.

"And I'm off, too," Cleve said, following him out the door. "Remember, just yell if you need anything."

"Thanks, I will," she lied.

FOUR

For the first time since the fire, Anneke slept without nightmares, although she woke with her hand on the fire extinguisher. Still, it was progress, she told herself, pushing the thing under the bed as she arose.

Friday morning dawned warmer, a relative term that meant the thermometer outside the bedroom window read fifteen instead of five. But she drove to work under a white and ominous sky, against which the trees stood out in sharp relief.

The offices of A/H, Inc., were in the Nickels Arcade, a glass-roofed corridor cut through the main campus-area business block linking State Street to Maynard Street behind it. Tiny stores lined the ground floor on each side, with a warren of offices above. A NATIONAL HISTORIC REGISTER plaque at the State Street entrance was testimony to at least one victory for preservationists.

Anneke stopped briefly at the pillared entry, noting two construction cranes marking new high-rises going up in the downtown area. Ann Arbor was undergoing one of its periodic building booms; the last one, she recalled, had cost the city a spectacular Victorian house next to the Arcade, razed to make way for a hamburger franchise. Well, at least the Arcade hadn't given way to "progress," she thought fondly. She climbed the worn stairs to her offices and pushed open the glass-paned door to the cheerful chaos that came with the territory of hiring only part-time student programmers.

"Ms. Haagen!" Marcia Rosenthal jumped up from her terminal, waving a sheaf of printouts. "I found the bug!"

"In the minimall program? Hooray." Anneke smiled at the girl's enthusiasm. "What was it?"

"Transposed loops," Marcia said smugly, leaning over to pick up the pencil she'd dropped.

"Good for you." Ken Scheede came in from the other room carrying mugs of coffee; he handed one to Anneke and perched on top of his desk with the other, feet on the chair. One knee poked through a hole in his worn jeans. "You got two calls from your insurance adjuster," he told Anneke.

"I'll call back later." She sat down at her desk and rummaged through the papers on it, seeking work-related tasks to bury her personal problems under. "Anything in the mail?"

"You mean besides bank calendars and Christmas cards from office-supply houses?" Ken grinned. "Not really. Except," he added, elaborately casual, "there was one new RFP."

"Oh? What's it about?" A new Request For Proposal might be just what she needed.

"City Council is thinking about a time-share system for all the Council members—scheduling, reports, word processing, city data, like that." He looked so eager that Anneke laughed.

"I take it you want a crack at that one?"

"I sure do," Ken said fervently. "I've been doing so much administrative shitwork, I think I've forgotten what programming is."

"How do you think I feel?" Anneke made a ferocious face at the mass of paperwork on her desk. "Sure, all right, consider it yours. But you get to do the paperwork. That way, if we don't get the contract it's your fault." She smiled, then leaned back and looked at him. "You're a local, aren't you?"

"Ann Arbor born and bred." He grinned. "Grew up over Scheede's Bakery."

"What do you know about Mackinac Court?"

"Ann Arbor history in microcosm," he rejoined. Anneke raised an eyebrow. "One of the earliest examples of developer's greed triumphing over city planning."

"Oh?"

"The original block was platted in 1870," Ken explained, "but the developer realized he could squeeze a couple more lots into the center. So he filed a revised plan creating that courtyard. There's some evidence that he may have bribed a couple of politicians to get it approved. Anyway, he got permission to build another two houses in the middle of the block.

"Then in 1912 the owners of those two houses decided they could make a nice profit by subdividing their lots to add a couple more houses to the court. And since one of them also owned Mackinac State Bank, getting approval wasn't hard. Finally, in the middle of the Depression, one of the owners got permission to squeeze in a couple of cottages to rent to visiting faculty. Back then, they'd have approved anything that meant a few jobs for a few workmen." He paused. "They still would."

"How on earth do you know all that?"

"Well, I had a girlfriend who volunteered with the Historic Preservation Society." He looked sheepish. "I helped them do some computer searches a couple of months ago, when they were trying to stop the Division Square project."

"What about Division Square?" Anneke vaguely remembered newspaper reports about the project, but she hadn't paid much attention at the time. "Do you think there's been anything . . . let's say, questionable about it?"

"Well, the society couldn't find anything. TGS Enterprises had all the right signatures and made all the right moves. None of the owners objected, and there aren't any other nearby residential neighbors to protest. They tried, but they couldn't document any historical value great enough to qualify it for Historic District protection. And there was no evidence of bribery."

"I'm surprised the Roper house didn't have enough historic value. And there's another Victorian there, too."

"Not enough." Ken shook his head. "A single house doesn't qualify for historic protection under state law; it has to be an area, at least a whole block. And they can't act on a whole block if only a couple of houses qualify."

"I'm going to hate to see it torn down, though," Anneke said.

"Sure, so will I. But you know, it's a tough place to keep residential. Those old Victorian houses are too big and too expensive to keep up for most families; and anyway, it's kind of a crazy place for families to live, right in the middle of downtown like that."

"I suppose," Anneke admitted, sighing and returning to the papers on her desk. "Now I'd better call the insurance company, and then I'm going to take off, and you two can do the same. After all," she realized suddenly, "it's New Year's Eve."

"That's okay." Ken grinned. "Karen and I are planning our own private celebration."

"All the more reason to go home early," she replied severely, hoping she didn't look as envious as she felt.

She didn't hope for much in the way of good news from the insurance adjuster, and her expectations were fulfilled nicely. No, the salvage operations hadn't made much progress yet against the ice; and no, they still hadn't found the cause of the fire. Not that that mattered much, Anneke thought gloomily. They needed an inventory of the contents as soon as possible, the adjuster told her; and did she have appraisals on those Art Deco antiques she'd mentioned?

She didn't want to think about her collection of Art Deco, a collection that included—that used to include—some surprisingly valuable pieces. There was—there had been—even a small ivory and bronze Paul Preiss statuette. Gone now, she assumed, along with the Chase chrome, the Eileen Gray tea cart, her one precious piece of Clarice Cliff. Well, no point brooding over it.

She called her daughters again—Rachel in Denver, Emma in Santa Cruz—although she'd talked to them the day after the fire. Both were gratifyingly matter-of-fact, paying her the compliment of assuming she could cope. Then for the rest of the morning, she ran more of the seemingly endless errands necessary to reconstructing a life—appraisers, banks, an hour in line at the Secretary of State's office to replace her driver's license, more shopping. At one o'clock she treated herself to lunch at Zingerman's, where she sat by a window with a bowl of beef barley soup. Outside, snow was beginning to fall onto the brick-paved street.

When she left the restaurant, the snow was coming down in earnest, fat white flakes that collected on her coat sleeve in clumps as she walked to her car. She ran more errands—computer store, groceries to get her through New Year's Day, half an hour in line at the post office to file change-of-address cards—driving through a curtain of white flakes that were piling up on the streets with ominous speed.

By the time she reached Mackinac Court it was after three o'clock. The snow was more than ankle-deep, and the courtyard was filled with children.

"We're getting a real blizzard!" Cashin called to her, pausing with a snowball in his hand. "An' I'm gonna get to use my new sled!" Ross peered out from behind a tree and waved a mittened hand at her, then ducked, laughing, as Marcella's snowball whizzed past his ear. Even to an incipient computer whiz, Anneke laughed to herself, a good blizzard beats a programming session. She waved back and mushed the remaining yards to her cottage.

The snow was now coming so thickly that she could barely make out the shapes of the children from her front window. She made coffee, feeling unexpectedly cozy, and curled up on the sofa with the latest Linda Grant mystery, an extravagance in hardcover that she rarely allowed herself. The snow was a benefaction that gave her, for the first time since the fire, permission to put all problems aside. It was impossible to get anything done in such weather; ergo, it was impossible to feel guilty for doing nothing. With a sense of comfort she'd almost forgotten, she snuggled deeper into the sofa and lost herself in an alternate world.

It was nearly six o'clock when she set the book down and went to the front window. It was still snowing; the cars in the parking area were entirely invisible, metamorphosed into hulking white mounds, the rest of the court a featureless landscape of white under the streetlamp. Eight inches at least, she estimated, and still coming down as furiously as ever.

She microwaved a frozen dinner of shrimp and rice, then turned on the television set, poured herself a brandy, and curled up to watch the news. It was full of weather warnings, business closings, and endless scenes of snarled traffic, and Anneke enjoyed the sense of cozy warmth always engendered by scenes of snow— for those safely tucked up indoors. The knock on the door, interrupting a report about a dogsled being used to rescue stranded motorists, was so unwelcome she almost ignored it.

"Hi! Come on out and play!" Cleve's face glowed red under the porch light, his habitual grin muffled by a long maize-and-blue Michigan scarf.

"C'mon out, Miss Haagen!" Marcella called, waving from the center of the court. "We're having a snow party!"

"We're building a fort an' we're gonna have a snowball fight an' when we're done we're gonna have hot chocolate! And cookies!" Cashin's flow was cut off by Barbara, coming up behind him and wrapping his scarf more firmly around his neck. Other bundled forms, unrecognizable beneath huge, puffy coats and hats and scarves, waved at Anneke. Two of them were already setting to work, shoveling snow into huge mounds in the center of the court.

Anneke's immediate response was a firm negative headshake. But before she could speak, the sound of a car caught everyone's attention. Slowly, creeping forward with agonizing caution, Brenda Roper's white Buick inched through the drifts into the turn from Division Street. Through the windshield, framed in the pattern of the wipers, Anneke could just see a man's taut face as he positioned the car, then gunned it slightly to leap the driveway into the court. The Buick moved forward, then slewed sideways; the driver wrenched the wheel, fighting the skid; Barbara grabbed children indiscriminately and herded them aside as the Buick bucked, swiveled, and finally shuddered to a halt, its wheels deep in a snowbank and its bumper against the hedge surrounding the court.

"Now you *have* to come out," Cleve said, drawing a long breath. "We'll need you to help push."

"I think you're right." Anneke discovered that she too had been holding her breath. "Give me a minute to get dressed."

But by the time she'd donned full winter gear—Joyce's borrowed parka rather than the red leather—Cleve and two other men, with Brenda steering, had succeeded in moving the Buick most of the way across the court. Anneke, knowing she wasn't really needed, nevertheless fell in with the men and together they pushed the car the rest of the way to the parking area, laughing and slipping in the snow as they went.

Brenda's elegant high-heeled suede boots sank to their tops in the snow as she emerged from the car.

"New Year's Eve," she said angrily. "Look at this." She glared around at the snow as if it were a personal insult. *"Nobody's* going to come, are they?" she demanded of the man who'd been driving. Only then did Anneke recall the party she'd been invited to.

"The governor's declared a state of emergency." The man shook his head. "All nonessential personnel are to stay off the roads. Everything's canceled, all over the state."

"My God, I've worked for *weeks* on this party," Brenda wailed. "Do you know that *Edward Pryor* was going to be here? And now look—*this* is my guest list." She looked around at the gathered court residents with an expression of disgust. "And another thing," she snapped at the man. "This is the *last* winter I drive this car. Next year we are getting a *BMW*, instead of these damn things that Detroit keeps foisting on people." She stalked toward her house, her attitude of dignified outrage marred by the need to wade ungracefully through the drifts.

"Thanks for the push," the driver said into the uncomfortable silence.

"De nada." Cleve smiled. "Anneke, this is Joe Roper," he said. "And this is Harvey Barlow." He indicated the other man who'd helped push the Buick.

"Glad to meet you." Joe Roper pumped her hand with cheerful energy. He was a big man with the look of an athlete gone comfortably to seed, his face round and friendly under thinning blond hair.

"And you're Ross's father, I take it." Anneke held out her hand to the other man, who hesitated for a moment, then jerked his own hand forward abruptly, resulting in an uncomfortable handshake that squeezed Anneke's fingers painfully inside her gloves.

"Uh, yes . . . Ross is . . . uh, I hope he hasn't been bothering you." He peered at her through round brown-framed glasses with a look of anxiety that Anneke guessed was more or less perpetual.

"Bothering me? Not at all," she protested. "He's delightful."

"Come on, you shirkers!" a laughing voice called from the center of the court. A down-muffled figure that Anneke just barely identified as female waved a hand furiously at them.

"Coming!" Cleve waved back. "Look here"—he turned to Joe—"why don't you change into something comfortable and come on back out. You look like you could use some fun."

Joe's face brightened. "I think I will at that. Give me five minutes. And thanks." Anneke wasn't sure whether he was referring to the push or the invitation.

Two down-coated figures were introduced as Gail Brenner and Cass Plawecki, two of James Kenneally's housemates. For the next hour they built fortifications, propelled themselves around on sleds, and hurled snowballs at one another with indifferent success. The snow and the dark combined to make visibility haphazard; only the lights from the houses and the streetlamp high overhead at the entry provided any light.

Harvey, rather surprisingly, turned out to have a natural flair for building snow forts; Joe, who was revealed to be a former Michigan football player, put his skills to use, throwing snowballs with such accuracy that he was disqualified. They were joined after a while by an elderly man introduced as Prof Carfax, who insisted on being referee, alternately issuing penalties and shouting advice.

Barbara appeared and disappeared, but remained spectator

rather than participant. Brenda did not appear; nor, to Anneke's relief, did T.G. She could see him through his living room window, picked out by the flickering light of a television set.

The snow continued; soon the tracks of the errant Buick had nearly disappeared. It was Barbara, finally, who called a halt, fussing over the children's soaking-wet mittens.

"Time for you lot to get inside and warm up. You got five minutes; I'll get some hot chocolate ready."

"And cookies!" Cashin called.

"How about coming back to our house?" Joe asked. Barbara looked at him consideringly. "Please. We need to do something with all the food we laid in for the party." Anneke expected Barbara to demur; instead, after a brief pause, she nodded.

"All right. I'll be along as soon as I talk to T.G."

"Wonderful," Joe said happily. "Why don't you all change into dry clothes and come by in about half an hour?" Anneke started to refuse, then decided refusal would look churlish; besides, why not? She might as well get to know her new neighbors all at once; she might even, she scolded herself, have a good time.

FIVE

• • • • • •

"C'mon, T.G., we're goin' over to Brenda's."

"Shit we're not." T.G. settled deeper into the big recliner, craning to see around her to the television, where Arnold Schwarzenegger was just about to blow the woman away. This was his favorite part.

"Marcella, you take Cashin upstairs and clean him up." Barbara turned to the children. "And put a clean shirt on him." When the children were gone she said, "You know I don't want language like that in front of the kids."

"Shit, they'll hear it sooner or later. Might's well learn it at home."

"Anyway, we got to go." She stood silent, watching him as he picked up the can of beer and drank slowly, looking at her over the rim. Shit, she's turned into a real ball-breaker. Not like when we was first married, when she thought I was somethin' special. Least, she always acted like she did, T.G. thought uneasily. Ain't even pretty no more, no softness to her, just all hard angles. No fun even in bed nowadays. Not like that little secretary, now.

Still, she was prob'ly right. Wouldn't do to offend the Ropers at this point—not after all he'd done to make sure this deal went through. Shit creek wasn't nothing compared to the mess they'd be in if Division Square went into the toilet.

Because they're just waitin' to take it away, he thought, welcoming the anger rising inside him because it displaced the fear. His list of Them was a long one, and sometimes, unless he was careful, it included Barbara.

"All right, all right." He levered himself out of the recliner. "But I ain't gonna dress up, not for no rich-bitch Ann Arbor snobs."

"I'll lay out your clothes," was all she said.

Not that she liked these Ann Arbor types any better than T.G. did. Intellectual bullies, is what they were, and damn fools besides. But then, most people were damn fools, in Barbara's experience. Mostly, they thought they could live their lives any which way they pleased—that the natural order of things didn't apply to them. And then of course they bitched and whined when it didn't turn out the way they wanted—as if you got what you wanted in this life. They lived their messy, disorderly lives and expected decent people to pick up the pieces for them.

Which we mostly do, Barbara thought acidly, because otherwise their messes screw up our lives, too. Trouble was, most people didn't want to take responsibility for things, not even themselves.

Thank the Lord her daddy'd made sure she grew up properly disciplined. Nowadays they'd probably call it child abuse, she snorted to herself. But she'd been a wild one, she remembered with a flicker of pride, and she'd been lucky to have a daddy who'd beaten the wildness out of her, even though he'd had to use his belt on her bare bottom to do it.

He'd seen to it that she got safely married, too, right out of Ypsilanti High School. All right, maybe T.G. wasn't no big romantic figure, ten years older than her and with his sparse hair and skinny body, but at least he'd never laid a hand on her. He'd turned out to be a pretty good provider, too, with the right kind of prodding.

It had been her idea to use his GI savings to buy that first crumbling old house near the Eastern Michigan University campus. They'd fixed it up just enough to meet the more obvious code requirements, then rented it to a gaggle of five undergraduate boys who didn't care—or didn't notice—that the refrigerator was broken, the plumbing corroded, and the mattresses rotting. Well, that's the way students wanted to live, she figured, the way they boozed and screwed all the time, and never bothered to clean house from one year to the next.

She, and T.G. of course, had used that rent money to buy the next building, and then the next, working the standard real estate pyramid scheme, moving finally into the even-more-lucrative Ann Arbor market. Done pretty well, too, until the recession, when prospective buyers suddenly weren't there anymore, and property that used to appreciate at ten percent a year was now actually dropping in value. Luckily they'd already put together the Division Square package, the big deal they'd been waiting for. But they'd had to sell everything else they owned to do it; that's why they'd had to move into the house in Ann Arbor, full of pretentious, irresponsible snobs who let their kids run wild, encouraged dope smoking, and drove nasty little Jap cars while decent men in Detroit went jobless and hungry.

Well, now that Rosa Barlow was finally dead, they were going to be pretty near rich. They could move way out into the country, get a couple of acres of their own. That'll show him, she thought obscurely.

"Joe, have you thought any more about that penthouse?" Brenda Roper asked her husband's reflection.

"Have a heart, love." He laughed, knotting his tie. "You only just told me about it on the way home from the airport. I haven't even seen it yet."

"Yes, but we have to move fast if we want it. They'll take a lot less for a quick cash sale."

"Aren't you jumping the gun a little?" he asked. "After all,

TGS hasn't gotten city approval yet. Maybe there's still a chance."

"Not anymore, now that Rosa's dead," she shook her head. "Harvey's already signed. Besides, I don't want to fight a public battle and lose; it would make me look very bad."

"I think I feel worse about this than you do," he said. "I know how much you love this house."

"Well, there's nothing we can do about it now." She looked around the huge master bedroom, with its marble fireplace and great crystal chandelier. Even as a child, she'd envied her parents this room. After they died, and her aunt and uncle moved into the house to raise her, she'd thrown such a tantrum they'd let her have the master bedroom for her own. They thought she wanted to be closer to the memory of her parents, but in truth she simply felt the room belonged to her.

"The penthouse has only two bedrooms, doesn't it?" Joe asked.

"Yes, but there's a huge living room, with a cathedral ceiling and a balcony, and a full dining room. And a spectacular view, all the way to the river." She'd leave the glass wall undraped, she decided, so people would see the view the moment they entered. It would be as impressive, in its way, as this house. Although she'd never be able to refer to "the d'Aumont house" anymore, she realized, her face clouding momentarily. Still, the big top-floor apartment in the downtown high-rise at least was officially called "the penthouse," even on the elevator board. People would have to refer to it as "the Roper penthouse," she thought, her normally sunny disposition returning at the thought.

"Well, if you really think that's what you want," Joe said dubiously. "It's awfully different from this."

"I know. That's exactly the point," Brenda replied. "If I moved into another big old house, I'd always be comparing it to this. This way, it's a whole new kind of place. I think it'll be fun."

"You really do amaze me sometimes." Joe smiled and bent over to kiss her, relief washing over him. He'd been prepared for a wash of hysteria when the Division Square deal was finally a reality. He should have had more faith in her.

I never do give her enough credit, he scolded himself. But then, he still could hardly believe his luck, that the beautiful Brenda d'Aumont had actually wanted to marry him. Her money was, then and now, meaningless to him; so was the house, except that she loved it, and anything Brenda loved, he wanted her to have. He would do anything, absolutely anything, to give Brenda everything she wanted.

"I'll meet you downstairs," he said to her reflection. He trotted down the wide staircase, past the big portrait of her father, Pierre d'Aumont. He had lived with the portrait for fifteen years, never noticing its striking resemblance to his own face.

His mother used to love Brenda's parties, Harvey Barlow recalled as he changed into dry clothes. Just a clean pair of jeans and shirt? He vacillated. Or a suit and tie? It was only an impromptu gathering, after all; well, not really, because of course it was still Brenda's New Year's Eve party, except it wasn't actually . . .

Frances used to hate Brenda's parties. "Getting all dressed up to sit around talking about getting all dressed up," she described them once. Whereas his mother had adored the chance to "put on some flash"; her one complaint about Ann Arbor had always been its aggressive informality.

It had been a mistake to live here; the two women were too different. It wasn't that his mother had interfered; the reverse, actually. She'd been delighted to turn over the household to her daughter-in-law, like a dowager duchess retiring from the role of chatelaine. Only, Frances never seemed to be the chatelaine type, the way his mother had been.

Rosa Barlow had been forty years old when she married, to her own vast surprise. She was tired out by then, after more than twenty years on the marginal fringes of show business, tired and getting frightened as she saw her looks and her energy fading away. She hadn't loved Wayne Barlow, but she was endlessly grateful to him, and when Harvey was born she determined to be

the perfect wife and mother. By her own lights, she had succeeded.

It's just that I was raised in a kind of time warp, Harvey thought
defensively, one where The Man of the House was king in his
castle. Intellectually, he knew that that sort of thing no longer ap-
plied; he just had never been able to figure out what other role
there was supposed to be for him.

When did they change all the rules? he wondered gloomily.
And are they ever going to tell us exactly what the new ones are?
Like for instance, just who *is* supposed to raise the children?

Because it's Ross who really matters, he thought, looking at the
boy as he always did, with a combination of wonder and terror.
He'd do anything in the world to give Ross the kind of life he
needed.

"Are you ready, Daddy?"

"Just about." Harvey grabbed the first shirt to hand and shoved
his arms into the sleeves.

SIX

• • • • •

A flocked Christmas wreath trimmed with red velvet bows adorned the Ropers' front door. Joe ushered the guests into a spacious hallway with a wide staircase curving upward under a crystal chandelier, and a heavy oak door directly ahead. To right and left, large, gracious rooms were visible through pairs of glass-paned double doors standing open.

Joe relieved them of their coats and led them to the right, into a room that ran the full length of the house. Anneke had an impression of soft reds and creams in rich, understated patterns, set off by the warm glow of polished woodwork.

Brenda was wearing dark blue satin pants and tunic, with pearl and sapphire earrings and a long, spectacular triple strand of pearls around her neck.

"Please, come in and have something to eat." She motioned with one hand toward a laden table standing against the wall; the other hand twisted the necklace at her throat. "I don't know what we're going to do with all this food," she said plaintively.

"I'll take what's left down to the St. Sebastian Center tomorrow," Joe said soothingly.

"May I have some caviar, Mum?" Victoria asked.

"Yes, you may." Brenda brightened at her daughter's question.

"I want some too!" Cashin cried. "What's caviar?"

"It's fish eggs," Victoria replied loftily.

"Yuck. Fish eggs? You're a liar," Cashin challenged. "Nobody'd eat *fish* eggs."

"Cashin, don't go around calling people names." Barbara came into the room without ceremony, with T.G. behind her. "You come over here and I'll fix you a plate."

Under Barbara's expert supervision, the complex occasion sorted itself out without fuss. The children were settled in a small back den with sandwiches and eggnog and television, while the adults arranged themselves around the coffee table with plates of food and their choice of drinks. Anneke thought it odd that Brenda would allow the other woman to usurp the role of hostess, but everyone else seemed to accept Barbara's authority without question.

Brenda drank champagne but ate nothing, sitting stiffly on the edge of a Queen Anne chair as if waiting for something. Joe poured mugs of eggnog and handed them around, then took up a position behind Brenda, one hand on her shoulder.

"Thanks for helping us out there." Brenda jerked her head in the general direction of the court, an oddly ungraceful motion. "I was . . . I guess I panicked, didn't I?"

"We had a hell of a time getting home," Joe said, patting her shoulder. "I was frightened myself. We shouldn't have gone at all."

"We had to." Brenda spread her hands. "Calvin Kendall's opening reception? How could we not show up?"

"Well, we're home now." Joe stroked her hair, and Anneke thought: Why, he really loves her, exactly as she is. To him, Brenda isn't a nagging, petulant, selfish woman, but a beautiful, demanding child, someone to be taken care of. Demanding because beautiful, or vice versa? Anneke mused. Beautiful because successfully demanding, perpetually smiling and satisfied because she perpetually receives everything she wants? Anneke filed the question away for future examination.

She had thought, when Joe invited them all back to his house, that he'd been reluctant to face Brenda alone; instead, he'd done it to give her a chance to apologize for, or at least get past, her outburst.

"Are you settling in okay?" Joe asked Anneke, drawing her into the conversation.

"Not too badly." She smiled. "Considering that I still have only half a dozen changes of underwear."

"Oh?" Brenda looked at her so oddly that Anneke found herself laughing.

"I'm here because my house burned to the ground last week," she explained.

"My Lord, really?" Brenda sounded more curious than horrified. "How awful."

"It was, rather," Anneke said as casually as she could manage. "Still, I'm having a good time shopping to replace everything." She kept her tone purposely light, reluctant to become the center of attention, and after a moment, as she'd hoped, the conversation became more general.

Anneke sipped champagne, feeling rather like an outsider, which of course she was. She leaned back in the crewel-upholstered wing chair and let the party flow around her, taking the opportunity to scrutinize her new neighbors.

Cleve and Joe were deep in a discussion of community schools in West Virginia; Cass and Gail argued the relative merits of graduate schools as they gobbled cheese puffs and shrimp; Harvey Barlow, Anneke noticed, ate ravenously but said nothing, every now and then glancing back toward the children in the den.

"If you want to sell out," Prof Carfax said loudly, "you'd be better off peddling your body to high rollers than peddling your mind to the Bus Ad boys." He was a big, rawboned man in a threadbare but carefully pressed plaid shirt, with sparse gray hair combed neatly back from his face. As he talked, he waved big, bony hands with bitten but almost painfully clean nails. In fact,

Anneke smiled to herself, he reminded her of a line from an old Beatles movie—"such a clean old man."

Gail Brenner, to whom his remark had been addressed, seemed unoffended.

"But suppose I enjoy business more than I enjoy sex?" Seeing Anneke watching, the girl grinned conspiratorially. She was small and blond, with huge blue eyes behind oversized pink-tinted lenses.

"Enjoy it!" Prof snorted. "As if that mattered nowadays. You're a generation of baby bureaucrats, hell-bent on becoming members of the Establishment."

"I haven't heard that word in years," Anneke said.

"Establishment?" He gave her a sharp look. "You think because the word's gone, so is the thing itself? That there is no Establishment anymore?"

"I don't think it's a conspiracy, if that's what you mean," Anneke said slowly.

"Conspiracy!" he sneered. "You don't know what you're talking about. It's a bloody machine, and the only way to stop a rogue machine is either by throwing a spanner in the works or cutting off its fuel supply."

"You can also climb aboard and take control of the wheel," Gail protested.

"Right," Prof said contemptuously. "You think you're going to change the world as third assistant vice president in charge of bribery at Conglomerate Oil Company. Let me tell you something: Once you're inside the machine, you become part of it. You don't run it—it runs *you*."

"Well, it's a little late to talk about moving into a commune and living on roots and berries," Cass interjected. She sounded angry for some reason. "What other choices do we have these days?"

"Choices? You can take risks. You can take direct action against the machine. Or, if what you really want is money, you can at least have the honesty to admit that you're willing to hurt other people to get it. Because that's the only way you *can* get it."

He began to cough agitatedly, bending forward against the

spasms, but before he did, Anneke caught a glimpse of something in his face that made her draw back sharply. Anger, she thought; no, rage, the kind you saw in the sixties, the cold, focused rage that toppled buildings and presidents.

"Here, drink this." Barbara appeared next to Prof's chair, thumped him none too gently on the back, and administered a glass of eggnog. "Silly old man," she said crossly. "Good thing for you the project's goin' through—get you into someplace where they'll make you live regular."

"Over my dead body," Prof declared between coughs. "I'm buying myself a downtown condo—in that posh new building, you know?—and I'm going to put a band together. We can practice right there. Won't that freak out all those old farts?" He rubbed his big hands together gleefully.

"Silly old man," Barbara said again, with no trace of warmth in her voice. She turned her back pointedly, and Prof chuckled.

"Don't you mind about the project?" Anneke asked him curiously. "I understood you've lived in that house nearly your whole adult life."

"You're a romantic." Prof gave an odd, rasping laugh. "Sure, I've lived there for nearly fifty years, getting older and colder and poorer. Now I've got a chance at the great American dream—instant wealth. Wouldn't you take it?" He leaned forward, peering at her. "No, maybe you wouldn't. You're old enough to be naïve. Not like this new crop we're growing."

Sounds of altercation from the den cut off further comment. Barbara stood up and strode toward the noise, which crescendoed and then stopped abruptly. When she returned to the living room, Harvey Barlow was on his feet.

"I'd better take Ross home," he said uncertainly, holding his plate in his hands.

"It wasn't anything," Barbara replied. "Leave the child be."

"But I hate to impose, uh, you know, with Ross always, well . . ." Harvey looked down at his plate unhappily.

"Harvey, for pity's sake, stop babbling and *sit*." The exasperation in Barbara's voice was palpable. "When Ross becomes a bother you'll be the first to know. Do I look like someone who lets herself get pushed around?"

Anneke, considering Barbara's last statement, decided it was a surprisingly shrewd self-analysis, and she tentatively revised her opinion of the other woman. A more complex personality, surely, than the only-a-housewife persona she seemed to attempt.

"Has Ross been okay?" Harvey asked.

"I'm glad to have him." Barbara answered his meaning rather than his words. "Especially during vacation—he keeps Cashin in line."

"Still . . ." Harvey said helplessly, then, with a burst: "This was supposed to be Frances's week for custody, you know, but she has a meeting with her dissertation chairman next week, so . . ." His voice trailed off.

"And of course *you* can just close up your dental office at her convenience," Barbara said acidly. Harvey remained silent, and after a moment Barbara made a face. "Have you gotten that furnace fixed yet?"

"Not yet." Harvey looked guilty. "I called one company, but they said they didn't handle those old converted coal furnaces."

"Crandall's does; I'll call Monday and get them out here next week." Barbara reached for a cheese puff, the furnace problem settled, and in Anneke's mind, the other woman suddenly fell into place. Barbara was the neighborhood administrator.

Lucky neighborhoods had them occasionally. They were everyone's primary resource—for service workers, for recipes, for emergency help. They were the ones who knew a good auto mechanic, or the one good fourth-grade teacher in the elementary school; their names were on everyone's school form under "Neighbor to contact." They were the ones who brought newcomers into the fold, whether they liked them or not, sometimes especially if they *didn't* like them. Because they understood that a neighborhood is a living organism, with a life of its own, as important in its way as the family itself.

Anneke sipped champagne, wondering if she was being merely fanciful. Well, in her experience all interrelationships among people, no matter how ordinary, were more complex than they seemed on the surface.

"Did I tell you the Warren deal went through?" T.G. interrupted, speaking around a mouthful of chicken.

"Your terms?"

"Better. I jewed him down another ten thou."

"Would anyone like some more food?" Brenda asked quickly, showing instinctively adroit hostessing skills.

"I'll take some more," Cass answered, reaching for a platter of smoked salmon cornets and grimacing at T.G.

"Undergraduates never get enough to eat." Cleve laughed, and Cass grinned at him unself-consciously, her dark pixie face cheerful once more.

"Makes a change from pizza," Gail said from around a mouthful of cheese.

"And *anything* beats cooking," Cass commented. "With Dennis and James out of town, we're on our own."

"Is James out of town?" Brenda asked.

"Yeah." Cass shook her head, black curls falling forward into her face. "He just took off all of a sudden yesterday."

"Well, with Dennis spending the holidays with his parents, he was probably sort of lonesome," Gail offered, then blushed slightly, her fair skin pinkly luminescent.

"Any time is a good time for them two to get themselves out of here," Barbara said acidly.

"Barbara, you're not only a jerk, you're a bad-mannered jerk," Prof snapped. "And I'm too old to have to put up with it." He rose to his feet with a grunt. "Good night, everyone."

"I think I'd better get home, too," Anneke said, more abruptly than she intended. She was suddenly exhausted, although whether from physical or emotional exertion she wasn't sure.

"I guess I better get the kids to bed," Barbara said after a poisonous glance at Prof. There was a general shuffling as people gathered themselves together.

"If you want to take some food back with you, please do,"

Brenda said. "There's plenty in the house, and you may not be able to get out much tomorrow." She glared out the window at the snow, and her fingers twisted angrily at her pearls. There was an audible *snap*, and suddenly small white beads cascaded through her hand onto the floor, where they rolled with amazing speed across the Oriental rugs and into every corner of the room.

"My pearls!" Brenda grabbed at her neck, fingers desperately scrabbling at the remaining beads. "Oh help, please. Careful! Don't step on them!" she said, her voice frantic. "Don't scratch them!"

Everyone fell to hands and knees, peering under furniture and running hands over the heavily patterned rugs which perfectly camouflaged the errant beads.

"Put them in here," Brenda ordered, holding out a cut-crystal bowl. "Gently!" Everyone did as instructed. They seemed not to resent Brenda's peremptory tone, as if making the same allowances Anneke had conjectured from Joe's attitude. Nothing personal in it; it was just Brenda's way. And of course the pearls must be extremely valuable. Anneke, reaching far under an inlaid mahogany buffet, retrieved a single white bead and ran it thoughtfully over her teeth, feeling its smooth roundness. Climbing to her feet, she deposited it in the bowl, which was filling rapidly.

"I think that's all of them," Joe said, looking around the room.

"Yes, I guess so." Brenda seemed to have lost interest in the chase. "If we missed any I'll find them later."

"There's an exact count on the insurance rider," Joe told her. "You can count them later to be sure, before you take them in to be restrung."

"You might ask to have them strung with knots between each pearl," Anneke suggested from hard experience. "That way, if they break again, you'll only lose one of them."

"I suppose you're right." Brenda favored them all with a brilliant smile. "Thank you for helping. More eggnog, anyone?"

There was a general shaking of heads; the impromptu party seemed to be over. They left the Ropers' house in a group, dispersing slowly through the white drifts to their own homes. The snow had finally stopped; the white landscape glittered slightly in the reflection of the house lights that lit their ways home.

SEVEN

* * * * *

The morning sun glittering off the snow was almost too bright to bear. Anneke squinted at the snow-blind world through her bedroom window, trying to decide if she should even bother getting dressed. The radio put the official total at eighteen inches of snow, congratulated itself on having scheduled its blizzard for a holiday, and reported please from state and city officials for all nonessential traffic to stay off the roads.

Still, the temperature had risen to twenty-six, balmy by Ann Arbor winter standards, and she found she had an urge to experience the silent white world outside—while it remained silent and white. Yielding to the impulse, she dressed in jeans and a new heavy sweater, made herself a quick cup of coffee, and headed out into the courtyard.

The flash of color caught her eye first. Not that it was bright; but the dark maroon made a stark contrast in the snow-covered landscape. Anneke detoured slightly across the courtyard to investigate, her boots crunching over the trampled snow.

She knew what it was, and who it was, long before she reached the spot. James Kenneally's body sprawled at the edge of the parking area, the long limbs flung sideways, looking as clumsy in death as he had in life. The maroon jacket was flung open and twisted under his body, and a pair of black leather gloves lay by his feet. His head was nearly underneath one of the cars—T.G.'s big Lincoln—its hulking shape barely recognizable under a foot of fresh snow. His face . . . Anneke forced herself to look at the terrible face, bloated and empurpled, automatically observing and analyzing even as her stomach heaved.

She looked around at the semicircle of houses, pulling Joyce's parka closer to her body to stop the involuntary shiver that had little to do with the cold. Snow lay thick on rooftops and along the sides of the houses, turning small bushes into sinister mounds. No lights showed; no children's voices broke the silence. They were sleeping in, of course; soon children would come boiling out, booted and mittened, to enjoy the gift of snow.

The image quickened Anneke's steps as she recrossed the courtyard to her cottage. Without removing her coat she reached for the telephone to call the police, then paused, keeping her hand on the instrument but making no immediate move to dial, forcing herself to take time to order her thoughts.

Damn Karl for being two thousand miles away, she thought unreasonably; what was the point of being involved with the head homicide detective if he wasn't there when you found a body? Why isn't there ever a cop around when you need one?

She fought back the giggles of incipient hysteria. Who should she call? Not 911; she didn't want to deal with a rookie patrolman. Luckily she knew, and was known in, the department; she'd been their computer consultant even before she met Karl. Well, Brad Weinmann, then; he was Karl's second in the Homicide Division, after all. If he's available, she thought grimly.

She shook her head in anger at her own indecision, picked up the receiver firmly, and dialed, fingers crossed. She breathed a sigh of relief to hear the voice of a desk sergeant she knew and liked.

"Linda, it's Anneke Haagen."

"Good morning," Linda Postelli's cheerful voice responded. "Started digging out yet?"

"I don't even own a snow shovel. Linda, is Brad Weinmann around?"

"Not at the moment." And then, as Anneke's heart sank, she added, "He's out checking on some downed power lines. Everybody's on blizzard detail today. Karl really knows when to take a vacation."

"Brad is on duty, then?"

"Yes." Linda's voice became more serious in response to Anneke's brusqueness. "You sound like you have a problem."

"It's more than a problem," Anneke said tensely. "It's a murder. Linda, can you dispatch Brad over here fast?" She knew she was pushing the envelope of police etiquette to its limits, but she didn't care.

"Yes, I think so," Linda replied after the briefest of pauses. "What's the address?"

"Thank you." Anneke let out her breath with a gust of relief. "I owe you one." She recited the address, then added, "Oh, and Linda, one other thing."

"Yes?" the sergeant asked warily.

"Would you ask him please not to drive into the court, and to look around carefully before he walks past the entry? Thanks." She hung up and, still in her coat, filled a mug with water, added a spoonful of instant coffee, and put it in the microwave oven. When it had heated, she took the dark liquid over to the window, where she could watch for the police. She waited anxiously, fearful that at any moment the children would come bounding out to play, so that when she saw the blue light of the police car winking through the hedge that barricaded Mackinac Court from the street, she hurried out toward it. Still, she was careful even in her haste to walk in the tracks she had made previously.

"Hi, Anneke. What have you got?" Detective Brad Weinmann, his youthful face serious and intent, greeted her from the sidewalk but made no move to step forward. The other man, whom Anneke recognized as a young black patrolman named Jim Zelisco, nodded to her soberly, his dark eyes already scanning the court.

"It's bad." Anneke, too, stayed where she was. "Before you come any farther, take a good look at the snow."

"I see." Brad looked around thoughtfully, then exchanged a glance with Zelisco.

The center of the courtyard was full of ruts and ridges and random mounds, beaten and trampled by last night's frivolity. Deep footprints led up to each house. But all the way around the edge of the court, along the sides of the houses, and particularly across the entry, the snow was absolutely virgin, save for a single set of footprints that crossed the entry and disappeared into the trampled area.

"All right." Brad took charge with brisk efficiency. "Let's go see what's happened." The two men entered the court now, stepping carefully in a single line along the side of the entry, avoiding the footprints already there. Anneke pointed wordlessly and needlessly; as soon as they broached the hedge they spotted the splash of color that had been James Kenneally.

Brad knelt beside the body but did not touch it. Zelisco looked at it only briefly, giving most of his attention to the surrounding scene.

"Dead, of course. Strangled." Brad spoke almost to himself. "Who is he?" he asked Anneke without turning.

"His name was James Kenneally; he lived in that house there." She pointed. "He was an architecture student." Brad nodded and stood.

"I'd better call in," Brad said to Zelisco. "You stay with the body. Anneke, why don't you wait inside; they'll want to talk to you." Neither of them mentioned Karl, but she knew they were both damning the circumstance of his absence.

"Of course. I'll put on some coffee." She started toward her cottage, then halted. "Brad, there are children here. They'll be coming out to play any time now."

"We'll take care of it. Nobody's going to be allowed out here until the Homicide team goes over the scene." His face was grim as he headed out of the court to the patrol car, placing his feet carefully in the tracks he'd made when he entered.

Anneke recrossed the silent courtyard, past still-curtained windows, sparing a sardonic thought for the unlikely emptiness, a white silence broken only by the chittering of a squirrel. From what she'd seen of them so far, Mackinac Court residents seemed to do a more than usual amount of milling, but thank God this morning everyone was apparently sleeping in. She wished she'd done the same; someone else would have found the body.

Inside the cottage, she took off her coat and filled the electric coffeepot, sure there would be need for more than a single cup. A glance at the clock amazed her; it was still barely 8:30.

Only then, having turned responsibility over to others, did the reality hit her. She stood still for a moment, shaken by the fact of James's death, but shaken even more by the implication of the footprints in the snow. Or rather, the lack of footprints around the edges of the court. Only one set of footprints led *into* the court from the street—presumably James's. Therefore, no one but James had entered the courtyard last night after the snow had stopped falling. And, therefore again, the murderer was still here, was one of them. James Kenneally had been murdered by one of the nine other adults who lived in Mackinac Court. Murdered by one of her neighbors.

She digested her conclusion slowly, wondering at her own reactions. She had been mildly fond of James, had respected his abilities and been amused by his unusual personality, but the fact of murder seemed more numbing than the fact of death. For the moment, at least, what she felt was anger rather than grief.

She poured herself a cup of coffee and took it over to the window, drawn in spite of herself to the scene outside. There was nothing in particular to see. Zelisco was still standing over the body; Brad was nowhere in sight. And then, abruptly, the courtyard was filled with blue-clad figures.

There seemed to be dozens of them, swarming aimlessly like so many angry wasps. But after a while Anneke could see patterns emerging. One group surrounded the body, another was fanned out across the courtyard, while still others tramped from door to door through the snow, knocking and talking to the residents. The impression of disorganization was spurious, Anneke realized; in fact, they were proceeding in a highly efficient and businesslike manner. She watched the spectacle, fascinated in spite of herself. The fact that she could see but not hear imparted a silent-movie surrealism to it all.

Two policemen knocked on the door of James's house, and Gail Brenner answered, her bright pink robe flapping open over bare feet. There was a moment of conversation, and the girl's body seemed to stiffen, then crumple. She backed away, and the two policemen disappeared inside.

Another policeman mounted the three steps to the Ropers' door, and in a moment Brenda answered their knock, in a long, sapphire blue satin robe. She listened for a few moments and then withdrew; Anneke was too far away to see any expression on her face.

Next door, the policeman detailed to the Smiths was having rougher going. Anneke couldn't see who answered the door, but she was close enough to hear sharp sounds. The policeman gesticulated feverishly before he finally nodded, shrugged, and left. The sound of a door slamming violently followed him.

Out of the corner of her eye, Anneke saw dark blue pass her cottage; this one must be going to inform Cleve. Others moved toward Prof's door and, to her left, toward the Barlow house.

Police continued to come and go from the court, and Anneke continued to watch, as, she was sure, did everyone else in the court. But most of their activity was incomprehensible to her. She found her eyes following one of them, a photographer, moving from point to point in the area, changing lenses, shooing people out of his way. He seemed to be photographing not merely the body but every part of the court from every possible angle.

She tore herself away from the scene finally with reluctance, poured another cup of coffee, and sat down at the desk, powering up the little laptop computer and opening her communications program. She dialed into the University computer system first, checked her E-mail and spent a few minutes with the electronic conferencing system. The on-line conversations, which ranged over every imaginable subject from philosophy to football, usually amused and entertained her, but this morning she had no patience for it. She logged off with a sigh, thought about dialing into her office computer and then decided against it, thought about starting a new world in SimEarth and decided against that also. She was relieved when the expected knock on the door arrived.

"Whew." Brad Weinmann stamped snow off his feet before entering. "Did you say you had some coffee?"

"I just made a fresh pot. Come on in." She poured them each a cup and filled a plate with the remains of the Pepperidge Farm cookies while he shed his coat and sank gratefully onto the sofa. When she joined him, he took a small notebook from his pocket.

"I need to get some preliminary information," he said. "Just a kind of debriefing."

"Of course. What did you want to know?"

"Well, just for form, I need to confirm that you didn't touch the body when you found it?"

"No. Not at all. It was obvious that he was dead." She shuddered at the memory.

"And you called the police immediately?"

"Yes."

"I know you've only been living here for a couple of days," he continued, "but I take it you met James Kenneally before you moved in?"

"Yes. I met him through work. In fact, he's the one who told me about this cottage being for rent."

"When did you see him last?"

"Thursday afternoon," she replied, remembering. "Just before he left for Chicago."

"Chicago?" Brad looked up from his notebook. "Any idea why he went to Chicago? Did he have friends or family there?"

"I don't know." Anneke shrugged helplessly. "I didn't know

him that well—we were just business acquaintances, really."

"And you didn't see him when he returned." Brad made it a statement rather than a question.

"No. I didn't even know he had returned. He wasn't around last night, at least."

"That's right." Brad looked at his notebook thoughtfully. "I understand there was some sort of outdoor gathering last night?"

"Yes. Very impromptu. We all just wound up outside playing in the snow." The bald words made the evening sound foolish rather than charming. "And a sort of rump New Year's Eve party afterward."

"Were all the residents there?"

"Yes, except for James, and his . . . oh, damn . . ." She fumbled for the proper word. "I don't know what the correct term is. The man he was living with. Anyway, one of their roommates said he was out of town."

At Brad's request, Anneke described the evening carefully, going over it twice as he questioned her about each person's comings and goings.

"You left the Ropers' at about ten o'clock," he mused when she was finished. "It had already stopped snowing. Do you think you'd have noticed the body if it was already there?"

"I doubt it," Anneke admitted after a pause. "I'd be walking in the other direction, with my back to the parking area. You'd probably have to ask Cass or Gail; they'd have gone right by the spot."

"We will, of course. I assume you wouldn't have noticed if there were footprints in the drive."

"I doubt it."

"Well, we know he was strangled," Brad said, "but it'll be a while before we know anything else."

"I know." Everything would go to the lab, of course—not just the body, but clothing, personal belongings, casts of footprints, everything found anywhere near the scene. She knew enough about Karl's work to be familiar with the drill. "Do you know who's going to be put in charge?" she asked finally.

"No idea," Brad said after a pause. "Right now it's all just routine." He paused again, and when he continued, Anneke felt sure there was something he had decided not to say. "Is there anything else you can tell me about James Kenneally?"

"Not really—nothing that's not on the record, anyway. I didn't really know him that well." And now I never will, she realized, feeling finally a real and profound sadness at the thought.

EIGHT

· · · · · ·

After Brad left she went back to work, wishing she had her CD player to block her mind from the activities outside. She dialed into her office and for the next few hours concentrated on debugging and testing the latest version of a retail time-share program. When she finally finished, she discovered it was past noon.

Looking out the window, she saw the police were gone. No, not entirely; she could see a dark blue figure standing just outside the entry. But the whole scene looked oddly empty; not only were there no children playing but there were no objects of any sort in evidence. The cheerful clutter of sleds and mittens and snow gear was gone. The police, it seemed, had swept the place clean.

She turned away from the window, sliced some cheese and wedged it into a croissant, eating more from habit than appetite. When she was done she wandered through the cottage, feeling physically cramped and mentally aimless. She looked out the window again, saw Prof wielding a snow shovel on his front walk, and on impulse decided to do the same.

There was an outbuilding between Cleve's cottage and the

Roper house, something halfway between a storage shed and a barn. There should be extra garden implements in there, Anneke reasoned, pulling on coat and boots and gloves. Trudging through knee-high drifts, she pushed open the door of the ramshackle structure and peered inside.

The interior was about as expected—a pile of bicycle parts on one side, a collection of sleds and snow saucers on the other, and a litter of other items shoved to the rear. Anneke could make out a beanbag chair spilling Styrofoam pellets, an oak rocking chair missing one of its runners, and an old power lawn mower with what she hoped was an empty can of gasoline next to it. Other unidentifiable detritus were scattered haphazardly about.

She found a collection of yard tools finally, selected the least bent and rusted of the shovels, and trudged back to her cottage with it, where she attacked the small walk, digging fiercely at the offending snow as if it were the enemy. As an afterthought, she trudged around the perimeter of the cottage knocking the heavy snow off the evergreens that edged the foundation. When she was finished, she crossed the courtyard to the parking area and began digging out the Alfa.

Prof and Barbara joined her almost simultaneously. Prof chipped away slowly with his shovel, while Barbara went to work on the area around the buried Lincoln, every now and then glancing around to locate the children, who had finally been released to the outdoors. Marcella, Cashin, and Ross popped in and out of sight as they raced around and behind the houses.

"I gotta get them out of the house, but I'm not gonna leave them alone out here," Barbara said, stabbing her shovel viciously into a mound of snow. "What with God knows who walkin' in off the streets, an' we're not even safe in our own houses."

Anneke sought for some noninflammatory response to Barbara's misinformation, but Prof was there before her.

"Barbara, I hate to burst your bubble, but the only person who 'walked in off the street' last night was James Kenneally." Prof thumped his shovel on the ground. "If the killer came from outside Mackinac Court, you better start believing in teleportation." So someone else had seen and understood the evidence written in the snow, Anneke realized.

"People like that. Didn't I warn you? Always causin' trouble, you read about it all the time—fightin' over each other in bars, gettin' themselves beat up and even askin' for it with all that leather-and-chains business and God knows what other sorts of things, and now they bring it into our own homes."

"Barbara, read my lips." Prof leaned forward. *"No one* entered Mackinac Court last night except James. There were no tracks in the snow except his. James was killed by someone in this court. One of *us.*" Prof seemed to exhibit a savage pleasure in the words.

"He's right, I'm afraid." Joe Roper came up behind Anneke, carrying a shovel and a broom. "That's why they're questioning us the way they are." He looked really distressed; his face sagged oddly, as if he could no longer make the effort to keep it firm. He's not going to age well, Anneke thought irrelevantly; that sort of youthful blond handsomeness didn't, in her experience, unless it contained a great deal of vitality.

"What'd they ask you?" Prof queried.

"The same thing they asked everyone, I assume." Joe began halfheartedly brushing snow off the Buick. "About the snow party last night, what time we went to bed, whether we heard or saw anything, how well we knew James."

"And of course no one here knew him more than casually, and no one could think of a single motive to murder such a nice, harmless boy," Prof sneered sarcastically. "Except Barbara, of course." He jerked his head in her direction.

"If I'd wanted to kill him," Barbara responded acidly, "I wouldn't of done it in my own front yard."

"No one would want to kill James," Joe said tensely. "Why would they? It's ridiculous."

"Is it?" Prof rasped. "Even though he'd sworn to stop the project? Suppose he'd actually found a way to do it?" He grinned wickedly.

"And suppose pigs could fly?" Barbara snapped. "That's about as much chance as he had of stopping the project."

"If they do think that's why James was killed," Prof said to Joe, "then you and Brenda are probably off the hook. You'd be the only ones here with a motive for keeping him alive. On the other hand, James and I weren't exactly buddies, *and* I'd have lost a bundle if he'd come up with a way to stop the project. So that gives me a couple of hefty motives, as the cops would be quick to notice. I imagine they'll want a real good look at the TGS books, too, won't they?" He shot the question at Barbara, grinning broadly.

"They can want all they please." Barbara refused to be drawn. "Our business is no business of anyone else's, and we're not living in a police state yet, thank you very much." She hurled a shovelful of snow high toward the fence. "They got no need to pester innocent people just because some of *them* bring their filthy quarrels into decent neighborhoods."

"So that's your story and you're sticking to it." Prof chuckled. "Hard to believe anyone can be that blind stupid."

But she isn't, Anneke mused. Barbara was rigid and bigoted, but she wasn't, in the normal way, at all a stupid woman. Which made her reaction to the murder distinctly odd.

They continued shoveling in less-than-companionable silence. *Was* the project the motive? Anneke wondered. It made as much sense as anything else, she supposed—certainly more sense than Barbara's stubborn fiction. The one certainty was that the murderer was one of *them*, one of her neighbors in this cozy little enclave. She eyed the others covertly as she shoveled, and then, afraid they'd notice her scrutiny, swung her eyes toward the center of the courtyard, where the children worked desultorily on an ungainly-looking snowman.

"Where's Victoria?" she asked Joe, noting the girl's absence for the first time.

"Inside getting an early start on packing." He paused in his shoveling, panting slightly. "She goes back to school next week."

"Still sendin' her to that place in Connecticut?" Barbara's voice dripped disapproval.

"I hate having her away," Joe said defensively, "but she seems to like it. Anyway, Brenda's flying back with her in a few days."

"Didn't the fuzz tell her not to leave town?" Prof voiced the question already in Anneke's mind.

"They never said." Joe looked surprised. "She'll only be gone a couple of days—drop off Victoria, see her broker in New York, and come straight back. Isn't it all right?"

"I don't know why it wouldn't be," Anneke said, shoveling up one final chunk of snow from under the wheels of the Alfa. If I had a child here, she thought, I'd be just as glad to have her out of the way for a while. She glanced toward the children again; Ross caught her eye, started to wave, and then checked the movement abruptly and lowered his eyes. Anneke felt a pang of conscience. She'd promised the child computer lessons and then had promptly forgotten about him.

"I think that's it for me," she said, stretching sore muscles. Shouldering the shovel, she waded through the snow toward her cottage, waving to Ross to join her.

"How about some computer time?" she asked when he caught up with her, a cautiously hopeful look on his face.

"Yes, thank you. If you're sure it's all right?" he asked anxiously.

"Absolutely," she assured him. "I'd be bored out of my mind otherwise."

Inside, she made hot chocolate and joined him at the keyboard, legitimately glad to bury her thoughts in soothing algorithms. For the next hour, they immersed themselves in programming, and Anneke was once more impressed by the boy's quick intelligence and intuitive understanding. She had him write a small BASIC program of his own, and when it didn't run properly he looked curious rather than disappointed. An excellent sign, she thought; the learning is more important than the ego involvement. Patiently she introduced him to the Trace command, showed him the essential elements of debugging, and was rewarded by his grin of pure delight when the program ran correctly.

"I think that had better do it for today," she said finally when the time neared five o'clock.

"Okay." He was disappointed but acquiescent.

"Look, tomorrow's Sunday," she said. "How about another session in the afternoon?"

"Okay." He looked happier at that, but still eyed the computer longingly as he put on his coat.

"And in the meantime," she said impulsively, "I want you to take this home with you." She dug into the desk drawer and pulled out an old DOS manual that had turned up in a box she'd brought from her office. "Read these two chapters." She pointed to the table of contents.

"You mean I can really take it home with me?" he asked, wide-eyed.

"Absolutely. I think you've got time for a little homework, don't you?"

"Oh, I do, I promise. And I'll take real good care of the book, too." He clutched the precious manual to his chest, his small face glowing. He'll probably read through the entire thing in one gulp and then sleep with it under his pillow, Anneke thought, smiling to herself as he left.

When he was gone she poured the remains of the hot chocolate into the sink and replaced it with a glass of sherry which she carried over to the sofa, switching on the television on her way. Outside, the sun was already setting, and darkness seemed to press against the small panes of the casement windows. After a moment, Anneke got up again and went through the cottage pulling drapes tightly closed and turning on lights, all the lights in every room.

As she emerged from the bedroom the television was blaring out "The Victors," and on the screen the blue-clad Michigan football team was pouring out onto the sunlit field in Pasadena for the Rose Bowl kickoff.

As the cameras panned the sidelines, she watched intently, searching for Karl's familiar form but not seeing him. Well, this was one of the few places where he'd look normal size. She laughed to herself; probably the TV crew would mention him at some point. He was one of Michigan's more famous football alumni, after all.

She succeeded in immersing herself in the game better than she'd expected. Throughout the first half, Michigan managed to contain Stanford's world-class quarterback, put one touchdown and a field goal on the board, and even get their passing game going. At the half Michigan led 14 to 10, and Anneke microwaved a frozen "gourmet" dinner and took it back to the living room as the second half got under way. The Michigan quarterback was just dropping back for a pass when the doorbell rang.

"Oh, damn," she muttered, backing toward the door to keep the screen in view. The pass floated downfield, drifting rather than spiraling, over the head of the receiver and into the hands of the Stanford cornerback for an interception. "Damn!" she said aloud, throwing the door open.

And stared dumbfounded, her heart lifting in absurd joy at the sight of Karl Genesko's enormous frame filling the doorway.

"Interception?" he asked, looking over her head at the instant replay, the smallest trace of a smile on his face.

"It's still not fair," Anneke said when they were curled together on the sofa. "They could have waited until tomorrow to call you back." She sat upright, pulling out of his encircling arm to face him. "I am assuming you didn't come back because of me."

"You told me not to, so I didn't," he replied calmly. "In fact, the chief called me this morning and told me to get the first flight back, crash priority."

"But why?" Anneke asked, puzzled. "Surely James wasn't as important as all that."

"No, that's true." Karl accepted her basic premise without argument, both of them acknowledging with uncynical realism that even in death, some people were more equal than others. "But the suspects are."

"I never thought of that."

"The chief did." He grimaced as the Michigan quarterback went down under a blizzard of red and white. "The Ropers alone would be bad enough, but T.G. Smith is a hotshot with the downtown crowd, and Bert Carfax still has a wide following among local radicals. Carfax alone could turn this into a real media circus if it's handled wrong."

"God, I never even thought about the press," Anneke said with dismay. "I'm surprised reporters and news photographers haven't been here already."

"They have," Karl said grimly. "We were able to keep them outside the court today on the grounds that it's a murder scene. And of course the blizzard helped—not only slowed them up but gave them plenty of other news to chew on. But I wouldn't make any guarantees about tomorrow."

"Still, the court's private property, isn't it?" she asked hopefully. "Can't we keep them out on the sidewalk at least?"

"What? Oh, yes, I should think so." He tore his attention away from the television set, where Stanford was completing a punt runback to the Michigan forty.

"Why don't you relax and watch the game for a while?" Anneke laughed. "And you probably haven't eaten all day, have you?" The question was irrelevant; she'd heard his views on airline food often enough.

"I can't stay." He sighed, one eye still on the television. "I came straight here from the airport; I've got to get over to the department right away."

"Do you want me to tape the rest of the game for you? Oh, damn, no, scratch that. I forgot, I don't have a VCR anymore." She grimaced. "One more thing to put on my list."

"You are all right, aren't you?" He looked at her closely, without touching her.

"I'm fine, honestly." She looked into his eyes, inches from her own. "I'm working it out."

"Are you sure?"

"Positive," she said firmly.

"All right." He nodded acceptance, but instead of rising from the sofa, he drew her toward him for a long kiss that had something of anger in it.

"I have to leave," he said finally, his mouth moving against the side of her neck.

"Are you sure?" Her voice cracked slightly.

"Positive." His hands moved against her back under her sweater, pulling her closer.

"Well, then . . ." She couldn't continue because he was kissing her again. Somehow, too, they were on their feet.

"Does this dollhouse have a bedroom?" he asked.

"Through there." She pointed. "What about the department?"

"They don't have a bedroom." He grinned down at her as he led her toward the doorway.

They made love with the happy familiarity of experienced lovers who have learned how to give and receive pleasure, and with the added intensity of a time apart. The passion between them was powerful but carefully controlled, leavened with humor; it didn't take itself too seriously. At least, she thought at one point, grinning to herself, she'd been wrong about one thing; the bed seemed to be big enough, after all.

"Now I really do have to leave," he said finally.

"I know." She sighed.

"I don't know what I'll be doing, but I'll call you when I can, all right?"

"Yes, all right." She held on to his hand as he slid out of the bed. "I'm glad you're back."

"I'd have come sooner," he said mildly as he dressed. "Never mind"—he stopped her response—"I know." He reached for his shoes, said "Ouch!" loudly, and sat down on the bed, massaging his toes. "What the hell is that?"

"It's nothing. Just . . ." Anneke felt her face flame with embarrassment as he bent down to peer under the bed.

"A fire extinguisher?" Karl pulled the thing from under the bed and, to her astonishment, looked at her with every indication of approval. "Good for you."

"I know it's ridiculous," she said angrily, not sure if she was angry at herself for needing it or at him for discovering it.

"It's not ridiculous at all," he declared. "It's an extremely intelligent response—exactly what I would have expected from you."

"Please don't patronize me," she said, now even angrier. She sat up straighter, pulling the duvet tightly around her shoulders.

"I wouldn't think of it." He sat down next to her. "I meant exactly what I said."

"But it's absurd," she insisted less forcefully. Karl always meant what he said. "Like . . . like changing your password after somebody's already rifled all your data."

"It's called a coping mechanism," he responded. "Look, cops have to know something about coping with disaster—God knows we see enough of it. The plain fact is that the people who recover best are the ones who refuse to see themselves as victims—the ones who do something to regain control of their lives."

"Can you ever really control your own life?" Anneke shrugged. "Now that I'm prepared for a fire, I'll probably be done in by a . . . a pack of wild dogs."

"The terrifying fragility of human life." Karl nodded. "I know —we try not to think about it, but when a disaster happens, it forces us to pay attention. The survivors are the ones who learn to look it in the face and accept it." He reached for his suit jacket. "That fire extinguisher tells me you're one of them."

"I don't know." She remained dubious. "Isn't it really just an emotional crutch?"

"Of course it is. Why is that a dirty word? If you broke your leg, would you consider a crutch to be merely a self-indulgence?"

"No, but . . ."

"Well, then." He finished knotting his tie and bent to kiss her once more. "I'll see you tomorrow."

After he was gone she wrapped herself in a bathrobe, dragged the duvet into the living room, and curled up on the sofa to watch the end of the Rose Bowl. Somehow, though, it wasn't as much fun anymore; she had missed Karl less when he was two thousand miles away than when he was half a dozen blocks away. When Michigan won on a last-second trick double reverse, she snarled at the television and snapped the dial to a nice, mindless sitcom.

NINE

• • • • • •

The first thing she noticed when she rose Sunday morning—after a nightmare-free sleep, thank God—was the fire extinguisher. Karl might be right, she considered, looking down at the ugly thing, but still . . . In her experience, crutches, at least emotional ones, too often became permanent fixtures in one's life. It was time for her to get rid of this one—first thing tomorrow, she told herself, pushing it under the bed with her foot.

She dressed in black jeans and a white silk shirt and walked barefoot into the kitchen to plug in the coffeepot. Then she went to the front door to get the Sunday paper. Which, she realized immediately, was lying in a snowbank just out of her reach.

"Damn," she said aloud, her bare toes clinging to the threshold as she stretched futilely toward the paper.

"Need help?" Cleve called from next door, where he was shoveling snow off his front walk.

"Can you hand me my paper?"

"Sure." He put down the shovel and slogged toward her through heaped drifts. "Here." He handed the paper to her, slapping chunks of snow off it. "Is it worth a cup of coffee?"

"Sure. Come on in," she said after only the briefest pause. She was only being neighborly, after all; it wasn't her fault that the neighbor in question was a good-looking man.

Inside, he shed his coat and wandered over to the computer while she poured coffee.

"I don't know much about computers," he said, peering at the little laptop, "but isn't it hard to do real work on one of these midgets?"

"Not on the new ones." She shook her head, setting coffee cups on the table. "But this thing's damn near an antique. I just haven't gotten around to replacing my desktop system yet."

"You've had about a year's worth of trauma in the last week, haven't you?" He sat down and took a long swallow of coffee. "James made page one, but only just," he said acidly, pointing at the newspaper. "After all, it was a football day."

She shook out the front section of the paper and looked at it. The entire top half of the front page was devoted to the Michigan Rose Bowl victory—screaming eight-column headline, six-column color action photograph, and an interview with head coach Ralph "Ro" Roczynski. James's death was reported in a two-column story at the bottom of the page, under the headline STUDENT FOUND STRANGLED IN SNOWBANK.

The story itself was long on details about James but short on information about the crime itself. James had been twenty-four years old, she read, originally from Cassopolis, Michigan, the son of a pharmacist. He had an older brother, an army tech sergeant currently stationed in Germany. There was a short sentence identifying James as the chair of the University of Michigan Gay Students' League, but not much else, only that "the police investigation is continuing."

"It doesn't say much, does it?" she said after reading through to the end.

"Well, what do you expect? He wasn't a hotshot jock, was he?" Anneke was startled by the vicious sarcasm in his voice. "Damn. Look, I'm sorry." He stood up, putting down his coffee cup with a clatter. "Thanks for the coffee. I'd better finish shoveling."

Now what was that all about? Anneke wondered when he was gone. She felt depressed and out of sorts, whatever gladness remained from Karl's return irretrievably gone. She turned pages of the newspaper idly.

To her surprise, Brenda Roper's face jumped out at her, under a short article about the art museum's upcoming costume exhibition. The opening-night benefit gala—tickets fifty dollars a head—was to feature "prominent local women" modeling various outfits. In the grainy picture, Brenda wore what seemed to be a long, dark cape, probably velvet, with a high stand-up collar and a tiny hat with feathery tufts at the sides. Even on Brenda it looks silly, Anneke thought, rising from the table to face the day.

The main streets, at least, were clear, thank God—much as she loved her Alfa, she had to concede it was a lousy snow car. She went first to her office, unsurprised to see Ken, Marcia, and a sophomore named Max Farber all busy at their computers on a Sunday morning. Students tended to grab work hours when and as they could, and the period between semesters offered them a rare stretch of free time.

"Hi, Anneke," Ken greeted her. "That's a hell of a thing about James Kenneally."

"I know," she said briefly, aware of three pairs of eyes on her.

"Right in your own front yard, too," Marcia said with a shudder that might have been ghoulish or sympathetic.

"Do you know where we stored all those old games?" Anneke asked repressively, repelled by their curiosity even as she acknowledged it as a normal human trait.

"I think there's a box in the Sun room," Ken said, casting a glance at Marcia.

"That's right, there is." She found the collection of discs, riffled through them looking for something to interest a nine-year-old boy, and took her collection with her, pausing only to give Ken instructions for tomorrow. Then she headed the Alfa south to Briarwood and more shopping.

She bought sensible things, like shoes and bath soap, and then splurged on a nightgown of foamy black lace. On impulse she stopped at the men's department and bought a black velour robe to replace the one of Karl's that had hung in her bedroom closet. He'd never stay overnight in the cottage, of course; that bed might be big enough for many things, but sleep wasn't one of them. Still, it would be nice for him to have a robe there. And possibly dinner tonight, she thought, making a final stop at a gourmet take-out shop before heading home.

There was a police car parked on Division, Anneke noticed when she turned into Mackinac Court. And Ross had apparently been watching for her, for he popped out of his house as she appeared, followed more slowly by Harvey.

"Hi, Miss Haagen," the boy said hesitantly, looking over his shoulder at his father.

"Hi, Ross." She paused to get a better grip on her parcels. "Would you like some computer time?"

"Yeah, that'd be neat. I guess . . ." His voice trailed off as his father caught up with them.

"Uh, Miss Haagen," he said fretfully, "are you sure that Ross . . . that is, he's spending an awful lot of time with you. . . . I mean, I don't want him to be a nuisance."

"He's not a nuisance," Anneke declared. "He's a delight. What's more," she added, grabbing the opportunity, "he's a natural programmer. He has enormous talent, and he really should have a computer of his own." She saw Ross's face light up.

"Still . . ." Harvey's voice was irresolute. "He's spending an awful lot of time stuck indoors with that thing, uh, that is, he's not doing anything else, is he? I mean, shouldn't he be outside playing baseball or something?"

"I'm sure he'll want to do that, too," Anneke soothed, "when it's the season for it."

"Well, but . . ." Harvey's further mutterings were halted by the arrival of two police cars. Two uniformed officers climbed from one of them and waited next to it; Brad Weinmann alighted from the other. Even before he had reached the center of the courtyard,

Prof appeared from the direction of the barn and stalked toward him; Anneke could swear she saw the light of battle in the old man's eyes.

"I'm glad to find you here," Brad greeted the small group, casting a slight smile at Anneke. "I'd like to ask each of you for your help. I'm sure you'd like to get this cleared up even more than we would."

"What sort of help?" Prof asked sharply. Harvey said nothing, but looked nervous.

"We'd like your permission to examine the contents of your medicine cabinets."

Whatever they had been expecting, it wasn't that. Even Prof was momentarily nonplussed, but he rallied quickly.

"You got a warrant?"

"No, sir." Brad was fastidiously polite. "That's why we're asking for your voluntary cooperation."

"And if we refuse, of course, we'll jump to the top of the suspect list."

"If you refuse, we just note the refusal," Brad responded matter-of-factly.

"I'll bet." Prof gave no quarter. "And I suppose there's a legitimate object to this fishing expedition?"

Brad hesitated, as if seeking the right word.

"We're searching for the murder weapon used to kill James Kenneally," he said finally.

"In medicine cabinets?" Anneke blurted in surprise.

"I thought he was strangled," Prof said in a more moderate tone, his hostility for once abated by curiosity.

"He was," Brad agreed.

"Then what the hell are you hunting for? Well?" He glared as Brad paused once more. "If you want to go rooting through my things, you're damn well gonna have to tell me what you're looking for."

"Okay," Brad said finally. "The lab says that James Kenneally was strangled with dental floss."

"With *what?*" "Dental floss?" "But that's ridiculous." They all seemed to be talking at once. Brad started to respond, then stopped, because as he opened his mouth to speak there was a kind of squawk from Harvey Barlow, and when they turned toward him his face had gone dead white.

"It wasn't me!" Harvey blubbed, staring around wildly. "Everyone has dental floss. Just because I'm a dentist doesn't mean . . . I know what you're thinking, that just because I'm a dentist I'm a failure, that I wasn't good enough to be a doctor. If I were a doctor you wouldn't try to pin this on me—oh no, you'd be all nice and polite and respectful. Well you're wrong, that's all. I hardly even knew James Kenneally, couldn't stand him, why would I kill him?"

"Oh, good grief," Prof muttered.

"Dr. Barlow, believe me, we don't suspect anyone yet," Brad said, irritation in his voice. "We're asking permission to examine everyone's medicine cabinets, not just yours. In fact, if you'll go along to your house with one of these officers, we'll get it done and you can stop worrying about it." He moved his head slightly, and one of the uniformed figures detached itself from the police car and drifted toward them.

"Harvey, hadn't you better take Ross back to the house?" Anneke saw the conflicting emotions on the boy's face, anxiety and concern mixed with embarrassed contempt.

"Yes, please, Dr. Barlow." Brad's use of his title seemed to calm Harvey somewhat.

"Ross, you come by later for a computer session, okay?" Anneke said. The boy hesitated and glanced at his father before nodding jerkily.

"I wouldn't have figured dental floss'd be strong enough," Prof said thoughtfully as the Barlows moved away, trailed by a young police officer. He flexed his strong fingers experimentally.

"And anyway, what's the point of searching for it?" Anneke asked. "Even if you find some of it, it won't prove anything, will it? I mean, everybody uses dental floss."

"It's just routine," Brad answered uninformatively. "Well, Professor Carfax? Do we have your permission?"

"If you take my dental floss, you better believe you're gonna pay me for it," Prof snarled.

"We will." Brad took Prof's demand for acquiescence. "Ms. Haagen? If we may?"

"Yes, of course." He was being professional and serious, and she was careful to respond in kind. For the first time it occurred to her that her presence here presented Karl with a potentially tricky situation.

"Officer Zelisco will go along with you." He handed her over to the young patrolman who had once been his partner, and who also carefully made no mention of their previous acquaintance until they were inside her cottage.

"Sorry, Anneke, but . . ." He spread his hands, looking uncomfortable.

"Don't be silly, Jim." She laughed and set down her parcels. "Go ahead—the bathroom is through there." He disappeared through the bedroom door and reappeared moments later. "Did you find it all right?" she asked.

"One container of dental floss, present and accounted for," he said with a smile.

"Like every other medicine cabinet in the world," she said, shaking her head. "What on earth is the point of a search like that? No, sorry." She withdrew the question hastily. "I didn't mean to put you on the spot." She changed the subject. "How are your classes going?"

"Pretty good," he said. "I should have my master's by next year." They chatted briefly, and when he left she unpacked her purchases, turned on the television set, and settled down to watch the San Diego Chargers lay out the Miami Dolphins in the second round of the NFL play-offs.

Damn this place. Albert Carfax aimed a vicious kick at the aged cabinet door, wishing it were that cop—the one with the shit-eating smirk just below the surface. The cabinet door retaliated by slamming against its jamb and caroming back, catching him neatly on the shin. He and Eleanor'd always meant to remodel the kitchen, but somehow they'd never gotten around to it. There always seemed to be more interesting things to do with their time and money.

Money. He kicked the cabinet again, more carefully this time, before he put the frying pan on the stove. While he watched the butter melt, he mentally subtracted the cost of a concert ticket from his January budget. He had a choice—the Dylan concert, or two biology department TGIF's at Dominick's, or one decent lid. Well, Dylan in Ann Arbor was a once-more-in-a-lifetime event; even if the guy's voice was gone, the power was still there, the poetry and passion still running pure and clear. Still angry after all these years.

Anger was something he understood. The anger was about all that kept him going these days; if he gave up, as he'd wanted to when Eleanor died, it would mean the bastards had finally beaten him. He no longer believed in the possibility of social change, in the value of political action, but activism had become a habit that was easier to continue than to break. Besides, he thought, the kids in the department need someone like me around to keep them from swallowing the nineties bait whole. On his better days, he sometimes believed that, just maybe, he'd be able to make a difference through one of them.

This wasn't one of his better days. He beat two eggs together briefly in a cup and poured them into the sizzling frying pan. He'd always been the pessimist in the family; it was Eleanor who'd been the optimist, the one who really believed that the marches, and the speeches, and the bumper stickers would actually change the face of the world.

He'd been an untenured assistant professor in the bad old days, when three tenured faculty members were sacrificed on the altar of Joe McCarthy. His parents had been General Motors line workers, but he was the first of his family to attend college, and he'd kept his head down and his mouth shut.

In 1968, he was a quietly respected full professor when the first Eugene McCarthy for President committee was formed, in a hotel room on the outskirts of Ann Arbor. He'd spoken of it, laughing, as "McCarthy to McCarthy in one generation," but it was an opportunity to atone for his earlier cowardice—and more, he discovered that he loved the action, the excitement of being at the center of major events, the swirling frenzy of Ann Arbor politics in the sixties.

He and Eleanor had been far older than their colleagues in the Movement, nearly fifty at a time when the kids didn't trust anyone over thirty. It amused them both, and pleased Eleanor immoderately, that they became a kind of role model for the kids around them, proof that it was possible to age without selling out.

If we'd sold out, I wouldn't be stuck in this crumbling pile of a house, he thought, scraping the eggs onto a plate and carrying them over to the threadbare sofa. More important than that—if we'd sold out, at least my life would be my own doing, my own creative act. Better to be a victimizer than a victim.

Once the cops left, he'd better make another trip to the barn.

TEN

· · · · · ·

Somewhat to Anneke's surprise, Ross showed up in the afternoon as promised, and as she had expected, he'd read his way through the DOS manual and was hungry for more. She worked with him for a while on the further mysteries of BASIC and then got him involved in an old version of Space Merchants. He seemed to have shaken off the scene outside; at least he made no mention of it, and Anneke was glad enough to know that it hadn't caused him to avoid her. She was, she realized, becoming alarmingly fond of the child.

He left finally, reluctant as always, when she shooed him home for dinner. The Chargers-Dolphins game had ended, and for a while she watched the San Francisco 49ers destroying the Chicago Bears, fascinated as always by the balletic spectacle. She had just about decided that Steve Young to Jerry Rice was the best combination in the history of football when there was a knock on the door.

"Hi." Karl came in stamping snow off his shoes. "Do you have a cup of coffee for a weary cop?"

"I think I could manage one," she said, smiling. "There's even some clam chowder and a couple of croissants."

"Sounds good. How's the game going?" He sat down on the sofa, setting his briefcase on the floor next to him.

"The Niners are up by twenty-one; they've just started the second half. Why don't you relax and watch while I get us some food."

They ate off trays on the sofa, watching the game and laughing when they discovered their drastically different takes on it.

"And they call themselves a great defense," Karl grumbled as Rice burned the Chicago cornerback for a forty-five-yard reception.

"No one has a defense good enough to handle that," she maintained. "I think I'm in love with Steve Young." She put her hand over her heart. "Did you see that pass? Scrambling backward out of the pocket, off balance, throwing across his body and still hitting his receiver twenty yards downfield? Absolutely fantastic. Besides," she teased, "he's gorgeous."

"You superficial fans always go for that quarterback tinsel-and-glitter, don't you? *Real* football people know that the defense is the most important part of the game. Oh, *tackle* the man, for God's sake," he growled at the television set.

As the game wound down, and Young hit Brent Jones in the end zone for one more score, Karl made a disgusted noise and turned away from the screen.

"Anyway, this isn't why I came," he said, reaching for his briefcase.

"Sore loser."

"Damn right." He looked at her oddly. "You know what they call a good loser? A loser." He extracted a file folder from the briefcase, looked through it for a moment, and then turned back to her. "What can you tell me about James Kenneally?"

"Not much." She spread her hands. "Nothing that's not on the record, certainly." She looked at the file folder.

"I don't mean that." He shook his head and replaced the folder in his briefcase. "What was he like? What kind of man was he?"

"He was . . . difficult," Anneke said slowly. "Very talented, of course; brilliant, really, and impatient with everyone else who wasn't. I suppose you could say he was arrogant," she concluded sadly.

"You liked him, didn't you?" That datum, too, he seemed to file away in his head. "Did he strike you as an impetuous person?"

"You're thinking about this Chicago trip, aren't you?" she said. "You mean, would he have gone haring off to Chicago on a whim?" She stared into space, trying to fix James in her mind. "Oddly enough, I'd say no. He *seemed* impulsive sometimes, but I think actually he was just terribly *focused.*"

"You mean he followed his own train of thought without worrying about other people."

"Yes, and that can look like impulsiveness because other people can't see the premises you're working from."

"It can also be dangerous," Karl commented. "It's easy to forget that other people aren't just props in your own personal script."

"Do you think this Chicago trip had anything to do with his murder?"

"Maybe. He doesn't seem to have planned it in advance—just picked up and left." He grimaced at the television screen, where various 49ers were celebrating rather calmly.

"Do you miss it?" she asked quietly.

"Only this time of year." He turned the ugly Super Bowl ring on his finger half-consciously.

"I still don't understand that search for dental floss," she said, trying to turn his thoughts. "Wouldn't you find some in nearly every medicine cabinet?"

"Ordinary floss, yes." He turned from the television set. "That's the kind you use. But what Kenneally was strangled with was the extra-thick, strong kind, called 'dental tape.' It was still there, wrapped around his neck—it had dug in pretty deeply." To Anneke's relief, he didn't go into further detail.

"Dental tape." Focusing on the weapon was a way to avoid thinking about the body. "I've seen it in drugstores—it isn't particularly rare, is it?"

"Not rare, no, but it's much less commonly used than the ordinary kind. We called one of the big drugstore chains, and they told us that dental tape accounts for only eighteen percent of all floss sales nationwide. Searching for it seemed worth a shot, at least. Unfortunately, all we found in the medicine cabinets was the ordinary kind."

"Even if you had found it, though," Anneke said dubiously, "it wouldn't really have proven anything, would it?"

"Not proof, certainly, but information. It's the sort of thing that has to be done, that's all. And in fact," he added, "the *absence* of dental tape is more interesting than its presence would have been. If there isn't any here, where did it come from?"

"Yes." She thought for a moment. "What strikes me most is, *why* dental floss? Or dental tape, or whatever? Why would anyone even think of such a thing?"

"I have absolutely no idea." Karl shook his head.

Uneasily, Anneke recalled Prof's hands, pantomiming strangulation. She mimicked the same motion. It's ridiculous," she remarked. "And besides, wouldn't it hurt your hands, pulling on it? And if he struggled, how could you keep a grip on something like dental floss, even the thick kind, without cutting your hands?" The mental images she conjured up were mildly sickening, visions of mad activity in a snow-covered landscape. "Oh, of course— gloves. You'd be wearing gloves anyway in this weather, wouldn't you?"

"Well, yes and no," he said. "We're assuming the killer used gloves, but to protect his hands from the floss, not from the cold. It's fairly certain that Kenneally wasn't killed where you found him, and most likely that he was killed indoors. For one thing, his jacket was open and his gloves were lying next to him, which seems unlikely if he'd been outdoors. And there were marks on his clothes that suggest the body had been dragged. We also think," he added, "that he was knocked unconscious before being strangled; we won't be positive until the full autopsy report comes in, but there were marks suggesting a blow to the back of the head."

"Hmm. James was no lightweight. If he was killed indoors and then dragged outside afterward, doesn't that mean it was probably a man?"

"Not necessarily. You'd be amazed at what a hundred-pound woman can do if she has to."

"Could he have been carried into the court from outside?" Anneke grasped at straws, hoping that perhaps it wasn't, after all, someone she knew.

"Possibly, although not likely, given the depth and definition of the footprints in the entry. But even so, the murderer couldn't have gotten *out* of the court or there would have been another set of footprints leaving. We examined the areas behind all the houses, along the fence, and the entire perimeter of the court was absolutely untouched snow. Whoever it was and however it was done, the murderer belongs to Mackinac Court."

Anneke sighed, recognizing facts when she saw them. "I take it he didn't have anything to indicate what he'd been doing in Chicago?"

"Not that we can see." He reached for the file folder again and extracted a sheet of paper. "Here, take a look at this and see if anything strikes you."

The paper was a list of the contents of James's pockets and backpack, and she read it first with a feeling of intrusion and then, as she concentrated, with growing interest. From his pockets, the normal things—wallet, a packet of tissues, and half a Tootsie Roll. From the backpack, more revealing items—one pair of soiled underpants, one pair of dirty socks, a plaid shirt, electric razor, comb, toothbrush, three paperback books (two science fiction, one Baudrillard), pocketknife, drafting tools, pens, the omnipresent notebook.

"Wasn't there a ticket stub?" she asked, rereading the list.

"No." Karl shook his head. "He must have thrown it away."

"Are you sure he didn't get back before Friday night?"

"Yes. We talked to the conductor of the Twilight Limited and showed him a picture of Kenneally. He remembered him very well, partly because he was so tall and partly because the train was fairly empty. It was New Year's Eve, after all. Kenneally was a passenger, all right. The train got in at eleven-forty-five Friday night, only a couple of minutes late. Kenneally got out at Ann Arbor. And what locks it in is that he took a cab from the station. He was dropped off at the entrance to the court around midnight."

"Did he? That surprises me a bit, even with the blizzard," Anneke commented. "Kids his age, boys anyway, don't usually spend money on cab fare if they can help it. And it had stopped snowing by then." She returned her attention to the list with the feeling that something else was missing. "The notebook. Was there anything in it to show what he'd been doing in Chicago?"

"If you're talking about that spiral-bound notebook that was in his backpack, there wasn't anything in it at all. It was nothing but blank pages."

"Blank? Nothing in it at all?" Anneke stared at him. "That's impossible."

"Why?" Karl looked at her alertly.

"You'd have to know James. He never went anywhere without a notebook, and he was *always* scribbling in it. Sketches, notes, ideas — that notebook was practically an extension of his body. He'd just spent the day in Chicago, and five hours on a train with nothing else to do? There's no *way* that notebook would be blank."

"Maybe he filled one in Chicago, decided he'd come up dry and threw it away."

"Never." Anneke shook her head positively. "He told me once he was saving them all so he could do a retrospective of his work in twenty years. He meant it, too." Poor James. He'd been so confident, so arrogant about his abilities. And from overheard comments in his office, Anneke suspected his talent might almost have matched his confidence. Now there would be no great works, no retrospective.

"Wait a minute." She had a sudden thought.

"What?" Karl waited expectantly, but she hesitated. She wanted to be sure first.

"Could I possibly take a look at something in James's room?" she asked uncertainly.

"Yes, of course," he said. Instead of asking questions, he stood up immediately and gathered up their coats.

"Kenneally's room is still exactly as he left it," Karl said as they crunched across the snowy courtyard. "It's been gone over, of course, but since I don't know what you're looking for, I can't tell you if it's there." It was the closest he came to asking any questions, and Anneke appreciated his forbearance.

A blast of sound greeted them as they opened the front door. Karl nodded briefly to the young policeman sitting on a folding chair in the tiny hall, then led her into the living room, where the source of the noise was revealed to be a big color television, tuned to MTV and blasting an anonymous rock video. Cass and Gail were sitting cross-legged at opposite ends of a dilapidated sofa, textbooks and papers spread around them. To Anneke's surprise, Prof was with them, sprawled on a chair and watching the televised gyrations with a sneer.

The television had covered the sound of their entrance, and both girls jumped when Anneke approached.

"Ms. Haagen! Come in. Sorry about the mess." Cass jumped from the sofa, scattering papers, and turned off the television, ignoring Anneke's protest.

"Please, don't let us disturb your studying."

"That's okay, I'm glad to get a chance for a break. Can I get you some coffee, or a beer? Oh, I guess not." Genesko's presence registered suddenly on the girl, cutting off her ebullience like an iron wall descending. "Did you want to talk to me?"

"No, we need to look at something in James's room," Anneke answered uncomfortably, feeling like an intruder. Which, after all, I am, she thought, looking around the shabby room. There were two overstuffed chairs along with the sofa, all so old that it was impossible to guess what their original color had been. Along one wall, books and papers and anonymous bits of clothing spilled across a scarred buffet and onto the floor. Against this squalor, a beautiful contemporary print in bold colors seemed to leap out at her from the far wall, and a handsome chrome floor lamp threw a glow over a fine stained-glass panel hanging against the front window. In other words, the usual student mixture.

"It's a real pit, isn't it?" Cass shrugged, following Anneke's gaze. "But the location's so great it's worth it for a year."

"I know. This isn't the time of your life for nest building, anyway."

"I wish my mother got that. She walks in here and she's like, how can you live like this? I don't know what I'm going to do if she finds out about James."

"Haven't you told her?" Anneke asked in surprise.

"No!" Cass said explosively. "And I'm not going to. She'd only try to drag me home, and I won't go." She looked at Anneke appealingly. "You know what parents are like."

"She'll read about it in the papers, you know." Anneke felt idiotically complimented to be included among those who "know what parents are like," rather than those who were like parents, even as she found her own parental mechanisms operating. "Won't it be worse if she finds out about it from someone else?"

"She won't. At least not until it's over, and by then it won't matter. Besides," Cass continued reasonably, "what about classes? This is our last semester. I'm all right. Really I am."

She was, too, Anneke concluded. Cass was one of the tough ones, the uncommon kind who give rise to the myth of youthful resilience. Gail, she thought, was different.

"How about you?" she asked the other girl, noting the red-rimmed eyes behind fashionable rimless glasses.

"I can't call my parents. They'd absolutely zone out." Gail looked seriously frightened at the thought of her parents' reaction. "I'd be dragged home tomorrow."

"Anyway, this *is* home," Cass interjected. "Besides, Prof says he doesn't mind spending the night here with us."

"Mind?" The old man was still capable of a healthy leer. "Best offer I've had in years." He looked at Anneke from under lowered brows, and she hesitated. Surely the girls needed . . . well, what?

She looked at them more closely. They were both pale and tired-looking; their shoulders were hunched tightly, and the muscles in Gail's back twitched with tension, but their faces were determined. They weren't yet quite all right, perhaps, but they would be. Besides, Prof wasn't the worst person to talk things over with.

"It's not so bad for us," Gail said, staring at the ground. "But Dennis is going to be totally blown, y'know?"

"Is he here?" Anneke asked.

"No, he's visiting his parents in Ohio." Cass's voice broke slightly. "I don't think he's going to come back."

"Oh God, it's so awful—how can he stand it?" Gail gave a rasping gulp. "Oh God, poor Dennis." She burst out crying, great harsh sobs that she muffled by burying her face in her hands. Cass stared into the distance, not touching her friend.

"They really did love each other." Cass spoke the words into the air, as if testing them. "It was . . . real, you know?" she said to Anneke, almost in surprise.

"I think I do know," Anneke answered, feeling a sense of enormous anger and wishing she had a target for it.

She followed Karl up the creaking staircase, past two closed doors whose surfaces were plastered with bulletin boards, posters, and cartoons clipped from newspapers, their edges curled and yellowing. Cass's and Gail's rooms, presumably. She got a glimpse of a black-and-white-tiled bathroom with an old claw-footed bathtub, and then they were standing at the back of the house, in front of another door. This one was covered with a single poster, announcing a Gay Pride march in San Francisco, the date more than a year old.

There was a police lock on the door to James's room. Karl bent to unlock it, pushed open the door and stood aside, allowing Anneke to enter first. She stood in the doorway for a moment, getting her bearings.

Clearly, this had once been the master bedroom. It was spacious and airy, with windows opening out on two sides. And it contained two of everything—twin beds pushed side by side, matching dressers, two identical desks, even two closets.

"I take it James and Dennis shared this room, and Cass and Gail had the two smaller rooms," Anneke said. Karl nodded, unspeaking, waiting patiently for her to proceed. But still she looked around, trying to absorb the room, to get some sense of James from it.

It seemed, at first glance, like any student room anywhere, a slovenly jumble of clothing, magazines, soft-drink cans, half-empty bags of unspeakable junk foods, and unidentifiable detritus. But that was only part of it, she realized. True, the beds and dressers and most of the floor were covered with litter, but desks and shelves, while crowded with items, were scrupulously neat. Books were lined on their shelves in military precision, pens stood at attention in mugs set precisely on the desks, and file folders were neatly arrayed in cardboard file boxes, their labels carefully facing front.

"This must have belonged to James," she said, moving to stand in front of a framed engraving. It was a tiny, almost miniature view of a Greek-pillared avenue, marching into the distance in a breathtaking tour de force of perspective. The paper was brown with age and frayed along the edges and Anneke was positive it was an authentic Renaissance work. She tore herself away from the tiny masterpiece with a sigh and turned to the bookshelves.

"This is what I was looking for," she said, kneeling in front of a row of spiral-bound notebooks. She pulled out several of them at random and looked at the covers. "They're all dated," she pointed out. "And they're sequential—day, month, and year, all in chronological order without any breaks between dates." She opened one at random, to a small sketch of a building she almost recognized. Under the sketch were notes in James's careful square handwriting. One of them said: "Space as conspicuous consumption."

"Are you looking for something specific?" Karl asked.

"Not exactly. I want to count the pages."

"I see." Karl took one of the notebooks from her and examined the cover. "These are all one-hundred-sheet notebooks. All right, let's count."

It was boring work, and Anneke had to force herself not to stop and examine pages; the small sketches, sometimes three or four to a page, were lively and incisive. When she had counted the pages in two of the notebooks, she looked at Karl.

"Well?"

"A full one hundred pages in the two of them I counted. How about yours?"

"The same. Is there a pattern to the dates?"

"I don't think so." He looked at the notebook in his hand. "March eighteenth to May fourth. And this other one is May fifth to July twenty-ninth. No, he just seems to have filled them up as he went along and then started on another. Excuse me." He moved to the small night table, swept a pair of socks aside with an expression of distaste, and picked up the phone.

"Put me through to Janet Ryan, please," he said into the receiver, then: "Jan, will you please get the notebook that was found in Kenneally's backpack and count the pages? And I also want to know the dates on the cover." He remained standing during the long wait, and Anneke passed the time browsing through the bookshelves. Dennis was obviously in anthropology; there were long stretches of books on Native Americans, on ethnobotany, on kinship rites. But his side of the double bookshelf also contained an array of philosophy texts and, surprisingly, several volumes of contemporary poetry. An interesting mind, she concluded.

"Thank you." Karl scribbled into his own small notebook and put down the telephone. Anneke looked at him expectantly.

"There were only seventy-three pages in the notebook he had with him—which means he used twenty-seven pages and someone tore them out."

"Even twenty-seven pages would be too few for five days in Chicago," Anneke said, thinking out loud. "I'd give long odds that there was another whole notebook that was also taken. What about the dates?"

"It had only one date. December twenty-sixth."

"Of course. He'd put the starting date on it, and then add the ending date when he put the notebook away. But December twenty-sixth? That was"—she did the quick calculation—"last Sunday, wasn't it?"

"Right. And he left for Chicago on the thirtieth."

"There's something else," Anneke said suddenly. "He was in my cottage on the afternoon of the thirtieth, and he was scribbling in his notebook while he was there. Whatever he wrote then would have been in this current notebook."

"Well, it's not there anymore." They looked at each other, neither feeling the need to fill in the verbal gap. Someone had removed those pages from James's notebook.

"It has to be something about Division Square," she said finally.

"Not necessarily."

"Not proven, but . . ."

"It could have something to do with the gay connection. It's possible that the notebooks contained a list of names that someone didn't want known."

"Not likely. Remember, he'd just gotten in from Chicago. It *had* to be notes from there, and that means it had to be connected to Division Square."

"Why?" He held up his hand as she started to protest. "I'll grant you that his notes from Chicago are gone, but remember, we still have no idea what he went to Chicago *for*. There's no proof that it didn't have something to do with his gay work. Whoever took the pages might simply have ripped out everything, just to be sure."

She could find no legitimate objection to his line of reasoning; she was simply sure in her own mind that Division Square was the key.

They walked back to her cottage in silence, and he picked up his briefcase as soon as they were inside.

"I'll be working late again tonight," he said. "If you think of anything more, let me know, all right?"

"Of course." She walked to the door with him, and he kissed her lightly before he left. Feeling rather abandoned, she sat down at the computer and hit her SimEarth world with a big, satisfying earthquake.

ELEVEN

Monday morning, Ann Arbor was a madhouse.

I should have expected it, Anneke told herself grimly, ramming the accelerator of the Alfa and hurling the little car in front of a station wagon crammed with furniture. The day after vacation, dorms reopening, students scrambling back into town, people anxious to make up for lost time—and all of them, apparently, out on the streets at once. She cut in front of a car with Virginia license plates and a mattress tied to its roof, then jammed on the brakes as a Cadillac from New York slowed to a crawl, waited for the green light to turn amber, and then jolted through the intersection, leaving her fuming at the red.

"My God, it's a zoo out there," she said when she finally got to the office.

"I know." Ken Scheede grinned at her. "But once the parents get out of town, it'll be okay."

"I suppose," she grumbled. "The students themselves aren't the real problem, I guess; at least they don't drive around town at ten miles an hour sight-seeing." She dumped her briefcase on her desk. "All right, what've we got on for today?"

"Three messages from LifeSites." Ken held out a sheaf of pink phone memos.

"Oh, hell, that's right." She'd managed to put the murder out of her mind, but now she remembered her last conversation with James. "They're having trouble with their plotter, aren't they?"

"It's worse than that," Ken said soberly. "They sounded really freaked; seems that James was the one doing most of their CAD work, and they've got a big project due."

"All right." Anneke sighed. "I'll go. Although in this traffic, it'll probably take me half the morning."

It took her, in fact, nearly twenty minutes to cover the four miles from the Maynard Street parking structure out to the south edge of town, where LifeSites, Inc., had its suite of modish offices. Inside, she strode to the flashy state-of-the-art reception desk and smiled at the receptionist.

"Hi, Felicia. Hear you've got some problems."

"Oh, Ms. Haagen." The receptionist looked relieved. "Mr. Seligson's been frantic. I'll ring him."

"Anneke, thank God you're here." Dave Seligson hurried out of a side door looking frazzled. "Isn't it awful about James?"

"Yes, it is." Anneke nodded soberly at the short, stocky man whose unprepossessing face gave no hint of his truly sweet nature.

"I hate like hell to worry about business at a time like this." He spread his hands, looking genuinely sorrowful. "But there are other people depending on us. And I'm no expert on CAD work, as you know. James was so damn good I didn't have to bother. And now . . ." He shrugged. "Think you can teach me the basics?"

"Not personally; I'm no CAD expert either. I can send you someone, of course, but won't you have to hire someone to replace James anyway?"

"We will, of course, but we need someone who's familiar with the project we're doing right now. Well, I guess I'm not that hopeless," he admitted. "Every architect's done some CAD work."

"I know. I imagine you're a lot better than you think. Anyway—" She was interrupted by the appearance of Chuck Diamond at the door to his office.

"Anneke, glad to see you. Come on in." The president of Life-Sites, Inc., wore his usual expression of leashed intensity, but there was humor in the quirk of his lips. "You too, Dave." He turned to the receptionist. "Felicia, would you get us some coffee, please? And then call Washington Peripherals and tell them they have exactly one week to deliver or we find another company to do business with. You know the routine."

He ushered them into his office, a whirlwind of activity, but when he sank into the huge leather chair behind his enormous desk, he contrived to appear relaxed and affable, the perfect host. Anneke recalled that he had built LifeSites entirely on his own efforts, from a one-man hole-in-the-wall office to one of the biggest architecture and planning companies in the midwest.

"Ah, good, thank you," he said to Felicia when she deposited a coffee tray and a pink message slip on his desk. He looked at the slip of paper, murmured something to the receptionist, and leaned back with his coffee.

"We're in something of a state of confusion, I'm afraid," he said, with no hint of apology in his voice. "It's not easy to concentrate on business when human tragedy intrudes—especially when it's one of your finest people."

"I hadn't realized James was quite so integral to your operation," Anneke said. "He was only part-time, wasn't he?"

"Some people accomplish more in less time than others. James was an intuitive. Know what I mean?"

"Yes." Like Ross at the computer, Anneke thought. There were intuitives in every field, the rare ones who grasped the essentials instinctively and moved on from there. "What exactly was he working on here?"

"It's a downtown shopping mall." Seligson leaned forward to explain. "We're designing an enclosure to cover three downtown blocks in Des Moines, make them competitive with suburban shopping centers."

"What was James's role?"

"Well, technically he was hired to do the CAD work for us, but he went far beyond that. We'd give him a design, and when we got the simulation back, he always seemed to've changed it, and he was always right." Dave Seligson's eyes glowed; where one might have expected jealousy there was only appreciation of ability. Anneke's already-high opinion of Seligson rose even higher. Chuck Diamond watched him with avuncular fondness.

"He was working directly for you?" she asked Seligson.

"Yes; I'm the project manager for the mall."

"Did he tell you why he was going to Chicago?" Anneke asked hopefully.

"He didn't even tell me he *was* going," Seligson replied, spreading his hands.

"So you don't know what the trip was for?"

"Not a clue." Seligson shook his head helplessly.

"Was there anyone else here he might have talked to about it?"

"No." Seligson shook his head again, firmly. "James didn't socialize much with many of the people here. I guess maybe . . ." His voice trailed away.

"Because he was gay?" Anneke asked.

"Partly that, I suppose," Seligson agreed. "But also because . . . well, you knew him."

"Yes. He wasn't the easiest person in the world to get along with."

"We didn't care about his personal life, you know," Diamond stated firmly, as if making an affirmative-action statement.

"Are you sure nobody here cared?" Anneke probed.

"If they did, they kept it to themselves," Diamond insisted, and Seligson nodded agreement.

"Even if they'd objected, James was so damned good, it would have backfired, and everyone knew it. I never heard of any problems. Even his manner was accepted; it was just how he was, and people respected him too much to object."

So they were one big happy family, Anneke mused as she drove back up State Street after reinstalling the plotter driver. Well, maybe in his work life James *was* less abrasive and self-absorbed than he was elsewhere. But, recalling the work she'd done with him at the LifeSites offices, she rather doubted it.

Back in the office, she sat down and looked mournfully at the clutter of papers covering her desk. The Quentin project, a fascinating LAN problem, beckoned seductively, and she reached for the folder, then withdrew her hand with a sigh and picked up the folder of billing statements, swearing under her breath.

Honestly, she thought, running her eye down the columns of numbers, I spend more time on this crap than I do at the computer. What she loved about her work was the programming itself, the creation of elegant algorithms that turned a collection of inanimate chips into a living entity. Instead, somewhere along the line she'd turned into an administrator, spending most of her time endlessly shuffling papers and filling out forms.

She was interrupted once by a call from the insurance company with news about the salvage operation, none of it good. They were writing off her house as totaled; they had recovered the remains of her small collection of Art Deco jewelry, now nothing but scrap metal. She told the adjuster to go ahead and take care of it all, then stared unseeingly at the papers in front of her for a while before bleakly returning to work.

At one o'clock, she looked up in surprise to see Karl standing in front of her desk.

"I have just about half an hour for lunch." He smiled at her. "Can you break loose and join me?"

"I think so." Anneke looked down at the Michigan tax forms she'd been struggling with and made a face. "God, yes, get me out of here." She looked around the office; Ken was gone, but Marcia was sitting at the Mac, looking at Karl out of the corner of her eye.

"Marcia, are you on for the rest of the afternoon?"

"Just until three." The girl tore her eyes away from Karl. "I need to get a class override this afternoon."

"Okay, I'll be back long before then." Anneke smiled to herself as she gathered up her coat and saw Marcia's eyes drift back to the big man standing relaxed by the desk; she forgot sometimes how impressive he looked.

"Is the Cottage Inn all right?" he asked as they descended the steps to the Arcade.

"Fine," she said, shivering as the cold struck her. "The closer the better."

When they were seated in the wood-paneled booth and had ordered their lunches, he took a small rectangular box from his pocket and handed it across the table to her.

"What is it?" she asked.

"Just something I thought you should have."

She lifted the lid of the box, drew in her breath sharply, and stared wide-eyed at him.

"You like it, I hope?" he asked.

"*Like* it?" She released the inner clasp and drew out the glittering wristwatch almost reverently. It was a small platinum and diamond rectangle by Vacheron & Constantin on a matching platinum mesh band; late twenties, she guessed from the superb Art Deco numbers. Two medium-sized diamonds at the top and bottom of the case were surrounded with smaller diamonds in a beautiful Deco pattern, and small diamonds edged both sides of the bracelet.

"It's fabulous. It's . . . My God, I can't accept this." She knew enough about Art Deco jewelry to have a reasonable idea of what the Vacheron had cost him.

"Oh? What a shame." He reached across the table calmly and started to take the watch from her, but her fingers tightened on it convulsively. "Well, you can give it back to me later," he said with the ghost of a smile.

"You bastard." She laughed. She removed the small Seiko she'd bought on one of her shopping expeditions and hooked the Vacheron around her wrist. "Just try to get it away from me."

"Well, that might be interesting," he said thoughtfully.

She swallowed her retort as the waitress arrived with their hamburgers, and Karl grinned slightly, and she felt such a flow of warmth that it dismayed her. How had he become such an integral part of her life? she wondered uneasily. She looked at him over her hamburger, searching for a way to put the relationship in perspective; not to distance it, exactly, but to put it in its place as merely one element of a well-ordered life.

"Can you come for dinner tonight?" she heard herself ask.

"I'm afraid not." He shook his head. "I have to meet with the DA."

"About James?"

"Yes." He made a face. "They want this one cleaned up fast, bless their hearts."

"Have you made any progress?" she asked sympathetically.

"Well, we haven't found any smoking gun yet." He reached into his briefcase and extracted a file folder. "This is what we've been doing so far."

"What is it?"

"Background checks on everyone living in Mackinac Court." He extended the folder toward her.

She started with the Smiths. Both born in Ypsilanti. Not childhood sweethearts, though—T.G. was ten years older than Barbara. Two years in the army, followed by several years in a local real estate office, and then he'd branched out on his own, buying and selling real estate during the boom years of the eighties and pyramiding his holdings into a small fortune. But when the bottom dropped out, T.G. hadn't pulled out in time, and now he was hurting. TGS Enterprises, she was unsurprised to learn, was financially overextended and absolutely dependent on the success of Division Square. The collapse of the project would mean bankruptcy.

"I wonder if Barbara realizes how close a thing it is," she remarked.

"I have a feeling she does, but no evidence to back it up."

"Mmm. I think I agree." Anneke picked up the next dossier.

Harvey Barlow, if anything, was in even worse financial shape than the Smiths. He was three months behind in payments to his ex-wife (which included alimony and court-mandated University tuition), and with a reputation as a second-rate dentist with a not-too-successful practice. His mother's estate consisted of less than five thousand dollars; the house was his only tangible asset.

Joe Roper had been born in Ohio and had come to Michigan on a football scholarship. He'd met the wealthy and beautiful Brenda d'Aumont at a Football Booster Club dinner hosted by her father.

"So she *did* marry the campus football hero," Anneke murmured.

"Not exactly," Karl explained, sipping at his coffee. "Joe was never more than second-string. He earned his keep, but he wasn't pro material and never expected to be. Football was just how he worked his way through college."

"You weren't ever teammates, were you?"

"No. Joe's a good ten years younger than I am."

Brenda's parents had been killed in a small-plane accident, and as the only child, she'd inherited the lot. Financially, the report was slim on specifics; the Ropers appeared to be wealthy, but since their finances were managed by a bank in New York, no details were available. Joe was a tenured professor with the respect of his colleagues, but Education School salaries were well below the big-money level. She moved on to the next report.

"Oh God."

"The report on Carfax?"

"Yes." Anneke kept her gaze on the paper, feeling her eyes swimming.

Twenty years before, Prof had authored a major biology textbook that had brought in fairly substantial royalties. Prudently, he'd banked the lot, saving for his retirement. Then his wife developed cancer, and lived on too long; the health insurance ran out, and the savings went after it. Today, all he had left was Social Security payments and his University pension. And his house.

"No wonder he's so angry."

"Yes. Of course, he was an angry young man back in the sixties, too. Or an angry middle-aged man, at any rate."

The report listed three arrests, one in 1968, two in 1969. Two of the charges, both for disorderly conduct arising out of protest rallies, had been dropped; the third—for possession of marijuana—had resulted in trial and acquittal. In addition, the report noted a search warrant issued for his address in 1971, the object of the search being a local member of the Weather Underground. And finally, the report announced triumphantly, he had once been an officer of the leftist Human Rights party.

"Obviously a dangerous character," Anneke declared, more sarcastically than she intended.

"A man accustomed to acting out his convictions, at any rate."

"I suppose." The next report was headed "Background Investigation, Grover Cleveland Marshall." Pinned to it was a report from the San Francisco police. And as Anneke read it, her eyes widened with surprise.

"Didn't you know?" Karl asked.

"That Cleve was gay? No, I had no idea."

"It's no secret, really. At least not in California. According to the San Francisco police, he's been married under their Domestic Partners Law for three years."

"That does explain why he reacted to James's death the way he did," she commented, aware of a certain inward embarrassment. And she'd been concerned about Cleve's possible interest in her; so much for egocentrism. She laughed grimly at herself and returned to the dossier. Reports on Cleve were all uniformly favorable—he was popular with his colleagues and students, active in University affairs, and a scholar of some note. His finances were in blameless order. In fact, a blameless life altogether.

"He's totally out of the closet, anyway," she said finally.

"In San Francisco, certainly."

"But not here? You don't mean you think it's a motive, do you?"

"It has to be considered, that's all," he said carefully. "We don't know what the relationship was between him and Kenneally."

"There's no reason to assume there was a *relationship*," Anneke said, more angrily than she'd intended. "Everyone says James and Dennis were a settled couple. Are you assuming that every gay man is automatically promiscuous?"

"Not at all. I'd have to ask the same question if they were both straight. And of course, there's the possibility that Marshall's sexual preference puts him at equal risk."

"You mean, if James was murdered because he was gay, Cleve might also be a target?" Karl didn't answer. "But you don't think that *was* the motive, do you?"

"Not really." He shook his head. "There are plenty of crazies out there who occasionally get tanked up and go gay bashing. But I don't think anyone living in Mackinac Court falls into that category."

"T.G. could," she said. "I saw them come to blows on Thursday." She described the fight in the courtyard, and Karl nodded thoughtfully.

"We know about T.G.'s attitudes, of course. He didn't make any secret of it when we questioned him. But that doesn't really change anything. It simply means that if T.G. is the murderer, he had two motives rather than one."

"True." She put down Cleve's dossier and picked up the next one, then looked up, startled, to see Karl grinning. The report was headed: "Background Investigation, Anneke Haagen."

"It never occurred to me." She grimaced at Karl's expression.

"Are you sure you want to read it?" he asked.

"Is there anyone in the world who'd pass up the chance to read a police report on themselves?" But she went through it quickly, aware of Karl's eyes on her, noting details of her divorce (amicable, the report said, with no alimony requested), the names and whereabouts of her two daughters, information about her home and her business, and a reasonably shrewd estimate of her financial situation.

"How boring it sounds," she said finally, feeling uncomfortable for no reason she could fathom. After all, there was nothing there that Karl didn't already know.

"It has its moments." He smiled.

There were three more reports, on the other residents of James's house, but they were sparse and uninteresting. Dennis had definitely been at his parents' home in Ohio. Cass and Gail had no conceivable, or at least discernible, motive; they were not gay, but they were vaguely leftish politically and found James and Dennis mildly romantic.

"It isn't really very helpful, is it?" She passed the sheaf of papers back across the table. "If you eliminate the three students, and the children, you've got eight suspects. And that's including me."

"I think we can both narrow the list down to seven." He smiled briefly as he returned the dossiers to their folder. "But I'm damned if I can narrow it down any further."

TWELVE

· · · · · ·

The icy wind that whistled across the Diag cutting through central campus ruffled the tail of the squirrel that stood aggressively on the path in front of the library, blocking Cleve's way. "Sorry, pal, I haven't got anything for you," he told the furry panhandler, who chittered angrily at him as he passed.

He huddled deeper into his jacket, sniffled as his nose began to run, and slipped on a patch of ice. He pulled the scratchy woolen scarf higher to cover the bottom of his face, then broke into a careful trot; he could cut through the Michigan Union and out the back of the International Center to Division, eliminating one frigid block at least.

He crossed State Street student-style, head down and oblivious to traffic, and plunged through the big oak doors in breathless gratitude for the warmth. God, how could people put up with this year after year?

In San Francisco, winter meant temperatures in the mid-sixties. Of course, summer also meant temperatures in the mid-sixties. Cleve stood in the middle of the lobby and fought back a wave of homesickness. Only another few weeks, he reminded himself; in the meantime, he'd go downstairs to the snack bar and warm himself with some espresso—bad, midwestern espresso, but better than nothing.

But the big poster at the foot of the stairs jolted him further. In screaming red letters, it read:

RALLY
FOR
GAY RIGHTS

and underneath, in scarcely less aggressive lettering:

The Police Don't Care;
We'd Better.

His stomach tightened and he turned away quickly, feeling a sense of vulnerability he hadn't experienced in a long time. In Ann Arbor, he was somehow more consciously—more *self*-consciously—gay than he ever was in San Francisco. There, he was a college professor, and a homeowner, and gay, and a runner, and a movie buff. In Ann Arbor, he was . . . gay, somehow entirely defined by this one aspect of himself.

He knew he'd been a great deal luckier than most gay men. He'd had (fairly) understanding parents (his mother had cried for only a couple of weeks), and he'd had the relative tolerance of San Francisco to ease his own acceptance. But still, there always seemed to be someone demanding something from him he didn't want to give.

Andy would probably have gone to the rally. Cleve thought about his partner, back in San Francisco, and a wave of homesickness washed over him. Right about now, Andy would be at his restaurant preparing for the evening rush, probably laughing at the posturing self-importance of his latest pastry chef. Andy would have gone to the rally and enjoyed it for the spectacle it presented, instead of feeling threatened. Andy made him feel accepted, whole; Andy made him feel safe.

James, on the other hand, had exacerbated his sense of vulnerability, Cleve mused over lukewarm espresso. James hadn't understood when Cleve had declined to join in the marches and the meetings, the demonstrations and support groups. He didn't want support, he shouted silently at the dead man. He only wanted to be left alone, to live his life the way he chose.

By the time Anneke got home, after a distasteful afternoon filled with still more paperwork, it was fully dark. Almost six o'clock, she noted, feeling a surge of pleasure as she checked the Vacheron by the light of the streetlamp. She crunched across the snow, her mind idly contemplating the sparse contents of her refrigerator, so that she didn't see the figure coming up behind her until a hand fell on her arm.

"Oh!" She jumped a foot and stared around wildly.

"I'm sorry." Cleve grinned at her. "I didn't mean to startle you."

"I guess I was on some other planet." Anneke forced a shaky smile, dismayed at the moment of real panic she'd felt.

"No, I really am sorry." He looked at her more closely. "You were really frightened, weren't you?"

"No, it's all right, honestly."

"It's not all right, though, is it?" he said soberly. "The world is a dangerous enough place these days without having to be afraid of your friends as well."

"I wasn't afraid of you," she protested. "I was just startled, that's all."

"Well, you should have been," he responded. "Afraid, I mean. Someone here"—he made a motion to encompass the court—"is a murderer."

"Well, I'm glad to see it was you, then." She smiled.

"Why?" he asked bluntly. "I could just as easily be the murderer as anyone else."

"Don't be silly," she said, hoping he didn't hear the uneasiness in her voice. Why not Cleve, after all? Could she eliminate him as a suspect just because she rather liked him? She felt her shoulders hunch as she fumbled in her purse for her key.

"You know, don't you?" He said it flatly, in a voice totally devoid of either apology or warmth, staring at her coldly in the dim light.

"Know what?" For a moment, she stared at him, confused. "Do I know who killed James, you mean? No, I haven't a clue. Why would you think I . . . Oh. That's not what you meant."

"No, that's not what I meant," he echoed.

"Yes, I know you're gay," she answered, striving for a matter-of-fact tone. "But—"

"May I ask you please," he interrupted, "not to spread it around?"

"Spread it around? Good God, of course not." She was really angry now. "What the hell do you take me for, anyway?"

"For a *het*," he said brutally.

"A . . . for a *what?*" As the meaning of the epithet penetrated, Anneke began to laugh, and after a moment Cleve laughed with her. "Look," she said, "come on in for a drink, will you? Please?" she persisted.

"Okay," he said after a short pause.

Inside, she switched on lights and poured them each a glass of wine, waiting until they were seated before she spoke.

"Look, I'm sorry if I seemed . . ." She made complicated gestures with her hands. "It wasn't what you think."

"That's okay." He shrugged. "I'm sorry I got all bent out of shape. I'm not usually so defensive—at least not back home."

"I guess back home you don't feel you have to hide anything," she said sympathetically.

"I think you misunderstand," he said, a frosty tone in his voice. "I'm not hiding anything here, either."

"Yes, but"—she sought for cautious words—"you asked me not to tell anyone."

"Tell me"—he shifted on the sofa to stare directly at her—"do you like to talk dirty during sex? Do you prefer to be on the bottom or on top? Do you ever do it doggy-style? Well?" he insisted into her silence.

"I deserved that, didn't I?" She grimaced.

"Yes, you did." His voice was still serious, but his expression had eased slightly. "It's a matter of privacy, not shame. I don't want to discuss my sex life with strangers, that's all, any more than you do."

"Point taken." She nodded. "I guess it's just that . . . well, I think the media accustom us to only two kinds of gay people."

"I know. You're either a terrified closet-dweller or a flaming queen. It's like you're some sort of traitor if you don't wear a Gay Pride button and go on marches. Nowadays, it seems like we're entitled to everything but our privacy. Don't misunderstand me," he added quickly, "I have enormous respect for guys like James Kenneally—respect and gratitude. I know how much we owe them. I just have to pay my dues in other ways, that's all."

"I know what you mean," Anneke said thoughtfully. "Just as I owe most of what I have to a couple of generations of feminist activists."

"At least you're not one of those parasites who says, 'Well, I'm not really a *feminist*, of course.' " Cleve raised his voice to a sarcastic falsetto. "The ones who think equal-opportunity laws were written by those nice guys in Washington out of the goodness of their hearts."

"I know. We owe a lot to the people like James," she agreed. "Did you know him well?"

"You mean were we getting it on together? No, we were not," he said forcefully. "Both of us have—had—good, long-term, stable relationships."

"That is *not* what I meant," Anneke snapped. "I meant exactly what I said."

"Sorry." He had the grace to look sheepish. "Getting defensive again. Really, I only knew him slightly; we were friendly acquaintances, not friends. He knew I was gay, of course—for one thing, I was a contributor to the local Gay Caucus—but really we didn't have much in common except our sexual preference. And I didn't kill him."

"I never for an instant thought you did." Which was as near to the truth as made no difference, Anneke told herself. Or at least, was what she wanted to be true, which would have to be good enough.

Tuesday morning, in among her E-mail was one message that made her quickly toggle her printer to get a hard copy. When the printer spit out the paper she reread the message with anticipation.

```
TO: ANNEKE HAAGEN
FROM: MICHAEL RAPPOPORT
DATE: MONDAY, JAN 3
SUBJECT: ART DECO FURNITURE

If you're still looking for Art Deco
furniture, take a look at the "Household
Goods" column in today's newspaper. I
know the house and it should have some
real quality things—if you can use the
word "quality" in reference to Deco.
```

"Now if I can just find yesterday's newspaper," Anneke murmured to herself, casting around the cluttered office.

"Sorry?" Max looked up from his terminal anxiously.

"Just talking to myself," Anneke responded, wishing the boy weren't quite so much the stereotypical—and in her experience atypical—computer nerd. Still, he was an undeniably brilliant programmer, and at eighteen he'd have plenty of time to grow out of it.

She found the paper finally, turned to the classified section, and ran her eye down the appropriate column. There it was—an estate sale in Barton Hills on Wednesday. The sort of neighborhood that, if it had Art Deco furniture, might just have the real thing, the kind of quality that was almost nonexistent outside of a New York or California auction house.

She entered the time in her appointment book. It was scheduled to start at 10:00 A.M., which meant she'd better get there by 9:30 to get in line. At most estate sales, she knew, only a certain number of people were allowed in at a time, and if she didn't make it inside with the first wave, there was hardly any point in bothering.

Michael had better be right about the quality, she thought, smiling to herself as she visualized his stupefyingly handsome face. He was an old, entirely platonic friend who chaired the Ann Arbor Antiques Association as well as running his own thriving business, specializing in Victoriana. Since he personally had contempt for anything made after World War I, he was always glad to steer her toward Art Deco pieces.

She cleared the rest of her messages and was checking her appointments for the day when Ken dropped a fat manila envelope on her desk.

"Oh, good, the resumes are in." She pulled a sheaf of papers from the University Student Employment Office envelope. "Anyone look good?"

"One or two," Ken said grudgingly. "And we only need a couple of new hires for winter term. I've scheduled interviews for later this morning."

"Carol Swann," Marcia blurted from her terminal, looking oddly defiant when Anneke turned to look at her. "Well, she's really good," Marcia said defensively.

"And of course, totally by coincidence, she also happens to be Allen's little sister." Ken winked at Anneke.

"Well, there you are." Marcia blushed furiously, spilled droplets of coffee on her desk, reached for the Kleenex to mop it up, and knocked her mouse off the desktop. "You know what a brilliant programmer Allen is." She made a futile grab for the mouse, swinging by its cord like a rodent with an elongated tail.

"Well, if computer smarts run in families, she ought to be pretty good," Anneke agreed. Allen Swann, now a computer-science professor, had been one of her first student programmers, and Marcia was obviously smitten.

"All right," she told Ken, "Let me know when they get here."

Carol Swann was hired after a brief interview—the girl seemed to have the same quick mind and sunny personality as her brother. The other resume, however, had a cryptic note in Ken's handwriting that said: "See what you think."

The applicant in question was a sophomore named Calvin Williams, who turned out to be well over six feet tall, black, and with a decided chip on his shoulder.

"You say you program in Fortran and C," Anneke read off his resume. "Who taught you C?"

"No one taught me; I taught myself. I got no credentials to prove I can do what I say." He put sarcastic emphasis on the word *credentials*. "I just got the books out of the library and went ahead and learned it."

"What computer did you use?"

"I got hold of a used XT back a few years ago."

"Which C compiler?"

"Actually, I did most of my work with C on a local mainframe, using the XT as a terminal."

"Oh? Whose mainframe?"

"Just someone around."

In other words, Anneke understood, he and his XT had been uninvited guests on some company's computer.

"Ever get caught?" she asked mildly.

"No, ma'am." The boy shrugged his shoulders irritably. "I never messed around with their stuff. I just borrowed some unused computer time." He reached down to pick up his backpack. "I take it the interview's over."

"I think so. Can you start tomorrow?"

"Tomorrow? You hiring me?" He looked so stunned that Anneke laughed.

"Look, Calvin, if I refused to hire every kid who'd ever done any unauthorized poking around, I'd have an empty office."

"Yeah, but I don't have any courses or grades or anything to show you."

"Nobody does at your age. Where the hell can a kid find someone to teach him C before he gets to college? Besides, I've always figured the ones who wait to be taught usually aren't worth much anyway. I ran the program you sent with your resume. It's pretty good; later on I'll show you a couple of tricks to tighten it up a bit."

She turned Calvin over to Ken and proceeded to the final interview. Lisa Barrow and George Oldenberg were A Couple, capital letters. They were both juniors, both computer science majors, and they were determined to work together.

"Eventually we want to form our own software company," George said.

"But we know we need experience," Lisa added.

"And it's not easy to find opportunities to work together," George continued.

"So we really jumped at this when we saw the posting," Lisa concluded.

"Well, I'm afraid we don't have any openings left," Anneke said, half-truthfully—they did actually need another person. But she could hardly imagine anything more tiresome than listening to this duo rattle on with their sequential conversations. She wished them luck, doubting in her own mind that they'd survive much more of such joined-at-the-hip togetherness, and thankfully returned to work.

The new computer equipment—Compaq, LaserJet printer, and assorted bits and pieces—arrived just as she was leaving for the day, and she had it loaded directly into her Alfa. She pulled into Mackinac Court before five o'clock, to be greeted by Ross scampering out to meet her as she pulled the Alfa up to the cottage door to unload.

"Hi, Miss Haagen," he greeted her, looking cautiously hopeful.

"Hi, Ross." She looked at his wistful face. "Want to help carry some things in exchange for some computer time?"

"Sure!" He took the bag containing several small peripherals and trotted toward the cottage. Anneke pulled the computer from the passenger seat.

"Can I help?" Joe Roper called, approaching on foot from the driveway.

"If you don't mind," she said when he reached the car. "I could really use a hand with the printer."

"No problem." He lifted the heavy carton out of the car and carried it to the door of the cottage. "You're a friend of Karl Genesko, aren't you?" he asked.

"Yes," she answered warily as she unlocked the door, reluctant to talk about either Karl or the murder. But Joe seemed to have other things on his mind.

"You know, I think I could have been a pretty good linebacker myself," he said, "only I wasn't big enough. Instead, I was a totally mediocre running back."

"Well, you were good enough to play for Michigan," Anneke replied, wondering why he seemed so glum about it at this late date.

"Only just." He carried the printer carton inside and deposited it on the desk. "I mostly warmed the bench for four years. Genesko was a two-time all-American, first-round draft choice, three Super Bowls . . ." His voice trailed off, sounding not so much envious as sad.

"You sound like you really loved playing football."

"Loved it? I hated it," he said, so fiercely that Anneke turned to stare at him. "I did it because it would get me what I wanted, that's all. Sometimes you have to choose between doing what you want to do and getting what you want to get. Only the really lucky ones have it coincide." The anger, if it had been anger, was replaced by pure sadness, an expression so at odds with his open, pleasant features that Anneke wasn't sure she was reading him correctly. And then the expression was gone, replaced by his customary cheerfulness. He smiled at Ross, who had followed them inside with the heavy shopping bag, riffled the boy's hair, and went back outside.

Now what was that all about? Anneke wondered, following him out to move her car. She saw him stop briefly to exchange greetings with Prof, who was crossing the court from the direction of the barn; when Joe turned away, his face was as placid and pleasant as ever, so that she wondered if the anger and the sadness had been merely her own imagination.

She pulled the car across the court into the parking area and trudged back to the cottage. Inside, she cleared space on the desk for the new computer and let Ross work on the laptop while she set up the new system and installed programs. He was working now with a simple BASIC textbook she'd bought for him, and all she had to do was answer occasional questions. She had, in fact, nearly forgotten his presence when she suddenly felt him peering over her shoulder at the high-resolution color monitor.

"Wow," he said, looking in awe at the graphic display—a full-color, hi-res picture of a jousting tournament, the title page of a role-playing game called Endor's Doom.

"Impressive, isn't it?" She smiled at him.

"The other one can't do stuff like that, can it?" He cast a disparaging glance at the suddenly discredited laptop.

"Well, it won't do ultra-hi-res graphics," Anneke admitted with a smile, "but it can handle the same games. They just won't look as good, that's all."

"Yeah, but . . ." Ross's voice trailed away as he stared covetously at the gorgeous display.

"Here, sit down." Anneke laughed and vacated her chair. "Give it a try."

"Are you sure?" But even as he spoke the boy was sliding into the chair and reaching for the mouse. Anneke handed him the game directions with a grin and left him to it while she gathered up boxes and packing material, filled out registration and warranty cards, and went to the kitchen to make herself a cup of coffee. Kids seemed to pick up the techniques of role-playing games by osmosis, she concluded, reaching for the television knob.

That was when she heard him scream.

THIRTEEN

It wasn't a loud scream—more of a wordless cry, followed by a thud, so that at first Anneke wasn't sure what she'd heard. But when she turned to look at him, he was standing up, the chair overturned, backing away from the computer with his fists pressed to his mouth and a look of such stark terror on his face that for a moment Anneke herself felt his dread like a kick in the stomach.

"Ross! What's the matter?" She jumped from the sofa and rushed to him, gripping his shoulders. His small body was rigid with fear, his face dead-white, small whimpering noises issuing from deep in his throat. And all the while his eyes were fastened on the monitor screen.

"Ross! Look at me!" She moved in front of him and took his face between her hands, feeling her own heart beat painfully in response to his terror. "Ross, look at *me*. It's all right, Ross, it's all right." She put her arms around him and hugged him to her, murmuring reassuring sounds and cutting off his view of the monitor, until at last she felt the small body begin to sag and then, finally, shake with sobbing.

She let him cry for a long time, holding him tightly in her arms with a rush of affection as he clung to her. She didn't move until his sobs began to subside; only when he hiccupped loudly did she loosen her grip and lead him gently toward the sofa, away from the computer.

"Now," she said as matter-of-factly as she could manage, "tell me. No, wait a minute." She made a quick trip to the bedroom and returned with a box of Kleenex. "Here, blow." While he did as he was told, obedient as ever, she tried to mobilize her rusty maternal skills. "Are you all right now?"

"I guess . . . I . . ." His face, blotchy with tears, started to break up again.

"It's okay," she said firmly. "It's all over. Now you can tell me about it, okay?"

"O-okay," he hiccupped, but then seemed to stick, unable to say any more.

"It was something you saw?" Anneke prompted, wishing, as she had so often in the past, that parenting didn't so often require mind-reading abilities.

"It was on there. It was in the second-level dungeon, and it jumped out at me—at Lars, my character—and it was going to take me away just like it took my grandma." His face crumpled again and renewed sobs obscured his last words; it took Anneke several seconds, as she reached for the Kleenex once more, to re-alize what he had said.

"Oh damn!" she said angrily, in sudden fury at the adults who were making such a hash of this child's life. "Ross, look at me." She waited until she had his attention, then spoke quietly and calmly. "Ross, nothing 'came and took' your grandmother. She was very old, and she died in her sleep quite peacefully. It's not a happy thing, but it was a very natural end of a good, long life. You have every right to be sad about it, but there's absolutely nothing for you to be frightened about. Do you understand me?"

"Yes, but . . ." He looked at her dubiously, fear still in his eyes. "But I *saw* it."

"Ross, it's just a picture on a computer screen. You know that."

"No, not *there*," he insisted. "I saw it come for my grandma."

"What do you mean? You saw what?"

"I saw the vampire. It came to my grandma's house that night, and then they said she was dead."

"You saw . . . Ross, you must be mistaken. You're old enough to know there's no such thing as a vampire."

"I know," he said solemnly. "But I saw it."

Anneke sat back and stared at him, her mind racing. Fact: His much-loved grandmother had died, and the adults around him had made no effort to help him come to terms with his grief and fear. It was hardly surprising that he would create nightmare images to fill in the blanks. Still, he was not a fanciful child; if anything, he was almost too owlishly serious.

But also, fact: There had been one unquestionable, undeniable murder in Mackinac Court. And Rosa Barlow's death was extraordinarily convenient for a number of people on the short list of suspects.

Had Ross actually seen something the night his grandmother died?

"Why didn't you tell anyone about this before now?" she probed.

"Like you said," he answered simply, "because there's no such thing as vampires." In other words—Anneke did a quick parental translation—no one would have believed him. In fact, he probably didn't fully believe it himself, there on the cusp between childhood and maturity—and so, unable to cope with the whole event, he'd simply repressed the memory until the computer image forced him to confront it.

Provisionally, she accepted the premise that he had seen something real. And decided quickly that questioning him further was a job probably better left to a professional.

"I'd like you to tell a friend of mine about what you saw, okay?" she said finally.

"No!" Ross blurted. "They'd just laugh at me."

"Am I laughing at you?"

"N-no." He peered into her face hesitantly.

"Neither will he, I promise you." Without giving the boy a chance to protest further, she went to the phone and dialed, fingers crossed. She heard Karl's voice at the other end with a gust of relief.

"Ross Barlow is here at my house," she said without preamble, "and I think you need to hear what he has to say."

"About Kenneally's death?" he asked quickly.

"No. About his grandmother's death."

"I'll be right there," he said after only the briefest pause.

While they waited, Anneke poured Ross a glass of milk. His hand shook at he took it from her—in fact, his whole body was shaking with reaction, she realized. Blood sugar, she thought, going to the cabinet and unearthing a small box of Godiva chocolates she'd been hoarding. And mine could use a jolt itself. They were each on their third piece when the doorbell rang.

"Karl, I'd like you to meet Ross Barlow." She introduced him with grave formality. "Ross, this is Lieutenant Karl Genesko. He's just going to ask you a few questions." Her careful reassurance was unnecessary; Ross's eyes widened as she made the introductions.

"Are you really Karl Genesko?" he asked, awestruck.

"Yes, I am." He met Anneke's eyes over the boy's head with an amused grimace. "I understand you have something to tell me." Ross didn't answer, but instead turned to look at Anneke beseechingly.

"Ross saw something the night his grandmother died," she helped out.

"Oh?" Karl was carefully matter-of-fact. "Can you tell me what it was?" Ross shook his head helplessly. "Well," Karl said patiently, "can you tell me what it looked like?"

"Like . . . like that." Ross jerked his head in the direction of the computer, acknowledging its presence for the first time since his outburst.

"Will you show me?" Karl waited until Ross nodded reluctantly, stood up, and led him to the computer.

"There." He pointed. Anneke moved to where she could see

the screen but remained a little distance away; Ross's face, she saw, was white but controlled, and she respected the effort it took him to confront the dreaded image.

"Hmmm." Karl studied the picture for a while in silence, with every appearance of serious consideration. It was a more or less typical dungeon scene, the stone walls lichen-covered, the window barred. There was a metal-bound treasure chest pictured in one corner, and a skeleton hanging from wrist irons clamped to the wall. All of it was clear and detailed and brightly colored, picked out in the superb high-res graphics like a fragment of a Hieronymus Bosch painting.

The figure in the foreground was even more finely drawn. This vampire owed little to the pseudo-romantic contemporary style, and more to the Nosferatu tradition—dark, twisted, head bent to one side, arms high over its head as it unfurled menacing bat wings. And every now and then it moved, darting forward toward the viewer with a jerky but oddly graceful motion.

"All right," Karl said at last. "Let's go back and sit down. I'd like to ask you a few questions, okay?"

"Okay." Ross moved away from the computer with unmistakable relief, sitting next to Karl on the sofa. Anneke busied herself with the coffeepot, out of sight but within earshot.

"Now," Karl asked when they were seated, "can you tell me when you saw this figure?"

"The night my grandma died."

"Do you know what time it was?"

"Uh-uh. I just woke up to—you know," Ross said shyly. "And I heard the TV from the living room, so I peeked over the banister."

"Do you remember what show it was that you heard playing on television?" Karl probed.

"Yeah, it was *Law and Order*. My grandma always watched it on Wednesday nights." So the . . . "sighting," for want of a better word, had been between ten and eleven, Anneke realized.

"Good," Karl said briskly. "And that's when you saw this figure?"

"Y-yes." Ross's face twisted again.

"Just take it slow," Karl soothed him. "Now, where was the figure when you saw it?"

"In the front hall." Ross's voice shook. "It was dark, see? But there was light from the living room, and it . . . it just sort of floated across the hall, like that"—he jerked his head toward the computer—"and into the dining room and I could see it start to spread its wings—it was going to turn itself back into a bat, y'know? And I knew if it saw me it would come after me and then I'd be turned into a vampire too—that's the way vampires happen—and I ran back into my bedroom and tried to hide only there wasn't anywhere to hide and I . . . and I . . ."

"Ross! It's all right!" Anneke hurried forward and took the shaking boy in her arms, sharing a look of angry sympathy with Karl. What a thing for a child to carry inside all by himself. "Ross, you said it yourself, remember? There's no such thing as vampires."

"But I *saw* it," he said, his teeth clenched in his desperate effort at self-control.

"Ross, if there are no vampires," Karl said calmly, "what else do you think it could have been that you saw?"

"But it looked . . . You mean," Ross blurted, twisting out of Anneke's arms to face Karl, "it could of been something else that just *looked* like a vampire?" Clearly this thought was a new one; just as clearly, Anneke could see an almost palpable wave of relief wash over him.

"What do you think?" Karl asked.

"I guess maybe," the boy said shakily, opening his mind to the wonderful, anodyne thought. "I guess it must of been, huh?"

"I think you're absolutely right." Karl nodded.

"Then my grandma *isn't* a vampire, she *isn't!*" Ross shouted joyously as Anneke and Karl looked at each other in sudden, horrified recognition of the ghastly secret imaginings the child had been concealing all this time.

"Now," Karl said to him, "how about if I walk you home and have a talk with your father?"

"D'you have to?" Ross asked anxiously.

"I'm afraid I do, you know."

"Well, but he may not be home," the boy said hopefully.

"We'll find him," Karl said, as grimly as Anneke had ever heard him sound.

FOURTEEN

• • • • • •

She didn't expect to hear from Karl any more that night, so when he rang the doorbell at eleven o'clock Anneke had already changed into nightgown and robe and settled down to watch the evening news.

"I saw your lights were still on, so I thought you'd like an update," he said when she let him in. Then he stepped back and examined her. "Auditioning for a revival of *Dynasty?*"

"It is a bit much, isn't it?" She glanced down at the robe she'd bought in a moment of mental derangement. The full, fitted swirl of emerald green velvet trimmed in beige lace hadn't looked nearly so . . . provocative in the store. "Have *you* ever had to replace an entire wardrobe at post-Christmas sales?" She folded her arms around herself, suddenly self-conscious, realized he was watching her with barely concealed amusement and threw up her hands in laughter. "All right, I give up. You're right, it's ridiculous."

"Is that what I said?" Behind his amused grin was an expression Anneke couldn't quite identify but that made her face grow warm.

"Would you like a drink?" She changed the subject.

"Brandy would be fine, thanks." He shed his coat and sat down with a sigh.

"Did you find out any more?" she asked, handing him a glass and joining him on the sofa.

"Well, I talked to Ross in more detail, and I talked to his father." Karl wrinkled his nose unconsciously. "I don't think there's much doubt that the boy did see something that night."

"You're sure of that? That it wasn't just a coincidental nightmare?" The thought wasn't new, but she herself had considered and rejected it during the evening. Karl, apparently, agreed with her.

"I'm positive in my own mind," he said, "but I can't begin to prove it. His father insists Ross must have been dreaming—in fact, he was almost hysterical about it." Again there was the slight twitch of his nose. "But the boy's description was too circumstantial for that—he described details of shape and movement too exactly."

"I assume he didn't get a look at the face?"

"No. He said its 'wings' were folded up and over its head."

"God." She shook her head irritably. "What the hell *did* he see? Did he see his grandmother's murderer?"

"Right now your guess is as good as mine," he replied grimly. "We don't even know that she *was* murdered."

"Of course she was." Anneke hadn't, in fact, been so positive herself until that moment. "Karl, what exactly did she die of?"

"Your guess is as good as mine on that too," he rejoined. "The death certificate," he anticipated her next question, "just said 'heart failure.' The doctor who signed it—a guy on the county staff—had never seen the Barlow woman before, and according to him it was strictly cut-and-dried. Just a seventy-eight-year-old woman quietly dead in front of her own television set."

"Wasn't there an examination, or an autopsy or something?"

"For what cause?" Karl shrugged. "The patrolman who covered the call swears there was absolutely nothing suspicious about it—no sign of a struggle, son all broken up, everything perfectly ordinary. According to the patrolman, the doctor barely looked at her before he scribbled his name on the certificate—anxious to get back to bed, I guess."

"And then they had her cremated immediately," Anneke pointed out.

"At her own request." Karl shook his head at her suspicious tone. "She made all the arrangements herself, a couple of years ago. The funeral director says she was very positive about what she wanted."

"Somebody said once that the perfect crime is the one nobody knows was even committed." Anneke made a face.

"And we can't really be sure a crime *was* committed. It's possible, you know," he forestalled her protest, "that what Ross saw was simply a friend dropping by for a visit. Rosa Barlow might still have been alive."

"Well, but you know the approximate time of this . . . sighting. Don't you know what time she died?"

"No. Look," he said in response to her expression of disbelief, "this was an absolutely ordinary event, the kind that happens all the time. Nobody paid much attention to details because nobody thought they'd matter. The death certificate was signed at 2:20 A.M., and the doctor barely even remembers the call, let alone the condition of the body. The best he could do was guess that she'd been dead 'more than a couple of hours.' " His voice was more resigned than sarcastic.

"So what happens next?" Anneke asked. "You're not going to just drop it, are you?"

"No." He smiled slightly at her challenging tone. "We'll re-open it—carefully—as part of the Kenneally investigation, and see what we can get."

"Is there any progress on James's murder?" Anneke asked.

"Well, we've got the final report from forensics."

"Anything significant?" For answer, he reached into his brief-case and handed her a sheaf of papers stapled together; she perused it briefly and handed it back to him with a shake of her head. "Too technical for me. Can you translate this into civilian?"

"It's pretty simple, really." He riffled through the report.

"First, on the medical evidence, he was killed somewhere between midnight and four A.M.—that's as close as they can put it. Stomach contents show he'd eaten a ham and cheese sandwich approximately five hours before death, but no one on the train remembers if or when they sold it to him." He shuddered. "I guess students can eat anything."

"And he really was killed with dental floss?" Anneke still found the idea hard to credit.

"Dental tape, yes," he corrected her.

"It's preposterous. Isn't it?" The weapon nagged at her. "I mean, *why* would anyone use dental tape to kill someone?"

"I haven't a clue." He shrugged.

"I take it you didn't find any of the right kind in Mackinac Court?"

"No. We didn't really expect to, of course, but we had to try. We looked in every medicine cabinet in the court, but we only came up with the ordinary kind of floss."

"It's still preposterous," Anneke repeated. She moved on to another subject, putting the question of dental tape aside. "I don't suppose he told any of his professional colleagues what he was looking for in Chicago."

"Not that they've told us, no."

"It's a shame Dennis was out of town. James would have told him, certainly. They seem to have been a very settled couple."

"As far as we can tell, they were. In fact, they were a kind of model to a lot of the gays here in town—sort of proof that gay people can live normal, sane lives. That's one reason there's been such an outcry about Kenneally's murder; he was important to them not just as a leader but as a kind of symbol. Both he and Dennis were HIV-negative, too, by the way. Everyone figured them for a couple of the lucky ones."

"Damn." The expletive was too weak for the enormous anger she felt. "I don't suppose anyone can be eliminated by alibis, can they?"

"No. For one thing, most of them live, or at least sleep, alone. The two girls who shared Kenneally's house have separate rooms.

Carfax and Marshall live alone. Harvey Barlow only has his son living with him. Even the Ropers have separate rooms."

"And Barbara and T.G.?"

"Oh, they alibi each other, all right. Both swear on a stack of bibles that they went to bed at the same time and were never out of each other's sight all night. In fact, they're positively insistent on it."

"And maybe the lady doth protest too much," Anneke said, pondering. Barbara's determination to believe in the outsider as killer, her refusal to accept the facts of the case . . . "Of course!" she said suddenly. "Karl, Barbara thinks T.G. did it."

"I think you're probably right." He nodded. "Although that doesn't necessarily mean he did do it."

"No, all it means is that he wasn't in bed all night."

"It also means he's the sort of man whose wife thinks he's capable of murder."

Anneke nodded, remembering the sense of suppressed violence she'd felt in her meetings with T.G. What must it be like to be married to a man like that? And, with Barbara's attitudes, feeling a lifelong commitment to that marriage? Anneke shuddered and shoved the thought away.

"What about the other end?" she asked, moving to another subject. "Is there any way to investigate James's movements in Chicago?"

"Not really." Karl made a face over his brandy. "We've telexed the Chicago police with a picture of Kenneally, but you know what the odds are on that."

"About as good as the odds of identifying Ross's 'vampire.' " She grimaced.

"Well, at least we'll see if we can find anyone who admits to being there the night she died. Of course, you do realize that if someone does admit it, it proves absolutely nothing."

"No. On the other hand," she said thoughtfully, "if *no* one admits it, doesn't *that* prove something?"

"What a devious mind you have," he said appreciatively. "Yes, that would at least indicate something—if you're willing to accept the word of a hysterical, traumatized eleven-year-old who was half-asleep at the time he thinks he saw a vampire."

"Which I am," she said firmly.

"So am I." He sighed. "Unfortunately." His attention was diverted momentarily by the television, where the news had given way to the sports report. He watched an interview with the Cincinnati Bengals' new head coach for a few moments, then reached into his briefcase again. "I almost forgot—I saw this earlier today and thought you might like it."

"Another gift?" She removed the white wrapping paper, conscious of his eyes on her, and stared first at the contents and then at him. "This isn't something you just happened to see," she said severely.

"Well, not exactly." His voice was bland. "Do you like it?"

"*Like* it? It's . . . fabulous." She picked up the silver box and looked at it. It was only three inches high but nearly twelve inches square, the top set with cabochon amethysts and rough turquoise stones in an intricate swirling pattern. She lifted the lid and saw that the inside was divided into four velvet-lined compartments, clearly intended as a jewelry box. "It's Spratling, isn't it? Yes, of course," she confirmed, turning the box over and examining the incised logo. Later than Art Deco, of course, but gorgeous nonetheless. "Karl, I don't know what to say."

"Say thank you." He smiled.

"Thank you doesn't seem to cover it."

"Well then, maybe this will," he said, pulling her toward him. It's too much—really it is, Anneke thought chaotically, not sure whether she meant the jewelry box or something else, finding it as always difficult to think straight while he was kissing her.

"It's too much," she said breathlessly when he finally released her.

"What is?" He kissed her again, expertly and for a long time. "Too much?" he asked.

"No. Yes. Oh, damn you," she said, feeling her face redden as he roared with laughter. "You know what I mean."

"I know that I'll continue to buy things for you occasionally, if I think you'll like them," he said seriously. "Unless, that is, you specifically order me not to." Which would, she knew, be the most ungracious thing she could do.

"You know, I'm afraid you could become habit-forming," she said at last, tracing the line of his ear with one finger.

"I'm counting on it." She saw the flash of a grin before he leaned forward to kiss her again, and something in her went cold even as she felt heat rise in her. Something important, she told herself as his hands moved over her body. I'll analyze it later, she decided, running her fingernails along his back, feeling muscles move beneath the fine cotton shirt as his arms tightened around her.

Only to find, much later, when he had left her bed, when the euphoria of their lovemaking had died away a little, that the cold feeling remained. And this time she had no trouble recognizing its source. It had been only an offhand comment, she tried to convince herself, and then damned herself for intellectual dishonesty. Karl didn't make offhand comments. Sooner or later, perhaps much later but inevitably sometime in the future, she would have to face the question of commitment.

Well, but he seemed content enough with their current situation, didn't he? Even as she posed the question, her analytic mind produced the answer: Not content, but rather patient.

When they'd first met, she had been coming off a failed marriage, one or two unsatisfactory casual affairs, and a spectacularly bad relationship. Karl had let her—no, had forced her to set the pace between them, forced her to admit and act on the almost immediate attraction between them. And he was doing the same thing now, waiting for her to take the next step. He would wait for a long time, she knew—but also knew, suddenly and with a sick certainty, that he wouldn't wait forever.

Did she want to marry him? Did she want to be married again? And were they different questions, or merely two ways of phrasing the same problem?

Damn it. She sat up in the empty bed and stared into darkness. All right, approach it from the other direction. Karl—Karl, who was passionate, intelligent, amusing, and supportive; who already shared her life and her bed; who made her feel alive, loved, and safe.

She didn't want to feel safe.

The realization hit her like a blow: She was afraid of being safe. She repeated the absurd oxymoron to herself, trying to make sense of it. Safe . . . domesticated . . . all those years of pale, safe domesticity, when she had been Anneke Mortenson.

Except she hadn't been safe. Not safe from the appeal of twenty-three-year-old graduate students to susceptible husbands, at any rate. Not safe from rejection, and failure, and humiliation. Only when she'd taken her life into her own hands, forced herself to take risks—only then had she been truly safe. Out of the dreary tragedy of her divorce, her subconscious mind had forged an imbecile link between risk taking and safety.

Marriage, any marriage, meant risking all that hard-won self-protection. But if that was the case, wasn't she denying her whole argument by refusing to take the risk of marriage? Somewhere in the middle of her third circuit of this hamster-wheel self-argument, she fell asleep.

FIFTEEN

• • • • • •

She dressed and headed out quickly Wednesday morning, determined not to worry further about indeterminate future problems. Instead, she concentrated on the beauty of the snow-covered landscape as she headed the Alfa north on Whitmore Lake Road to the estate sale.

Barton Hills is a small, private enclave just outside the city. Anneke steered through the stone gates and followed the bright red ESTATE SALE signs along winding blacktopped roads, viewing the great houses on either side with appreciation. Out of her price range, of course, but handsomely done, with taste as well as money.

She had no trouble locating the sale; cars and vans already lined the narrow road on either side of the house. She maneuvered the Alfa into a small space between a van and a converted pickup truck, careful to avoid digging herself into a snowbank, and trudged up the long driveway to the house, shivering in the cold. Although it was still twenty minutes before ten o'clock, there was already a small crowd, and Anneke took up her position at the end of the line. She counted the heads between her and the door and was unsurprised to see Michael Rappoport first in line. She was relieved to note that there were only sixteen others between them. They'll certainly admit at least twenty in the first wave, she thought, leaning her head back to examine the huge house.

It seemed promising, at least for quality, but there was nothing in the least Art Deco about it. It was a sprawling, very contemporary-looking ranch house, with a greenish metal roof, the whole looking deceptively simple from the front. But by craning her neck, Anneke could see a long wing sweeping away on one side, and she guessed there was another to match it on the opposite side. This was a *big* house.

By the time a frazzled-looking white-haired woman opened the front door, Anneke was chilled through and wondering if even a Deskey breakfront would be worth pneumonia. Behind her, the line of antique-hunters stretched around the curve of the drive and out of sight.

"We'll let the first twenty-five people in," the woman at the door announced. The groans from the people at the back were drowned out by the eager chattering of the ones in front, and in a moment Anneke found herself inside, in the biggest living room she had ever seen.

There was a sweeping expanse of glass at the back, giving onto a broad terrace lined with small trees. There were walls lined with built-in cabinetry of a pale, beautifully grained wood. And throughout, it was furnished with soft beige-upholstered modular seating of no design merit whatsoever.

"Terminally tacky, isn't it?"

"Hi, Michael." She wrinkled her nose. "The earth-tone brigade strikes again. You've found something worth buying already?"

"Maybe." He held up a small pitcher of thick, lumpy-looking clear glass, with a wide, flaring lip. She stared at it in amazement.

"Surely that can't be real Stiegel?"

"Maybe," he repeated, his grin widening. "At two bucks it's worth a try. Now," he said briskly, "before you OD on beige, there *is* something here for you." He handed her a numbered tag.

"What is it?" She peered at the price tag. "For four hundred dollars, it better be gold leaf."

"Better than that. Come on." He led her down a long corridor and into a room that was clearly the master bedroom. Mirrored closet doors lined one whole wall; the rest of the room was nearly filled by an enormous king-size bed and a pair of ugly blond night tables. Half a dozen people were pawing through odds and ends scattered on the bed.

"There." Michael pointed unnecessarily; Anneke had already spotted his find, a geometrically simple chiffonier—simple, that is, save for the fact that it was faced entirely with fine peach-colored mirror.

"It's gorgeous," she said appreciatively, opening drawers that glided silently at a touch. Inside, she could see the hardwood construction and the careful dovetailing of the joints. "But four hundred dollars?"

"What would a brand-new bedroom dresser cost you?" he asked reasonably. "And what would it be worth in six months? And what is this worth now?"

"I know, I know." She recited the calculations. "If I paid two hundred dollars for a cheap dresser now, it would be worth maybe fifty next week. Whereas if I bought this and shipped it to Christie's tomorrow, it would probably go for close to a thousand." She answered his questions as much for herself as for him. "In which case, I'd be an idiot to pass it up. Except . . ." Except, she realized suddenly, when she looked at the chiffonier, nothing happened. She looked at it again, waiting for the lift of the heart, the surge of adrenaline that every true collector recognizes. It didn't come; the chiffonier remained merely a beautiful piece of furniture that she admired without in the least coveting.

"Well, even I make mistakes sometimes," Michael said philosophically, seeing her almost subconscious shake of the head. "You lost your whole collection in that fire, didn't you?"

"Every single thing." She nodded.

"It happens sometimes—collectors who lose everything and never quite regain the feeling. Don't worry about it." He patted her hand consolingly. "You'll either get it back or you'll move on to something else." Then he looked at the hand he held more closely. "At least you saved that watch—what is it, Patek Philippe?"

"Vacheron," she said absently. "And it wasn't saved from the fire; it was a . . . recent acquisition." She found herself reluctant to admit having accepted so extravagant a gift. Idiotic, she told herself, turning to avoid Michael's too-sharp eye.

And then the dresser caught her eye—well, actually it would be called a semainier. It was a beautiful rosewood piece about five feet tall but only about eighteen inches wide, with seven drawers, one for each day of the week. It had, Anneke decided, a kind of masculine elegance that was nearly irresistible.

"Michael, what do you think of that piece?" she asked, elaborately casual.

"Too pricey for me to make a decent profit on it," he said, looking at her quizzically.

"Yes, but is it good?" she persisted.

"Very good, assuming it's authentic. Want me to check?"

"Would you please?" She waited while he removed and examined drawers, peered at carved corners through a small loupe, and ran his long, delicate fingers over the hardware.

"Almost certainly British," he said finally. "Somewhere between 1800 and 1840. Two of the drawer pulls are modern reproductions, and one of the drawers is a replacement—not the front, luckily, just the inside sections."

"Is that bad?" she asked anxiously.

"Not hopelessly." He steepled his fingers and stared at her. "Obviously the modern repairs reduce its value, but they're well done, and on a piece this old it doesn't absolutely disqualify it. I'd say the price allows for the condition; you certainly wouldn't get burned, although I couldn't resell it for enough to make it worth it for me. But are you sure you want to abandon Art Deco for Regency?"

"It's not for me," she said finally, after a long hesitation. "It's a gift."

"My dear Anneke, have you looked at the price tag?"

"No." She did so now, and blanched. "My God, is it really worth eight hundred dollars?"

"Oh, it's worth a good bit more than that. At the right New York auction, it might go as high as twelve or fourteen hundred. I'll tell you what. If the recipient doesn't like it, I'll take it from you on consignment. I think I can promise that you won't lose money on it."

"He'll like it," Anneke said absently, doing a quick mental run-down of her checking-account balance. "Michael, I'm going to buy it." She pulled the tag off the drawer handle quickly, before she could lose her nerve.

"My congratulations," he said seriously.

"For what?"

"It's about time you found a man worth buying a gift like this for." And then, while she fumbled self-consciously for a response, he changed the subject. "Now, there's one more thing I want you to buy. This." For the first time, she noticed the lamp he'd been carrying tucked under his arm.

"That?" She peered at it dubiously. It was a dull brownish metal, probably bronze, in a reeded pattern. The shade was com-posed of four trapezoidal slabs of dull, streaky brown-and-white glass framed in reeded bronze. It was heavy and stolid-looking and entirely unappealing.

"I think I'll pass," she said after examining it. "It's Art Deco, of a sort, but it's really too early for me."

"Buy it anyway," Michael said firmly.

"Why?" She looked at him curiously. "What's so special about it?"

"Humor me. Please? It's only fifty dollars."

"Michael, fifty dollars doesn't qualify as 'only,' especially after I've just committed to eight hundred." She looked at the homely lamp again, then back to Michael. In the years since he'd started in the antique business, his eye had become legendary. And he'd never yet steered her wrong. "Oh, all right," she capitulated fi-nally.

"Good. Did you want to look around any further?"

"You tell me. Is there anything else worth bothering with?"

"No. The rest of it is entirely unimpeachable and totally uninteresting contemporary. Come on, then, let's check out."

At the table by the front door, Anneke wrote out the check and handed it to the bored woman manning the cash box. Then she looked up in dismay.

"Oh! Michael, I just realized something." She couldn't believe she hadn't thought of it before. "All I've got is the Alfa. Is it going to fit?"

"I think so, if you put the top down." He laughed at her look of horror. "I'd give you a hand, but my van is in the shop. I don't think you'll *quite* freeze to death."

"Well, at least the lamp will fit in the front seat."

"No. Let me hang on to it for a while." Michael shook his head. "I want to take it back to my shop and clean it up for you."

"I wish I knew what you saw in it." Anneke handed it to him without regret.

"So do I," he said, peering at it with a mixture of irritation and fascination. "I'll let you know." He waved a hand and disappeared.

She drove the three or four miles back to Mackinac Court erratically, torn between high speed—to get out of the cold quickly —and slow, to minimize the icy wind. Every now and then, she caught sight of other drivers, huddled inside heated cars, shaking their heads at the sight of the lunatic woman driving around in a convertible with the top down and a large piece of furniture propped against the passenger seat. By the time she turned off Division she was in a state of half-frozen hilarity.

As she coasted to a stop, giggling, Brenda Roper approached the parking area and peered at her oddly for a moment. But when she saw the contents of the Alfa, her eyes lit up.

"It's beautiful," she said appreciatively. "British?"

"Probably." Of course, Anneke realized, Brenda would be something of an expert on antiques; they went with the lady-of-the-manor persona.

"I didn't know you collected antiques." Brenda seemed to be revising her opinion of Anneke.

"Actually, I collect Art Deco," Anneke replied, taking off her gloves to warm her frozen fingers. "Or at least, I did until my collection went up in flames."

"What a shame." Brenda didn't sound like she thought it was much of a shame. "Still, if you can move up to pieces like this . . ." She ran a hand over the smooth wood.

"Well, I'm not sure I'd have voluntarily traded an anonymous dresser, however handsome, for a Priess sculpture." Anneke matched Brenda's casual tone with an effort of will.

"Did you really lose an original Priess? How awful." Again Anneke could see her adding points to some invisible score.

"Along with a Clarice Cliff pitcher and an Eileen Gray tea cart," Anneke added, half-amused, half-repelled by her own name-dropping.

"You sound like an expert," Brenda said, rather sharply, Anneke thought. "Still, at least you saved that beautiful watch." Unknowingly she echoed Michael, her eyes traveling to Anneke's wrist. "Baume et Mercier?" she pronounced in the French manner.

"Vacheron," Anneke said shortly, suddenly disgusted with the game. "I think I'd better get this chest inside before I turn blue from the cold. Except . . ." She hadn't considered the logistical problem at this end when she'd had it loaded into her car. Besides, she realized suddenly, she didn't want simply to dump the chest in her living room for Karl to see the minute he walked in; she wanted its presentation to be an *event*. And there was certainly no place to hide it in the tiny cottage. "Would it be all right if I put it in that barn for a couple of days?" she asked.

"If it's really just for a couple of days," Brenda agreed dubiously. "You know what cold and damp will do to fine wood."

"Yes. Just until the weekend," Anneke stated firmly. "Now if I can just figure out how to get it in there."

"Well, good luck." Brenda waved a hand negligently. "I have to get to my museum board meeting." Anneke hadn't really expected her to offer help, and she wasn't disappointed.

As Brenda glided the Buick out of the court, Anneke ran the options through in her mind. Well, first get it as close to the barn as possible, she decided, climbing back into the Alfa and maneuvering it carefully across the courtyard. Now, she thought as she opened the door of the barn, if I can tip it out over the back of the car, I can probably walk it inside.

"Need help?"

"Hooray." She greeted Cleve's arrival with relief.

"I saw you pull up," he said, zipping up his jacket as he covered the few feet from his cottage to the barn. "What are you trying to do?"

"I want to store this in here for a couple of days." She indicated the chest. "It's a gift." Somehow she felt no discomfort revealing the fact to him.

"Lucky man." He rewarded her with a matter-of-fact tone. "Where do you want to put it?"

"I'm not sure." She wondered what masculine quality the chest possessed that everyone automatically assumed it was intended for a man. "I need to keep it off the damp floor, at least," she said, staring dubiously around the dirty structure.

"How about up here?" He moved toward the rear, where a stack of wooden pallets formed a kind of platform.

"What's goin' on?" The voice echoed loudly enough in the reaches of the barn to make Anneke jump. She turned to see Barbara's silhouette in the doorway, sharply outlined against the bright sunlight outside. The shape was larger than she would have expected, somehow menacing in the gloomy building.

"Phfah, what a mess." Barbara came toward them out of the light, shattering the illusion. "Got to get this place cleaned out, come spring." She wrinkled her nose. "That dresser in your car? You sure you want to put that in here?"

Anneke nodded. "It's just for a couple of days."

"Well, if you put it up here, it should be okay." Barbara climbed onto the pallets, removed a rusted hubcap, and tossed it to the ground. "You two bring it in," she said, locating a broom from somewhere in the recesses of the barn, "and I'll sweep off a place for it."

Meekly, Anneke and Cleve did as they were told, deferring, as everyone seemed to do, to Barbara's authoritative expertise. The chest, small as it looked, was surprisingly heavy; Anneke breathed a sigh of relief when they maneuvered it finally onto the pallets without scratching the fine patina.

"Here, throw this over it." Barbara had found an old blanket, threadbare but reasonably clean, and under her direction they wrapped the chest carefully, tucking the blanket corners under its legs. Barbara stepped back finally and nodded approval. "That should keep it okay," she said. "Long as nobody steals it," she added darkly as they exited from the barn. "I don't suppose that policeman boyfriend of yours is any further along on findin' out who killed James."

"I . . . really don't know what sort of progress the police have made." Anneke fought to keep her voice level, aware of Cleve's amused expression. Damn the woman!

"Well, they got no call to go botherin' Harvey," Barbara said acidly. "Damn idiots they are, goin' around makin' trouble just because a fool of a kid has a nightmare." So she knows about that, too, Anneke thought; so did Cleve, she realized, seeing his jaw clench angrily.

"How is Ross?" she asked.

"He's okay." Barbara shrugged. "Least, he will be once he gets this vampire nonsense out of his system." She glared at Anneke accusingly. "Kid always was too nervy; last thing he needs is someone to encourage it." She stamped away toward her house, leaving Anneke sorting and discarding half a dozen angry retorts.

"Well, I'd better move my car," she said finally to Cleve. "Thanks for the help."

"*De nada.* I hope your 'policeman boyfriend' appreciates that chest." He grinned.

"God." Anneke cast her eyes upward. "How the hell did she know?"

"Our Barbara knows everything that goes on in Mackinac

Court," Cleve said solemnly. "Not much happens here that she misses. Especially," he leered cheerfully, "nocturnal visitations."

"Oh shit," she exclaimed forcefully, not sure whether to laugh or kick something.

"Don't worry about it." Cleve laughed. "Consenting adults, remember?"

"Right." She laughed with him, sharing absurdity, and climbed back into the Alfa, thankfully pushing the button to raise the convertible top.

SIXTEEN

Still, she thought as she drove to the office, Karl would have to be told. He might think it best to restrict his visits to Mackinac Court to purely professional errands, at least until James's murder was cleared up. If it ever is, she thought dismally; it had already been five days, and if the police had made any real progress, she certainly didn't know what it was.

"Ms. Haagen, did you want me to work on this public-school survey?" Calvin asked as soon as she pushed open the office door.

"No. You don't have enough statistics yet." She crossed to her desk.

"I thought I could use him on the preliminaries of the city council project," Ken offered.

"Good; that's UNIX-based, and I think he's pretty good at C," she agreed, looking at Calvin. "Let Carol handle the survey." For the next while, she sorted out work assignments, read through the mail, and concentrated on work. When she finally leaned back, stretching, it was after one.

On the way to lunch, she picked up a newspaper, and over a tuna sandwich she read the day's report on the murder with growing consternation.

It was no longer old news; today it took up nearly a quarter of page one in the morning paper. Under a large photograph of Mackinac Court, and a smaller one of the leader of the University's Gay Students' League, the headline read:

LOCAL GAYS PLAN PROTEST RALLY

In the wake of the murder of university student James Kenneally on New Year's Eve, local gay activists are planning a march on Ann Arbor City Hall Friday afternoon, following a memorial service for the slain architecture student. The memorial service is scheduled for 3:00 P.M. at Huron House, the nondenominational student chapel.

Kenneally, a former chairperson of the University of Michigan Gay/Lesbian Students' League, was found strangled near his rooming house in Mackinac Court Friday morning.

David Arneson, current chairperson of UMG/LSL, announced the march last night, in a statement that included accusations of police indifference and community persecution of homosexuals.

"There is a very strong, very active, and increasingly violent antigay underground in the city of Ann Arbor," Arneson charged. "The police are very much aware of this, but have refused to take any firm action because they hope it will drive gays out of town. It's time to put this city on notice that we are not going to go away, that we intend to stand up for our rights as citizens, and that, if necessary, we will fight back against antigay violence whenever and however it is necessary.

"If James Kenneally had been heterosexual," Arneson continued, "the police would have his killer in custody already. We do not intend to allow open season on gays in the city of Ann Arbor.

"Everyone who cares about civil liberties in Ann

Arbor should be concerned about the life and death of James Kenneally. We call on those people—gay or straight—to join us Friday afternoon at four o'clock to march to City Hall to protest the unequal protection of the law provided by the Ann Arbor police."

Lt. Karl Genesko, heading the investigation into Kenneally's murder, said that while he is aware of, and deplores, antigay violence, the police at this time do not think that was the motive for Kenneally's murder.

"We believe the murderer was someone Kenneally knew," he said, "and we think that the killing was motivated by reasons that have nothing to do with Kenneally's sexual orientation."

A department spokesperson strongly denied Arneson's charges of police indifference to violence against gays, and he announced that they planned to put on extra personnel for Friday's march. "We do not expect any difficulty protecting the demonstrators," he said.

Anneke put the paper aside with a sigh. If she weren't in the middle of it, she knew, she would have had a certain amount of sympathy for Arneson's anger. But she felt an absolute conviction that in this case, at least, they were wrong—that James's sexual orientation was irrelevant to his murder.

For the rest of the afternoon she kept busy working, putting off the call to Karl, and in the end he called her, just as she was about to leave for the day.

"I should be getting a couple of hours off for good behavior this evening," he said. "Can you join me for dinner?"

"I'd love to."

"Good. Shall I pick you up around seven?"

"Why don't I meet you at the restaurant?" she said after a pause. "I'll explain when I see you."

"All right." His voice held only the mildest interrogatory note. They settled on a Chinese restaurant on the edge of town, and

Anneke gratefully powered down her terminal and headed home to change.

"Have you made any progress?" she asked him when they were seated and had ordered.

"Well, negative progress." He smiled a trifle grimly. "No one admits having visited Rosa Barlow the night she died—not the neighbors, or any of her friends, or any of the people in the Theatre Guild."

"Theatre Guild?" Anneke looked at him in surprise.

"Yes, didn't you know? She was very involved in theater work. She was an actress as a young woman—first in vaudeville, then in silent movies. She married late, at forty, and quit show business, but she stayed active in local dramatics. In fact, she was supposed to do *Arsenic and Old Lace* this spring."

"At seventy-eight? How marvelous. I wish I'd met her." Anneke recalled Cleve's fondness for the dead woman. They paused for the arrival of their food, and over orange-spiced pork and General Tso's chicken, she followed a new train of thought.

"Could any of the people in Mackinac Court definitely *not* have been Rosa's visitor?"

"Nobody has an ironclad alibi, if that's what you mean. We checked them out, of course, but it's all pretty inconclusive." He maneuvered pork deftly with his chopsticks. "T.G. and Barbara Smith, home all night together. Carfax, home all night alone. Marshall, in the library until it closed at midnight."

"Any witnesses?"

"He says he saw several people he knew at different times, but there's nothing there that would really lock him in at the relevant time. Joe Roper," Karl continued, "was home alone with his daughter, who had a stomachache. Brenda Roper was at a Museum Associates meeting; according to her, the meeting broke up around ten o'clock but she spent another hour or so there on paperwork for the acquisitions committee, which she chairs. She says when she got home around eleven, Joe was already asleep."

He paused and sipped his beer. "And finally, Harvey Barlow says he was in his office until after one A.M."

"What on earth was he doing in a dental office for half the night?" Anneke asked in surprise.

"Cooking his books, is my guess," Karl said sardonically. "He's being called in for a tax audit next week. Oh, and by the way," he added, "Frances Barlow says that she, like Marshall, was in the library until closing time."

"I never thought of her," Anneke admitted. "But really, you know," the thought struck her, "it couldn't be her. Or Harvey either, for that matter."

"You mean because Ross would have recognized his own parents?" he asked shrewdly.

"Well, wouldn't he?" she countered.

"Maybe." Karl shook his head dubiously. "But remember, the boy was sleepy, and then terrified, and whoever he saw was pretty thoroughly covered up. What's more, Frances Barlow has a pretty good motive. Harvey is behind in both alimony and tuition payments; if he gets a windfall from the sale of the house, she shares in it."

"Yes, but remember, she couldn't have killed James," Anneke persisted. "She wasn't in Mackinac Court that night."

"That's true." He looked at her quizzically over his beer.

"All right," she capitulated, "I know you can't prove a connection. But two murders by two separate murderers in one court in one week?" she said scornfully.

"Are you sure we even have two murders?"

"Yes! And so are you."

"I know." He sighed and spooned fried rice onto his plate. "But I've got to tread very carefully on this one. I'm up to my shoulder pads in press and politicians. Especially now that the gay activists have decided to stick their considerable two cents in."

"In a way," she said thoughtfully, picking up a last piece of chicken with her chopsticks, "I'm kind of glad to see gays beginning to get themselves some political clout."

"Well, I wish they'd learn to use it more intelligently," he said sourly.

The waiter arrived with their check. As Karl signed the charge slip, Anneke turned reluctantly to the subject she'd been avoiding all evening.

"There's something else I think you'd better know about," she said awkwardly.

"Oh?" He looked up.

"Not about the murders, really. About . . . Barbara saw you leaving my house last night and drew her own conclusions," she said in a rush.

"I see." The corners of his mouth twitched faintly. "And what exactly did the saintly Mrs. Smith conclude?"

She recounted her conversation with Barbara, repeating the words "policeman boyfriend" with such loathing that he started to laugh.

"All right, all right." She made a face. "But it really isn't funny, you know."

"Well, if you object to the term *boyfriend*,"—he grinned— "there's always . . . Never mind." He brought himself up short. "I'm sorry if I've caused you problems with your neighbors," he said seriously.

"Good Lord, you can't think I'd care about that," she protested, stung. "I'm merely concerned that it could put you in a very difficult position in regard to your work." The words sounded stilted even to her; worse, she was only half-sure they were true.

"If you'd rather I stayed away . . . ?" He let the sentence trail off.

"Do you really think," she said stiffly, "that I'd let an appalling, narrow-minded, self-important woman like that dictate my behavior?"

"Not for an instant," he said, in an entirely serious tone that didn't quite mask the amusement in his eyes. "Shall we go? I have a meeting with an assistant prosecutor in half an hour. Unfortunately, I'm afraid Barbara Smith will watch from her window in vain tonight."

Anneke thought later, walking into the empty cottage and flicking on the television set: well, if Karl isn't going to worry about Barbara, I certainly won't. Still, it was probably just as well that he was busy tonight; she'd get undressed, watch television for a while, and go to bed early. The thought of this thoroughly rational plan for the evening gave her no pleasure whatsoever.

In the nightmare the smoke was featherlight, curling around her face in pearly luminescence. It insinuated itself under her eyelids, in her nostrils, its touch so gentle that she didn't realize, at first, that she could no longer breathe. She tried to brush it away, but it wrapped itself around her hands, her arms, her face, insistently caressing. Then the fear began, spiraling to panic as she fought for breath, fought to draw air into her lungs. . . .

"No!" Anneke came awake to the sound of her own cry, leapt from the bed and grabbed for the fire extinguisher, fumbling her arms into the sleeves of her robe as she jammed her feet into slippers. . . .

"Oh shit." This time she could laugh at herself, she decided. After all, she hadn't had a nightmare in several days; she'd have to expect them to recur occasionally, for a little while longer. In the meantime, brandy was definitely called for. She pulled the robe around her and turned to set down the fire extinguisher.

That was when the smoke alarm sounded.

The insane scream of it was shocking, unbearable; she felt the adrenaline rush of sheer, atavistic terror, the ancient primate fight-or-flight response. The agonizing cacophony was a physical pain, not a warning of danger but itself the enemy. With a sob she raced for the kitchen, for the source of the assault, wanting only to put a stop to the hideous din.

Smoke was curling up from the floor behind the kitchen counter.

The smoke detector clung to the ceiling like an evil slug. Its light had come on, illuminating the living room in odd patterns of light and shadow. If she climbed onto the kitchen counter she could reach the thing, yank its battery, silence the endless, appalling, nerve-shattering scream.

Smoke was curling up from the floor.

She stared at the foggy wisps for the space of several heartbeats. The smoke was real. Forget the shrieking horror of the smoke alarm and concentrate. The smoke was real—she could smell it now, taste it—but there were no flames. Odd; it seemed to be coming up through the floor, from the basement. Only, the cottage had no basement, not even a crawl space—it was simply a frame structure set on a concrete slab. She peered more closely through the smoke, seeking its headwater, its source. There! At the base of the wall the white paint seemed to be moving, oozing, changing color like a monochromatic kaleidoscope. Outside, then; the source of the smoke was *outside* the cottage.

For a moment the closely reasoned deduction gave her such satisfaction that she simply stood and watched the smoke eddy along the floor, marveling at her own cleverness. A random wisp reached out toward her, curling up and around her face; she inhaled, coughed. And then finally, as if someone somewhere had thrown a switch, her mind kicked out of panic mode.

"Oh shit!" She looked around frantically. She was still holding the fire extinguisher; she started to aim it at the base of the wall and then stopped herself. No—the fire was *out*side. She raced for the door, flung it open and sped around to the side of the cottage.

At the back of the narrow space between her cottage and Cleve's, so narrow that she could have stood with arms outstretched and touched both buildings, a tapering pillar of flame licked the sky, engulfing what had once been a tall, thin hemlock. The fire danced and leapt and swirled, and every now and then a shower of sparks shot forth, like spores seeking new sustenance. As Anneke watched, momentarily frozen, a tongue of flame detached itself from the parent blaze and descended on a clump of juniper growing against the wall of her cottage. There was a dull, whooshing thud, she jumped back, and the small bush simply disappeared in a ball of flame.

Cleve. She should wake Cleve. But even as the thought came she discarded it, her mind sorting options with preternatural clarity. So far, the blaze itself was actually more or less confined to the masses of shrubbery; the cottage walls themselves were starting to scorch but were not yet burning.

She raised the big fire extinguisher. If she acted now, her mind reasoned coldly, it could probably handle the fire, whereas if she wasted time rousing Cleve, both cottages would inevitably be lost. Now: Hold it upright; aim at the base of the fire. Good; swing it back and forth; get maximum coverage from the foam. *Don't waste it.* There; flames were licking at the bottom of that yew. Got it! Got it; nearly under control now. Only, she wished that whoever was making that small, continuous, intensely irritating whimpering sound would for God's sake shut up. . . .

"Anneke! Jesus Christ! Here, let me help." It was Cleve; he grappled for the fire extinguisher but she hung on to it grimly. Hold it upright; swing it back and forth; aim low.

"Anneke, it's all right!" Cleve shouted in her ear. "Let me help —the fire department's on the way!" She heard it then, over the hissing of the nozzle, over the spitting and crackling of scorched wood, the gloriously rising wail of sirens, the finest sound in all the world.

She released her grip on the fire extinguisher so abruptly that Cleve staggered slightly under its sudden weight. She backed away unsteadily, out of the narrow channel between the cottages, turning to scan the night beyond the courtyard. There—there came the pulsing red lights, moving up Division. She raced toward the entry drive and out onto the sidewalk, waving frantically as the big yellow trucks approached.

"In there! Hurry!" she shouted as the first of them cut its siren and rumbled through the hedge opening. The driver nodded once, reassuringly, and eased the huge vehicle forward. Cleve was standing there waving and pointing, she saw; a second fire truck followed the first; it was all right now. It really was all right.

Only then did she start to shake.

SEVENTEEN

• • • • •

She found herself finally, with no clear idea of how she got there, standing next to one of the fire engines, with a strange, rough wool blanket wrapped around her, watching men in black, rubbery-looking coats stamping around her cottage. She looked around, trying to get her bearings; the continuous pulsing of the red fire-truck lights gave the scene an evil, unearthly appearance.

There were two—no, three—of the huge yellow trucks. Cleve stood off to one side, in quiet conversation with one of the firemen. Barbara and Prof stood a little away, bundled in coats, Barbara with an expression of outrage on her face. Anneke saw other faces then—Gail and Cass, flowered nightgowns showing underneath long down-filled coats; Joe Roper, his round face worried; T.G. standing on his porch, black topcoat over plaid pajama pants, looking oddly uninterested. Not Brenda, though, and not Harvey, although when she glanced toward the Barlow house, Anneke thought she saw a face at one of the bedroom windows. Another neighborhood get-together, she thought, choking back laughter.

The blanket itched intensely; she started to throw it off and then stopped quickly as the cold hit her. The green velvet robe, ridiculous to start with, was no outfit for a January night in Michigan. Why the hell hadn't she grabbed a coat before tearing outside like a demented lunatic? Well, at least she could go back inside now and change into something decent.

She started to edge toward the cottage, obscurely worried that someone would stop her, when the sound of another siren made her pause. She turned in time to see Karl's new Land Rover leap the edge of the drive at such speed that the small knot of onlookers jumped back in alarm. Karl was out of the car almost before it skidded to a halt inches from the nearest fire truck; he strode forward, gave her one long, comprehensive look, and then turned to one of the firemen.

"Get these people out of here," he snapped, jerking his head at the onlookers. "You, all of you," he barked. "Please go back into your homes at once."

"I got a right to be here," Barbara retorted, undaunted. "That's my property that's burnt."

"Mrs. Smith, this is a crime scene," Karl declared tightly. "Any of you who refuse to return to your homes"—his gaze raked the assembled spectators—"will be placed under arrest at once and charged with interfering with the police in the performance of their duties." As if to add point to his words, a maroon-and-blue police car pulled into the drive.

If any more vehicles show up, Anneke thought hysterically, Mackinac Court will be in gridlock. She watched as people drifted away. Cleve started toward her, glanced at Karl, and stopped; then he gave her a quick smile, sketched a salute and disappeared into his cottage. Now what's the matter with him? Anneke wondered, turning to look at Karl.

The expression of cold, concentrated anger on his face staggered her. She had never before seen him so angry—in fact, she realized, she had never seen him angry at all. Karl didn't *get* angry. But now he was so coldly furious that the fireman he was talking to had backed away from him uneasily, leaving a gap between them that Karl's raised voice had no trouble bridging.

"Christ, of course it's arson," she heard him say, his voice carrying above the rumble of the fire trucks like a whip crack. "This is officially an attempted murder and you'd fucking well better treat it like one."

The fireman said something Anneke couldn't catch. She'd never heard Karl swear like that, either, she thought irrelevantly.

"I expect a complete investigation report on my desk by noon tomorrow. No, I don't give a shit what time it is. *Or* how dark it is. Jesus, haven't you people ever heard of portable floodlights?" Karl motioned over his shoulder, and a figure moved hastily toward him from the police car. "One of my people will stay here and work with you." There was another murmur from the fireman.

"Just *do* it!" Karl shouted, and then, shockingly, he raised his arm and hurled something with all his strength against the side of the nearest fire truck. It was a flashlight, Anneke saw in the split second before it smashed against the truck; it hit with such force that the side panel of the truck dented under the blow.

For a moment nobody moved, frozen in a kind of insane tableau; then Karl turned his back and retreated to the Land Rover, while the others continued to stand and stare at him. What on earth is wrong with him? Anneke wondered, shocked by his outburst. And what did he mean, "attempted murder"? She saw Brad Weinmann move finally, approaching one of the firemen and whispering something in his ear. The fireman shrugged and nodded, seeming to take it in stride.

She wished they'd turn off the flashing red lights; the constant flicker was interfering with her mental processes, making it hard to concentrate. There was something she should be figuring out, but she couldn't figure out what it was. As she worked on it, Brad approached and put a hand on her shoulder.

"Anneke, you must be freezing," he said quietly. "Why don't you come inside?"

"Yes, all right." She sagged against him, suddenly exhausted, giving up her mental effort. "The fire's completely out?"

"Absolutely," he reassured her. "Thanks to you—the firemen

said if you hadn't had that fire extinguisher and known how to use it, both cottages would have been totaled."

"How much damage was there?"

"Nothing structural," he answered, pushing open the door. "See for yourself."

She stood for a moment inside the doorway and looked around, marveling at how normal the cottage looked. There were dark splotches on the kitchen wall which she assumed were water damage from the fire hoses, but other than that there were no visible signs that anything out of the ordinary had happened. Just another day in Mackinac Court. She laughed aloud and Brad looked at her anxiously.

"No, I'm not going to get hysterical." She laughed. "It's just . . . oh shit."

"Why don't you sit down and let me get you some brandy," he suggested, still looking concerned.

"Best offer I've had all day." She sat down on the sofa finally. Muscles twitched in her arms. She'd be sore tomorrow, she realized; the fire extinguisher had been heavier than she'd thought.

"Here you go." Brad handed her a glass of pale gold fluid. "Drink it slowly," he warned.

"I know." She took a small sip of the brandy, feeling its warmth gratefully. For the first time, she began to relax. *I didn't do too badly at that*, she thought with a glimmer of self-satisfaction.

"Brad, will you please get the interrogation going?" Karl entered without ceremony and stood in the doorway, biting off terse sentences. "Now, while everyone's still awake. There's a search crew on the way; we'll need to brief them when they get here. I've assigned Eleanor Albertson as liaison with the fire-investigation team; make sure she understands the drill. Oh, and don't forget to cordon off the site—all of it." He looked meaningfully at Brad, who nodded once quickly and left the cottage. Only then did Karl turn to her.

"If you're planning to make a habit of this," he said, "you might want to start buying your fire extinguishers wholesale."

Anneke looked for the half smile that should have accompanied the bantering words, but it wasn't there. His face was tight and peculiarly expressionless; after a moment, he crossed to the liquor cabinet and poured himself a brandy.

"Now," he said, glaring at her, "will you please tell me—no, wait." He strode to the bedroom and returned with her white-covered duvet. "Here," he said angrily, "get rid of that goddamn blanket."

"I forgot I still had it," she said in surprise. The blanket, recalled to notice, began to itch furiously once more, and she yanked herself free of it and threw the disgusting thing to the floor. She reached for the duvet, but stopped when she saw the expression on Karl's face. "What's the matter?"

"You'd better take that off, too," he said in a strained voice.

She looked down, with a sense of shock, at the remains of the green velvet robe. It was no longer provocative. The hem was torn and ragged, filthy with dirt; one large chunk, and several smaller ones, were charred into ugly, pitted masses where fire had melted the nylon; the lace trim hung in tatters; and everywhere were smears of ash and dark, matted splotches still damp from foam.

"Well," she forced a laugh, "I guess I'll never replace Alexis Carrington in this."

"No." He didn't smile. "Take it off, please," he said, with such seriousness that it didn't occur to her to object. She unbuttoned the remains of the robe and dropped it to the floor alongside the blanket, shivering in her thin nightgown. The look on his face was entirely devoid of sexual awareness, yet she felt a sudden, rare moment of self-consciousness; she took the duvet quickly and huddled into the corner of the sofa.

"Now," he said savagely when she was seated, "will you please tell me why the bloody *hell* you didn't call the fire department?"

"I didn't . . . but Cleve called them," she said, nonplussed by his anger.

"Yes, *after* you went rampaging out there like a road-company Red Adair. Fighting fires is a job for professionals, not idiotic amateurs."

"Now just a minute," she flared, "in case it escaped your attention, I *put out* the damned fire. If I'd stopped to call, this cottage would now be a mass of smoldering timbers."

"So you risked you life to protect eight hundred square feet of woodwork?"

"No! It wasn't like that, damn it. Besides, I didn't 'risk my life.' I got the hell out of the house, just like I did before. I did just what you're supposed to do."

"Right," he said scornfully, glancing so pointedly at the rag of green velvet that Anneke felt her small store of self-satisfaction leak away as though it had never existed. The fact is, she confronted the truth dismally, I didn't call the fire department because it just plain never occurred to me. In fact, I panicked. Again.

"All right, maybe I should have called," she admitted, trying to shrug it off. "All I can say is that it made sense at the time. Besides," she added, caught between anger and self-ridicule, "I'm damned if I'm going to buy a *second* new wardrobe in two weeks."

His face struggled visibly for a second as he tried to maintain his anger; then he gave up and burst into laughter.

"My God, you *are* an idiot." He sat down next to her finally and put his arms around her, duvet and all. He held her more tightly than usual, his face against hers; the roughness of his unshaved cheek felt oddly comforting against her face. "Don't you *ever* do anything like that again," he said, raising his head and staring down at her with a look of such intensity that a shiver went through her. But before she could respond he shook his head and released her, his face composing itself into its familiar, calm expression. "Now," he said briskly, "tell me everything you can remember about the fire."

"There isn't much *to* remember." She sighed, pulling the duvet more tightly around her. "I woke up, the smoke alarm went off, and I ran outside with the fire extinguisher."

"Repeat that, please?" he said sharply. When she did so, he asked: "In that order?"

"What do you mean?"

"You woke up first, and *then* the alarm went off?"

"Yes." She thought back, checking her memory of events that seemed a lifetime ago. "I had a nightmare," she admitted uncomfortably. "I think that's what woke me."

"Can you recall the events of the nightmare?"

"Why on earth would you want to know that?"

"Just humor me, please?"

"All right, but . . . no, sorry." She shook her head after a brief pause. "It's gone."

"Never mind. Did you hear anything when you woke up?"

"You mean before the alarm went? Not that I can recall, no. There really wasn't much time; it seems to me that the alarm sounded almost immediately."

"Did you see or hear anyone, or anything, while you were"— he paused deliberately—"fighting the fire?"

"No." There was a point to all his questions, but she couldn't quite pin it down. She tried to shake off exhaustion, forcing her mind to function. "It was purposely set, wasn't it?" she asked finally.

"Oh, no question about it." He nodded. "The shrubbery between the two buildings was drenched with gasoline." He picked up the rag of green velvet and held it out to her. "Here. You can still smell it."

"Is it . . . connected to the murder? Murders?" She tried not to think about the implications of standing practically on top of a fire in a gasoline-soaked robe.

"I have no idea. Yet," he said grimly, giving her a quick, light kiss as he got to his feet. "Now, I think it's time for you to get some sleep. If you'll get dressed and throw some things into a suitcase, I'll take you back to my place. You can spend the rest of the night there."

"But . . . your place? Why?" Anneke looked around, suddenly nervous once more. "Brad said the fire was out, that there was no structural damage."

"There isn't. That's not the point."

"Then why do I have to leave?" She shook her head in confusion. "I don't understand."

"You really don't, do you?" he said soberly. "You *must* be exhausted. Anneke, think—someone tried to murder you tonight."

"Murder? Me? But . . . that's ridiculous," she blurted.

"I wish it were," he said tightly. "But someone in this delightful little enclave sneaked out in the middle of the night, poured gasoline around your house, and set a match to it. And until we find out who it was, I want you where I can be sure you're safe."

"Karl, that's absurd." But even as she spoke the words her mind was analyzing data. "Why me?" she asked. "I mean, why not Cleve? The fire would have taken both cottages, wouldn't it?"

"Good point." He nodded approvingly. "But unfortunately, the evidence contradicts it. Gasoline was poured on the bushes and on the side of your cottage, but not on his. Whoever did it obviously didn't care if the fire got Marshall, too, but you were the primary target."

"But *why?*" For a moment the reason seemed more important than the fact. "Why on earth would anyone try to kill me? *I'm* not involved with these people. Unless . . ." She stopped and stared at him in horror. "My house. The other fire. Maybe it has nothing to do with Mackinac Court. Maybe it's someone else entirely, someone who . . ."

She didn't realize she was shaking until he moved quickly to her and wrapped his arms tightly around her. She huddled against him, absorbing comfort like physical warmth from his body, feeling her terror subside. No, not subside exactly, merely withdraw to a deeper recess of her mind—not gone, just crouched and waiting. She fought against the renewed shivering, the assault on her self-control.

"I don't think the two fires are connected," Karl said soothingly when her tremors at last stopped. "Remember, your house went up very quickly, all at once—it couldn't possibly have been caused by an arsonist as amateurish as this one."

"Still . . ."

"We'll check it out," he reassured her quickly. "But in the meantime, you'll be safe at my apartment."

She would be safe with him, she knew. She could stop fighting the fear, all the fears. Safe . . . the word brought her up short. She would be safe, yes; but it would be his safety, not her own. No one could give her that, she had learned laboriously; she could manufacture it only within herself, layer by painful layer, like an oyster toiling over its pearl. She couldn't leave, didn't dare leave. Any single surrender to fear, she knew suddenly, meant complete surrender.

"I can't," she said at last, pushing back nauseating dread. "I have to stay here."

"Anneke, don't be silly," he said sharply.

"I have to," she insisted, as much to convince herself as him. "Don't you see? I can't let someone frighten me out of my own home."

"You're being ridiculous," he declared angrily. "Someone is trying to kill you, for Christ sake."

"I know." She shrugged miserably. "And yes, I'm scared. But it's just something I have to deal with by myself. Please understand," she said when he didn't speak, "this is just the way I have to do it—on my own."

"Yes, I think I do understand," he said at last, and Anneke thought he sounded tired and oddly sad. "The cat who walks by her wild lone can't afford to need other creatures. And yes, I'll admit you've never given me the right to worry about you. Very well," he said briskly, striding to the door and taking his coat from the hook. That isn't what I meant! she started to cry out, only to wonder if perhaps it was. "There'll be a police guard outside for the rest of tonight," he said as he left. "Otherwise . . . take care of yourself."

She looked at the blankness of the closed door, frozen by the ambiguity in his parting words. Was he merely warning her to be careful, or was it something more final than that? She remained where she was, huddled on the sofa wrapped in the duvet, for a long time before finally dragging herself to bed. To her surprise, she fell asleep almost immediately.

EIGHTEEN

• • • • • •

It was late in the morning when she woke, all at once with her heart pounding. She'd been dreaming the college dream, the one where you're in a classroom taking an exam, only you've never been to any of the classes or read any of the material; it took her several long seconds to get her bearings, to register the duvet around her, the sun streaming in the window.

The faint smell of burnt ash.

Reality flooded in, unwanted, a heavy weight settling in the pit of her stomach. The fire, the fear. Someone trying to kill her. Karl leaving . . .

Stop it. She sat up quickly and swung her legs over the side of the bed. Once she was up and dressed and fully functioning, she'd be able to sort it all out.

Only, there were no data *to* sort, she concluded a while later. Even a long, hot shower, clean clothes, and two cups of coffee couldn't create sense out of nonsense. And the notion that someone had tried to kill her was nonsense. She hardly knew the people in Mackinac Court; she was entirely irrelevant to Division Square or anything else in their lives; she hadn't seen or heard anything that she hadn't already passed on to the police. It was ridiculous; evidence or no evidence, Karl *had* to be wrong.

Karl . . . She ran over his parting words for the tenth time. Well, it will be all right, she assured herself. And damn all messy emotionalism anyway, she thought fiercely; I don't *want* to have my life screwed up by sloppy, uncontrollable feelings like fear, and love.

Her mind scurried away from the word, and she stood up quickly. There was always the good old basic prescription for emotional distress—work. And she'd slept so late that it was already after ten o'clock. She drained her coffee cup, picked up her briefcase, and headed for the door.

Outside, the smell of damp, burned wood was stronger. There was yellow police tape across the area between the two cottages, and, she noted in surprise, the splotch of bright yellow catching her eye, police seals on the door of the barn. And, everywhere she could see, the ground had been beaten into a wet, soggy mess.

Only then did Anneke register the ambient temperature, cool and clean-feeling against her face—forty degrees at least, possibly higher. The January thaw had come at last.

For a moment she simply stood and breathed in the lovely air, reveling in the sense of pure, physical euphoria familiar only to cold-climate dwellers. Then she slogged across the courtyard to her car. Even the presence of a police cruiser in the parking area couldn't dampen her rising spirits as she climbed into the Alfa and, in a gesture of idiot bravado, pressed the button that retracted the convertible top.

I'll call Karl later and sort things out, she thought, smiling in response to the smiles of passersby as she drove to work. The streets and sidewalks were crowded with people, coats thrown open, grins on their faces as they splashed laughing through widening puddles. Impossible to feel gloomy on such a day.

When she pushed open the door to the office, the first thing she saw was Marcia Rosenthal standing on a chair in a corner, stretching to reach the ceiling.

"What's going on?"

"I found this at a little shop on Liberty. Isn't it great?" Anneke peered dubiously; "this" was a construction of circuit boards and chips and electronic oddments, linked together into some sort of mobile.

"There!" Marcia said triumphantly, before Anneke could comment. She jumped down from the chair to admire the addition, which twisted in the air over a bank of filing cabinets whose tops were covered with stacks of printouts. Well, one more thing littering the office won't make all that much difference, Anneke thought wryly. And at least it was sufficiently out of the way that it wouldn't fall on anyone or get tangled in their hair.

Then she looked at it more closely and winced—Marcia had hung her treasure from the ceiling with a long strand of dental floss. Something clicked in Anneke's mind, and she stood for a long moment staring at the nearly invisible strand. Something about dental floss . . .

"Ms. Haagen? Is it all right?"

"It's fine, Marcia." Anneke sighed and shook her head; the random notion, whatever it was, had disappeared. "Where is everybody?" she asked, suddenly aware of the empty office.

"Ken and Max both called to say they wouldn't be in till this afternoon. Actually, I thought I'd cut out a little early too, if that's okay?" Her voice trailed upward hopefully.

"In other words, everyone's getting a jump on spring fever." Anneke laughed. "Sure, go ahead." She watched the girl gather up her book bag, grab for her purse as it slid off the desk, and bump into the door as she left. Why not? Anneke thought. I'll go through the mail, then call Karl. Maybe we can drive out to Island Park and feed ducks.

But when she called the police desk and asked to be put through to Karl, it was Brad Weinmann who answered.

"Hi, Anneke. Karl's in a meeting, so he asked me to fill you in." His voice sounded vaguely uncomfortable, Anneke thought, but when he continued he seemed straightforward enough. "First, we got the report on your house fire, and it definitely wasn't arson."

"Are you sure?" she asked anxiously.

"One hundred percent positive," he assured her. "The fire started inside one of the walls—fused wiring. There's absolutely no question about it."

"Then the two fires weren't connected."

"No. Last night's fire *was* arson, of course. Someone splashed gasoline on the bushes and on the outside of your house and put a match to it." Well, she'd known that, of course, but hearing it repeated gave her an unpleasant jolt nonetheless. "We think," Brad continued, "that the gasoline came from that barn there in the court. We found a couple of nearly empty cans in there, next to a power mower, and it looked like they'd been moved recently."

So that's why the barn was sealed off, Anneke realized. But it didn't help, of course; everyone in the court had access to the barn, and most of them used it at one time or another.

"I assume there weren't any fingerprints on the cans," she said.

"Nothing usable." She could almost see him shaking his head. "And it really wouldn't mean anything if there had been—anyone there could have a plausible reason for messing with them, even just moving them to get to something else. The place is a mess, after all." He sounded offended by the barn's disorder.

"I know." With a start, Anneke recalled the chest she'd stored there. She wanted to ask Brad if it was all right, but couldn't figure out, quickly enough, how to phrase the question. Well, she'd check on it later today—maybe give it to Karl tonight, as a kind of peace offering.

". . . all trampled down, unfortunately," Brad was saying.

"Sorry? I was out of phase there for a minute," she said hastily. "What did you say?"

"Just that there weren't any usable footprints," he repeated. "The fire was started at the rear of that alleyway, and presumably the arsonist went around behind one of the cottages after he torched it. But the ground around there is all beaten flat, and of course the fire hoses turned the whole thing into a complete mess."

"And this thaw probably finished the job." Anneke sighed.

"Thanks, Brad. Would you ask Karl to give me a call when he gets out of his meeting? I'm at my office."

How the word *mess* did keep cropping up, she thought unhappily, looking around the unnaturally empty office. Without the usual cheerful bustle, the untidy stacks of printouts, used coffee cups, and discarded wads of paper made the room seem suddenly, unbearably chaotic. Well, screw it, she told herself savagely, reaching for the power switch on her terminal; thank God for cool, orderly algorithms.

Programming was soothing, mind-filling; the necessities of pure logic drove out extraneous stimuli, drove out emotion. Only the ache between her shoulder blades forced her, finally, down from the pure Platonic plane and back to messy reality. She was surprised and a little dismayed to discover that it was past one o'clock. Surely Karl should have called by now.

She dialed the familiar number, but once again it was Brad who answered.

"Hi, Anneke. I'm sorry, but Karl's out of the office." This time, he sounded definitely constrained.

"Oh, well, never mind." Anneke fought to keep her voice level, unrevealing.

"Anneke, is everything all right?" Brad asked awkwardly.

"You mean aside from two house fires in a week?"

"I just meant . . ." His voice trailed off, and Anneke felt guilty for her sharp tone. Brad wasn't just prying; he was honestly concerned.

"Other than that, Mrs. Lincoln, how did you like the show?" She forced a laugh, trying to defuse the uncomfortable moment.

"Yeah, well . . . There's one other thing," Brad continued, sounding relieved to be back on professional topics. "We'd like to use your place for a stakeout tonight, if it's okay with you."

"A stakeout?"

"Yeah. Just on an off chance, of course," he said hurriedly, "but we thought it'd be worth a try. If it's okay, Eleanor Albertson will set up there sometime this afternoon. You won't have to do anything, just let her keep watch."

So. Point to Karl, she conceded with angry admiration. She could have rejected a guard for her protection, but how could she be so churlishly selfish as to refuse to cooperate with the police investigation? No wonder he was refusing to accept her calls.

"Certainly," she yielded with as much grace as she could muster. "Tell her to come ahead." She rang off quickly to avoid saying more, then stared around the messy, empty office for a minute before standing up abruptly and grabbing her purse. Screw it all, she thought again; I'm going to go feed ducks.

Outside, the temperature had climbed still further, and the red shearling coat suddenly felt intolerably hot. I'll go home first and change clothes, she thought, looking enviously at the swarms of students wandering State Street in a happy daze of light windbreakers and sweatshirts. Most of them seemed to be in arm-and-arm pairs, making the most of the rare, cherished April in January. Anneke found herself elbowing them aside fretfully as she walked to her car.

The continuing thaw had turned Mackinac Court into a morass of mud, puddles and chunks of weirdly shaped, blackened snow. Anneke picked her way across the courtyard, intent on keeping her suede boots as dry as possible; not until she had nearly reached her doorstep did she become aware of the sound.

It was an odd, muffled thumping that seemed to be coming from Cleve's cottage. No, beyond that, she decided—from somewhere around the barn. Police activity of some sort? She took two or three steps in the direction of the sound and then stopped and looked around.

The yellow barricades and seals were still in place, but the police car was gone from the parking area. The court seemed ominously empty. Nonsense, she told herself, of course it's empty, it's the middle of the day. Still, she probably shouldn't go haring off like a gothic heroine. At least see if I can bring along reinforcements, she jeered at herself as she crossed to Cleve's cottage and knocked on the door.

"Hi. ¿Qué pasa?" he asked, opening the door in bare feet. His eyes looked red and puffy.

"Well, I just . . ." Now that she'd got her reinforcements, she felt stupidly embarrassed. "How are you?"

"About as tired as we both look." He eyed her. "Thank God for smoke alarms. Is something else wrong?"

"I don't know," she said, now more dubious than ever. "Do you hear something odd?"

They both stood silently for a moment, listening. The thumping sound continued, halted, came again.

"Wait here while I get some shoes on." Cleve disappeared inside and reappeared a few seconds later, tennis shoes thrown on over bare feet. "Come on."

He led her to the door of the barn, its bright yellow seals still firmly affixed. There was no question now—the thumping sound was emanating from behind that sealed door. They looked at each other, perplexed.

"There's a window around back," Cleve said. "Let me go take a look."

"Be careful," she said, glad she'd had the sense to bring him along. Of course, he still had to be accounted a suspect, she reminded herself, even for the arson. After all, he hadn't called the fire department until after the fire was nearly out.

"Come on." He reappeared around the corner of the barn at a run, splashing heedlessly through ankle-deep puddles.

"What is it?" she asked as he tore at the strips of yellow plastic across the door.

"It's Prof."

"Prof?" Whatever she'd expected, it wasn't that.

"Yes. I think he's hurt. Damn this stuff." He yanked the plastic tape free finally and hauled open the door, and they both peered forward into the darkness.

"Over here! Jesus, it's about time." Prof's voice was weak but as irascible as ever. "I've been banging on the wall for half of forever. I thought I'd be stuck here all night."

Anneke turned toward the voice, her eyes still accommodating to the darkness. She finally saw him, over in the corner to her left, lying on the floor against the back wall. Above him, the dirty window was propped open. His body was crooked over a rolled-up carpet, there was a rusted bicycle over his legs and chunks of what seemed to be a broken table were scattered around him.

"Good God, are you all right? Here, let me help you." She reached for his arm, but Cleve stopped her.

"No, don't," he said grimly.

"He's right." She noticed now that Prof's voice sounded hoarse, and as her eyes adjusted to the gloom she realized his face was covered with a sheen of sweat. "I think . . . I broke something." He pointed down along his body, and Anneke saw his leg twisted through the structure of the bicycle. "You'd better call . . . medics." She looked at Cleve, who nodded.

"I'll stay here with him," he said.

"Right. Hang on, I'll be right back." She wasted no further time on commiseration, but raced back through the puddles to her cottage and dialed 911, giving them the vital information as economically as possible. She took a few seconds for thought—a blanket, and some sort of stimulant. Not alcohol, she knew; perhaps hot milk. She ran a cup through the microwave, grabbed a blanket while it heated, and made her way back to the barn.

"They're on their way," she said, wrapping the blanket around him. "Here, can you drink this?"

"Don't want it." Prof waved the cup away angrily. "Just want to get the hell out of here."

He looked worse—gray and drawn and, worst of all, frightened. She sought for something to say but could think of nothing reassuring; at his age, broken bones could be disastrous. In any case, prolonged conversation would probably just tire him even further. She heaved a sigh of relief when the wail of sirens penetrated the barn, and she ran outside to direct them.

"In here." She waved to them.

"For Pete's sake, what's goin' on now?" Barbara appeared on her porch. Anneke motioned toward the barn.

"It's Prof," she called. "He's had an accident."

"Bad?" Barbara called back.

"I don't know." Anneke shook her head and waved her arms to

indicate ignorance, then turned to follow the two paramedics who jumped out of the ambulance. But once inside, there was nothing she and Cleve could do but stay out of their way as they knelt over Prof and performed their complicated tasks. She stood aside, feeling worried and helpless.

"Crazy old man." Barbara was still zipping up her coat as she hurried into the barn. "What's he doin' muckin' around in here, anyway?" She craned her neck to see over the paramedics, but their backs blocked her vision. "Prob'ly went and broke something, and I'll have to take care of him the next two months." She would, too, Anneke knew; she'd carp and complain and nag, but she'd see that Prof was well cared for.

The paramedics straightened up, and Anneke saw that Prof was now secured to a stretcher, blankets tucked around him. His eyes were closed, whether in pain or sleep she couldn't tell.

"Are you takin' him to the hospital?" Barbara asked.

"Yes, ma'am. Are you a relative?"

"No, thank goodness," Barbara answered crossly.

"Is there someone we can notify? Someone who can be at the hospital with him?"

"No, he's got no relatives." Barbara shook her head, looking worried. "I'd go with him, but I've got a houseful of kids comin' home in a little while."

"I'll go with him," Anneke said after a momentary pause.

"I'll go too," Cleve volunteered promptly.

"Good. You can check in at Emergency," the paramedic said, carrying the stretcher toward the ambulance.

The ambulance, siren wailing, disappeared quickly. Anneke climbed into the Alfa and put the top back up and Cleve squeezed into the passenger seat with a grimace, his legs folded at an uncomfortable angle. Anneke made a gesture of apology as she put the tiny car in gear; the Alfa really was a one-woman vehicle, her own personal capsule. That may be why I love it so much, she mused, driving out Washtenaw toward the hospital.

NINETEEN

* * * * * *

By the time they got to the hospital Prof had been engulfed in the medical process, and it was more than an hour before they were directed into a small room where the old man lay. His face still looked pinched and drawn surrounded by hospital white, but his color was better and his temper was as surly as ever.

"Come to take a look at the old crock?" he grunted.

"Something like that." Anneke smiled at him. "How are you feeling?"

"About the way you'd feel with a broken ankle and twenty pounds of plaster on the end of your leg." He motioned to the foot of the bed, and Anneke saw with relief that the cast extended only as far as his knee.

"You were damned lucky," she said sharply, aware of a growing fondness for the testy old man. "That could have been a full-body cast. How long are they going to keep you here?"

"Dunno how long they're gonna try, but I plan to be home in a couple of days."

"If you stage a breakout, Barbara'll never let you forget it." Cleve grinned a warning at him.

"Humph. Damned woman thinks I can't take care of myself."

"Well, I'm not so sure you can," Anneke asserted. "What on earth possessed you to climb through that window into the barn, anyway?"

"None of your business."

"The hell it isn't," Cleve declared. "If it weren't for her, you'd still be lying there. The least she deserves is an explanation."

"Well, she's not gonna get one." He glared at both of them impartially.

"You've been in and out of there several times lately, haven't you?" Anneke said suddenly, remembering his shambling form coming from the direction of the barn on more than one occasion.

"So?"

"So, that's where the gasoline came from." She looked at him directly, seeing now not the cranky, rather endearing old man but the bitter, hostile ex-radical, ex-activist.

"Ah shit," he snorted, meeting her eyes squarely. "You really think if I wanted to torch a building I'd do such a piss-poor job of it?"

"Then what *have* you been doing in the barn?" she persisted.

"Like I told you"—he shook his head stubbornly—"it's none of your business."

"Perhaps not. But it *is* mine." Karl stood in the doorway surveying them for a moment; when he moved forward to stand by Prof's bed he seemed to fill the small room.

"Hah. I wondered how long it would take the fuzz to get here." Prof looked more pleased than disturbed by Karl's arrival; he seemed to gather himself together, the light of battle in his eyes.

"All nine-one-one calls from Mackinac Court are reported in," Karl said mildly. "I'm sure you realize, Professor Carfax, that I need to ask you some questions."

"I think that's our cue to split," Cleve said hastily. "Anneke?"

"Hey, stick around," Prof protested.

"I've got to get to the library." Cleve shook his head.

"Well, you stay then." Prof turned his head toward Anneke.

"I've got a right to have a witness present." There was an odd sort of urgency in his voice.

"If it's all right?" she asked Karl.

"Oh, it's perfectly all right with me," he said, in a tone so wholly neutral that Anneke felt a sudden chill. "However, Professor Carfax might prefer to have an attorney present."

"Attorney." Prof spat the word. "I don't need an attorney, because I'm not going to tell you anything."

"Well, if you'll excuse me, I think I'll grab a cab home." Cleve left the room hurriedly, and Karl closed the door behind him.

"Now, Professor Carfax," he returned to the bedside, "perhaps you'll tell me why you broke into a sealed crime scene."

"And perhaps I won't," Prof mimicked Karl's even tones.

"You realize I can have you arrested for criminal trespass, interfering with a police investigation, and suspicion of arson?"

"And *you* realize I'm eighty-three years old." Prof hitched himself up on one elbow, clearly enjoying himself. "Y'know," he said conversationally, "in general, old age sucks, but there's an element to it that's very . . . empowering. Women have the same advantage, sometimes," he said to Anneke. "If the culture perceives you to be weak and powerless, you're immune to certain of its mandates. For instance," he continued didactically, "thirty years ago if a kid on a bike nearly ran me down, I didn't dare flip him a bird; he might've stopped and decked me. Now I can do it without fear of retaliation. Women can, too, in normal middle-class circumstances."

There was something to what he said, Anneke mused, struck by his shrewd comment. She forgot sometimes, she realized, that he was an academic, with the academic's habit of analysis.

"Now, you can threaten all you want," Prof continued to Karl, "but we both know that nobody's going to jail an old crock my age for procedural nonsense like that—not unless you can connect me to a crime a lot more tightly than you can at the moment." He leaned back against the pillows with a satisfied grin.

"I take it, then, that you're refusing to explain why you broke into the barn," Karl commented, unruffled.

"Got it in one."

"Very well." He looked down at the old man. "If you were merely being contrary, you've punished yourself sufficiently." He glanced pointedly at the cast on Prof's leg. "If you're involved more deeply than that . . . well, you're not going anywhere. Now, if you'll both excuse me?" He turned toward the door and, to Anneke's dismay, favored them both with an impassive, unsmiling nod.

"Will you be—" She broke off, aware of Prof's eye on her.

"I'll let you know, of course, if we learn anything further about the fire." His expression was entirely courteous and entirely distant. "And thank you for your cooperation on that other matter," he added, with such polite formality that her stomach turned to ice. He closed the door quietly behind him, and she stood and stared at its blank surface.

"You're better off without him," Prof spoke acidly behind her.

"It's not . . . never mind. How are you feeling?" Anneke moved hastily around behind him and fluffed pillows.

"Love's nothing but trouble anyway," he continued as if she hadn't spoken. "Look at me—thirty-five years of marriage and this is what I have to show for it. What's the point of being happy for thirty-five years if you end up miserable anyway?" He twisted around to look at her. "You're better off learning to be unhappy from the beginning, right?"

"Don't be silly," she said sharply.

"That's the other thing about being old," he replied. "You're allowed to make outrageous statements—once you're over sixty you automatically become either profound or senile. Did you know that swans mate only once, for life? No one's ever figured out how they decide which mate is right for them. Stupid birds, swans." His head went back against the pillows and his eyes closed.

She stood and watched the rhythmic rise and fall of his chest under the gray hospital blanket, unsure whether he was asleep or merely ending the one-sided conversation. After a while she picked up her coat and tiptoed from the room.

She thought about his ramblings as she left the hospital and climbed into the Alfa, dumping her coat on the passenger seat, spreading out now that she was alone in the car. Wheeling out of the parking lot, she turned left, on impulse, toward Huron River Drive, and for a while she simply drove, speeding west in the little car along the twisting, treacherous road. She drove as fast as she dared, forcing herself to concentrate on the road, forcing herself not to think about Prof's enigmatic—sardonic?—comments, about murder, or arson, or fear. Especially she didn't think about Karl, or the icy weight that remained in her stomach.

Somewhere out past Barton Dam she put the top down again, trying to savor the sense of pure, solitary, unalloyed freedom she usually felt, alone in the tiny car. And then, as she reached the entrance to Delhi Park, she knew what she had to do.

She pulled into the entry drive to the park, past dripping, snow-weighted trees, and sat and stared at the frozen, tumbled rapids. After what seemed a long time, she spun the Alfa around, floored the accelerator, and hurtled back toward town.

It was past 5:30 when she got back to Mackinac Court. The three children—no, in fact today there were five of them, Anneke noted—stamped and shouted in the sloppy puddles, their galoshes sending sprays of water skyward to glitter in the twilight. As she detoured around them to avoid being splashed, Joe Roper hurried across the court to intercept her, ignoring the wetting he received.

"I just heard about Prof," he said, his round face worried. "Is he all right?"

"He's fine," Anneke reassured him. "He broke his ankle, and they're going to keep him for a few days, but it's nothing serious."

"Thank God," Joe said fervently. "Does he need anything? Is there anything I can do for him?"

"I don't think so, at least while he's in the hospital. Why don't you drop in on him tomorrow?"

"I'll do that. What the hell was he doing in the barn, anyway?" he peered at Anneke anxiously.

"I don't know." She spread her hands. "He refused to say." She stepped aside for the small gray Toyota which pulled into the court, Harvey Barlow's discontented face just visible behind the wheel. One of the childish figures detached itself from the group at play and took one or two reluctant steps forward before pausing.

"Come on home, Ross," Harvey called, slogging through the melting snow. "This used to be a nice, safe place for kids," he said sulkily, coming up to Anneke and Joe. "Now we get murders, and fires, and God knows what else—no wonder kids get nightmares." He glared at Anneke.

"Hi, Miss Haagen." Ross's dragging feet finally brought him abreast of the adults. "Is the computer okay?"

"Don't bother Miss Haagen anymore, Ross," Harvey said quickly. "I don't think she'll want you messing around in there after everything that's happened."

"Of course I do," Anneke said sharply. She wasn't sure whether Harvey meant the fire or Ross's own experience, but she was moved by the unhappy resignation on the boy's face, and repelled by Harvey's air of peevish satisfaction. "He hasn't been 'messing around,' " she said pointedly. "He's been learning computer programming—and at an amazing rate, by the way. The computer's fine, Ross; the fire didn't hurt it at all. Anytime you want to get back to work, just let me know."

"Are you sure?" The boy looked cautiously hopeful.

"Absolutely. Only—" The stakeout, she remembered suddenly; it was probably already in place. "I'll be busy tonight, but how about tomorrow afternoon, after school? Unless, of course," she directed the challenge toward Harvey, "your father has some reason to object?"

"I suppose not." Harvey shrugged, but there was hostility on his face. "As long as you don't get him all upset again."

"I'll see you tomorrow then," she said to Ross, refusing to dignify Harvey's comment with a response. Now why, she wondered as father and son trudged away, does Harvey want to keep Ross away from me? Ordinary parental concern, or something else? Or is Mackinac Court turning me hopelessly paranoid?

"Poor Harvey." Joe shook his head sympathetically. "He's never been very good at coping, if you know what I mean."

"Yes, well . . ." Anneke let the sentence trail off, feeling her own sympathies engaged elsewhere. All very well, but it was Ross who paid the price for Harvey's personality flaws. And perhaps Rosa and James, as well? She shook her head irritably. "I'd better get home," she said abruptly, turning toward her cottage.

When she pushed open her door she found the promised stake-out already in place.

"Ms. Haagen?" The woman who stepped forward, hand out-stretched, was small—barely over the minimum height require-ment, Anneke guessed—and petite and darkly beautiful, with huge brown eyes and curly masses of dark brown hair. "I'm Elea-nor Albertson." She pulled her wallet from her purse and flipped it open expertly to display the police shield. "I hope you don't mind my being here," she continued formally, with no hint of apology in her voice. "Karl—Lieutenant Genesko—told me to come in when I was sure no one would see me."

"I don't mind in the least." Anneke smiled brilliantly. Eleanor Albertson's use of Karl's first name had been no accidental slip. "I won't be here tonight in any case." She started toward the bed-room. "Just give the key back to Karl tomorrow," she tossed over her shoulder.

One of the things she had done after leaving Delhi Park was to buy a small suitcase. Now she packed clothes and makeup and nightwear and, for good measure, the latest Gillian Roberts paperback. She might have a long wait.

"You're welcome to anything in the refrigerator," she told the policewoman when she returned to the living room. "I imagine a stakeout must be pretty boring."

"Are you leaving town?" Eleanor Albertson eyed the suitcase with barely concealed curiosity.

"Leaving town? No." Anneke went to the door and donned her coat.

"Will . . . the police know where you are?"

"I don't think that will be a problem," Anneke replied ambiguously. "Good luck with your stakeout." And she closed the door gently behind her, savoring the range of emotions on the other woman's baffled face.

She went first to her office, where she found Max and Calvin hunched over their keyboards. She worked contentedly for a couple of hours, then ate a late dinner at a nearby coffee shop. It was after ten o'clock when she let herself into Karl's apartment.

It was empty, of course; she'd seen the vacant parking spot reserved for the new Land Rover, purchased when Karl decided Thunderbirds were too small for him to drive comfortably. She knew that major cases always meant late nights. She poured herself a glass of sherry, flicked on the bedroom television set, and curled up on the king-size bed with her book, perfectly content to wait.

The bright overhead track lighting penetrated her light doze. She opened her eyes to see Karl standing in the bedroom doorway regarding her somberly.

"What are you doing here?" he asked, and Anneke could discern no trace of welcome in his voice. She sat up, blinking against the light; well, she hadn't really expected any better. She took a deep breath to get her over the first difficult moment.

"I'm here because I love you," she said with utmost seriousness.

"Even assuming that's true," he replied, unmoving, "it just isn't good enough."

"I'm here because I need to be here."

"That makes it worse, not better." He shook his head. "You don't *want* to need me. You think that anything you can't cope with alone is a kind of defeat. Anneke, I don't want to be the continual instrument of your defeat. We want different kinds of relationships, different—"

"I sold my car."

"—levels of commitment. I don't—what did you say?"

"I sold the Alfa. Traded it in. It took some fast work, too."

"For what?" He asked the question intently, as if it mattered.

"A Firebird."

"A *what?*"

"The new Pontiac Firebird. Well," she said, half-defensive, half-amused by his look of disbelief, "it's the only interesting car I could think of that's big enough for you. You'll love it—two-seventy-five horsepower, V-eight engine, *six*-speed transmission, at sixty-five miles an hour the engine is barely moving." She subsided, aware that she was babbling.

"Oh shit," he said with quiet violence, sitting down at the foot of the bed and staring at her. Emotions flickered over his face so quickly that Anneke couldn't read them; well, at least there *are* emotions, she thought, holding her breath. "You loved that damned car," he said at last.

"Yes, I did," she agreed with a pang. "But I didn't *need* it." She met his gaze squarely; at least she knew he understood her quixotic gesture.

"I don't know if that's true," he said slowly. "Sometimes symbols can be more powerful than reality. Are you so sure of what you need and don't need?"

"Sure?" she flung the word back at him. "Of course I'm not sure. I'm not sure you won't fall for a twenty-five-year-old rookie a month from now, either." She allowed a smile to play over her face. "You've got to learn to take some risks, Lieutenant."

"Take risks . . . ?" he choked. "You know," he surprised her by taking her seriously, "you could be right. Maybe," he regarded her thoughtfully, "I *have* been too cautious." He stood up, took off his jacket, removed his tie. "Just remember," he said, his eyes glittering as he flicked off the overhead lights, "it was your idea."

This time when he made love to her it was not with sophisticated, half-amused skill, but with a raw passion that seemed to explode between them. There was too much undeclared emotion between them, too much dormant tension; it erupted all at once, in a single fierce detonation that left her shaken and gasping.

They made love again then, more slowly this time, with a rich, creamy sensuality that was almost unbearable. She cried out once as the spiraling crescendo of sensation caught her, and he looked at her with a feral grin and said mockingly, "Anytime you want me to stop, just say so," and she disgraced herself by gasping out, "Don't you dare!" so that he laughed aloud in a kind of triumph.

Is this the man I thought was too safe? she wondered through the roaring in her ears, and the notion was so absurd that mirth bubbled through her, and this time it was she who laughed. And *that* surprised him, she saw with enormous satisfaction as they came together at last with an explosion of passion.

A long time later, he lay propped on one elbow looking down at her.

"Well?" he said at last, and the single word had the quality of a complex question.

"Yes," she replied, not entirely certain what she meant but certain that it was the right answer. She turned and curled herself against him, to sleep with his body next to hers.

TWENTY

• • • • •

When she woke Friday morning, from a sleep so deep that waking was a kind of decompression, Karl was already gone. She sat up and looked around fuzzily, feeling disoriented. The digital clock radio on the bedside table blinked 8:36; next to it was a chrome carafe and a large black footed mug. When she opened the carafe the aroma of hot, strong, fresh-brewed coffee was almost mind-expanding.

Any man who can make coffee like this is worth giving up a sports car for. She smiled to herself, downing one mug of the wonderful liquid before getting out of bed. She showered and dressed and made the bed, then took the rest of the coffee into the living room. There, she sat at the round Queen Anne dining table in a state of tranquil euphoria and surveyed the room with the mild wonder Karl's apartment always engendered. Not that the elegant, mostly British antique didn't suit him; what surprised her was how comfortable she always felt in an environment so alien to her own personal tastes.

Less alien than the Firebird, at least, she realized when she stood in the parking garage staring at the huge metal-flake blue beast crouched in its slot. Although she had to admit, as she pulled out of the garage and launched herself into traffic, that driving the gorgeous monster did offer its own kind of high. She drove directly to her office, nearly sideswiping two parked cars and once jumping the curb on a tight turn. Still, she got a kind of weird delight out of the impressed looks of pedestrians—although most of those who stared, openmouthed, were pubescent males. When she reached her office finally, after a taut several minutes maneuvering the Firebird into her suddenly narrow space in the Maynard parking structure, she was already in love with the car.

The afternoon entry in her calendar brought her out of euphoria with a thud. She'd completely forgotten the memorial service for James. She thought briefly of not going, but rejected the notion, not entirely sure why. A sense of obligation to James, perhaps; and also, she admitted sourly to herself, pure, damnable curiosity.

She read through the mail and was working with Calvin on the outlines of the City Council program when Michael Rappoport called.

"I want to return your lamp."

"I'm not even sure I want it," Anneke replied, recalling the clumsy piece he'd made her buy at the Barton Hills sale.

"Oh, yes you do. When can I bring it over?"

"Well, I need to go home and change clothes later today anyway," she said, feeling that the blue jeans and sequined denim jacket she wore were inappropriate for a memorial service. "Why don't you meet me there around one o'clock?"

"Good. What's the address?"

She gave him directions and returned to work, but her concentration was broken; besides, she was hungry. She gave up and powered down her terminal.

"I'll be back later this afternoon," she told Ken Scheede. "Anything you'll need me for before then?"

"Don't think so," he replied cheerfully. "We should be ready to install the minimall program early next week."

"Good. I'll be glad to get that out of our hair. How's the school survey coming?" She ran through the day's operations with him briefly, wondering how she'd ever have gotten along without him in the last couple of weeks. But when she tried to express her appreciation he waved it away.

"Where else would I get a chance to do so many different things?" He grinned.

"Well, you've got a raise coming anyway," she said decisively.

"Now *that's* the kind of gratitude I like," he said as she picked up her coat.

Outside, the weather remained warm. She stopped at a nearby shop for salad and a turkey croissant to go, picked up a newspaper to read with lunch, and headed home.

The cottage bore no traces of Eleanor Albertson's presence. Anneke wondered briefly if the woman had snooped through drawers and cabinets, decided that of course she had, and found that she was laughing softly to herself. Smugness, she told herself severely, was very unbecoming.

She read through the newspaper while she ate, paying close attention only to the small article about the scheduled memorial service. The Gay Students' League was still planning to march on City Hall; in addition, the Detroit Gay Activist Coalition was sending several carloads of participants to support their Ann Arbor allies. Anneke sighed and moved on to the Lifestyle section. She was reading a review of a new television sitcom when the doorbell rang.

"Here it is." Michael entered with the lamp held triumphantly aloft. It had been cleaned and burnished, and looked a great deal better than it had, but Anneke was still not enthralled. "I knew my instincts couldn't be wrong," Michael said with more than a little smugness.

"I still don't know what you see in it." Anneke shook her head dubiously.

"Not even now?" he looked at her archly. "Well, you, my dear, are now the proud owner of an authentic, original Frank Lloyd Wright desk lamp."

"You're joking." She stared at the chunky artifact in disbelief.

"I never joke about something that could be worth upward of ten thousand dollars," he said loftily. "Here," he grinned at her dumbfounded expression, "let me plug it in."

He set it on the desk, looked around for an electric outlet, and spotted the built-in banquette for the first time. He stopped abruptly. With a grunt, he got down on the floor, turned over on his back, and wriggled under the banquette. He emerged finally, stood, brushed off his immaculate gray trousers, and strode without comment into the bedroom. He was there for several minutes; when he came out, his expression was awestruck.

"Why didn't you tell me?" he demanded.

"Tell you what?" She looked at him, confused.

"You mean you don't know? Jesus, how could you miss it?" Michael waved his arms with angry enthusiasm. "Look at that banquette, and the clerestory windows, and this paneling. And if you missed all that, how the blazing hell could you miss that hexagonal pattern in the bedroom?"

"Michael, will you kindly tell me what on earth you're blithering about?"

"Blithering, am I? Blithering?" His voice rose to a squawk. "When you're sitting in the middle of a Frank Lloyd Wright house and don't even recognize it?"

"What?" Anneke gaped at him. "Are you sure? Oh, Michael, it can't be."

"It can, and it is. I don't make mistakes about something like that," he insisted grandly.

"But . . . then . . ." Anneke sank weakly into a chair as the full implication of Michael's announcement hit her. "My God," she breathed, "so *that's* what James found out in Chicago."

Michael looked at her uncomprehendingly, and she realized with surprise that he was entirely unaware of Mackinac Court affairs. She'd been so involved in it all, she'd somehow assumed everyone else was, too. Briefly she sketched the whole story for him; when she was done he rubbed his hands together, the light of battle in his eye.

"The Frank Lloyd Wright Foundation is in Oak Park; that

must be where Kenneally went. I'll get in touch with them tomorrow. Somebody there is bound to remember him. And then I'll get in touch with the Historic Preservation Commission. We can now document historic value for four of the seven houses in this court, and that's enough for them to act on. Those damned sharks can kiss Division Square good-bye; nobody's going to tear down those two great Victorian houses now."

"So that's why you're so excited." She laughed at his single-mindedness.

"Of course." He looked at her in surprise. "You don't think I care about these gimcrack little cottages, do you?"

So now we know for sure why James was murdered, she thought as Michael departed, rubbing his hands together glee-fully. Or at least, close enough to certainty—she hedged her bets in deference to the demands of pure logic.

And also, she realized suddenly, we know the motive for Wednesday night's fire. She'd been right all along, then—no one had tried to kill her; it was the cottages themselves that had been the target. Except in that case, why did the evidence suggest that the arsonist had concentrated so carefully on her cottage alone?

Shaking her head, she strode to the phone; Karl needed to know about this latest development. But when she called the department, she was told that both he and Brad were out. Well, at least this time I know it's true, she smiled to herself; she left word for him to call, then went into the bedroom to change clothes.

The best she could do for funeral clothes was a light gray tunic over matching pants. And she had her choice between the wildly inappropriate red shearling coat and Joyce's equally inappropriate green parka. The shearling, when she had selected it and stepped outside, was also still too warm; the thaw was continuing, although the sky was now overcast. She mentally put a lighter-weight coat on her still-extensive shopping list and, before heading to her car, detoured toward the barn to check on the antique chest. The yellow police tape, she noted, was gone.

The chest was still in its place on the rough platform, she saw as she stepped into the darkness of the barn, but the blanket over it

• 177 •

had been disarranged. The police—or someone—had un-wrapped it, then. I'd really better get it out of here, she thought. Perhaps tonight would be the time to present it.

She moved forward, sidestepping a large carton that rested against the platform, and her eye was caught by a pale glitter. Jewelry? No, sequins; she bent to examine the contents of the carton, an amorphous mass of discarded clothing. There was a torn peasant dress; a feathered hat with half its feathers missing; a flapper dress, once sequin-covered, whose delicate fabric crumbled under her fingers as she touched it.

"Lookin' for somethin'?" The sound of T.G.'s voice was so shocking in the silent barn that Anneke felt as if she'd been jolted by an electric current. Her whole body jerked in galvanic protest as she spun around, her heart pounding, to see him standing there laughing immoderately at her reaction.

"Got ya good, didn't I?" His laugh was a series of high-pitched, staccato sounds—"he-he-he"—that bounced disagreeably off the rafters. "Funny, you don't look like the kind of gal that'd scare easy."

"I was just . . . checking on the chest I stored here." She backed away from him and clambered onto the platform, getting her breathing under control with an effort.

"You really go for that old stuff?" He eyed the chest disparagingly as she rearranged its covering. "I'da thought you'd like somethin' more spiffy and modern." The look on his face was unpleasantly close to a leer.

"Like a sixteen-story high-rise, you mean?" she retorted acidly.

"It'll sure be an improvement over these drafty old houses," he replied, unoffended.

"You really believe that, don't you?" Anneke asked curiously.

"Sure I do. Nobody really wants to live in these big old eyesores anymore, they just got some idea that anything older's gotta be better." His sharp-featured face grew animated. "S'pose nothin' ever got torn down, what kinda world would you have? You gotta keep movin' forward, that's all. That's what progress is all about, right?"

"Is it 'progress' to destroy neighborhoods and replace them with office space that nobody wants, just to make a profit?"

"If nobody wanted it, it wouldn't *make* a profit, would it?" he answered shrewdly. "Division Square is gonna make a lot of money for a lot of people."

"Don't start counting your money yet," she snapped—and then could have bitten her tongue.

"What does that mean?" Was she merely imagining an undertone of menace in his voice?

"Just that . . . there are still people trying to stop this thing." She stepped down from the platform and moved as casually as possible toward the door. Stupid, stupid to allow herself to be alone with him in this dark, deserted place. She was almost violently relieved to hear his sarcastic laughter.

"Those bleedin'-heart preservationists? They got two chances —slim and none." He snorted. "Nobody's ever stopped progress yet." She heard his laughter once more as she quickened her steps out of the barn.

Huron House was quartered in a converted house near campus. By the time Anneke arrived crowds were already gathering; she drove around several blocks, mournfully passing half a dozen parking spots that would have been big enough for the Alfa, before finally finding a place for the Firebird.

Inside the chapel, there had been only the most minimal remodeling. The interior still consisted of a series of rambling interconnected rooms, randomly furnished and, given the crowds, badly overheated. Anneke stood in the entry hall for a moment getting her bearings, looking through wide archways into the various rooms.

Each room appeared to contain a discrete cluster of people, each cluster oddly separate from the others. Not a function of architecture, she concluded; the small rooms merely gave physical point to the essential separateness of the groups within them.

It was a metaphor of James's life, Anneke thought; each group represented a part of that life, yet each of them stood apart from the others, a kind of symbol of the difficult compartmentalization of James's life. More than ever Anneke felt respect for the dead man, who had walked a tightrope among these disparate groups with apparent success.

She picked out the Mackinac Court contingent first, in a small alcove off one side of the front room. Well, *contingent* was perhaps too grand a word—besides herself, only Cass and Gail, and the Ropers, were in attendance. Brenda, looking appropriately solemn, wore a creamy silk blouse beneath a tailored navy blue suit that was a masterpiece of expensive simplicity. She also wore the triple strand of pearls, now restrung, and still straight rather than knotted, Anneke noted. At her ears were diamond solitaires ringed in gold.

Neither of the Smiths were there, of course, nor was Harvey. Nor Cleve; Anneke thought it must have been a difficult decision for him. She wished momentarily that he'd had the courage to attend, then admitted that she had no way of understanding the pressures he must live with every day. She had no right to make judgments about his behavior, she told herself, looking around at the other mourners.

It was easy to pick out James's gay friends, who more or less filled the big front room. Not because they looked or acted like stereotypical homosexuals, but because they looked and acted like stereotypical undergraduates. Most of them, male and female alike, wore blue jeans and parkas or heavy windbreakers, the standard student uniform. She spotted only two ties and one dress in the group. Two or three, in angry defiance, were tarted up in the kind of gay regalia that Anneke felt sure was more parody than reality. The Ann Arbor gay community didn't often go in for that sort of display.

Unlike the older mourners, they chattered among themselves rather than maintaining the pseudo-respectful silence adults learn to consider appropriate funeral behavior. Anneke recognized David Arneson from his picture in the newspaper; he seemed to be the center of the group, waving his arms in animated conversation.

She spotted a group that she mentally tagged the professional contingent, in the room to her left. Chuck Diamond and Dave Seligson were there, along with two other men she didn't know. All were dressed in sober business suits; they had clearly gravitated toward one another, like to like, and now stood making awkward conversation. There were also several men with cameras and notebooks, presumably from area newspapers, standing around looking bored.

Anneke found herself moving almost automatically toward the Ropers, but before she had gone more than a few feet, the crowd seemed to eddy forward, the groups breaking apart slightly as they flowed toward the center hallway. She found herself being herded down a narrow flight of stairs that debouched into a large, open basement room. She took a seat in the back row of rickety folding chairs and arranged her face into appropriately solemn lines.

The room, big as it was, rapidly filled to overflowing, and the temperature climbed from sultry to stifling. Anneke tried to concentrate on the young minister, standing behind a makeshift pulpit at the front, but found her mind wandering. At least there's no coffin, she thought, obscurely grateful; James's body had been returned to his parents for burial. Poor James, who'd been brilliant, amusing, infuriating, stimulating. She'd been fond of him without truly realizing it; there were things she still wanted to say to him . . .

She came alert with a jolt and looked around quickly, hoping no one had noticed her lapse into semisomnolence. The heat was making her feel light-headed; well, maybe physical and emotional fatigue had something to do with it, too, she admitted to herself. Too many alarums and excursions in her life. She heard the minister's closing words with a gust of relief and pressed through the crowd as fast as she decently could, going straight up the stairs and out of the house to breathe in gulps of cool fresh air.

"Anneke, are you all right?" Joe Roper stood beside her, looking concerned. "Can we give you a lift anywhere?" He motioned toward the curb, where Brenda stood waiting next to the white Buick. How *did* she manage to get the most favored parking space? Anneke wondered. She nodded a polite greeting; Brenda seemed as placid as ever, but Joe looked white and drawn, a caricature of his normal, round-faced cheerfulness.

"Thanks, I'm fine," she told him. "I think the heat got to me a bit. My car's just around the corner, and I think the walk will do me good."

"If you're sure." He patted her shoulder. "I want to get out of here before . . ." He gestured vaguely, and Anneke realized for the first time that the crowds pouring out of the chapel were not dispersing, but were in fact coalescing. Of course, the march on City Hall.

She noted the police presence, recognizing one or two of the resigned-looking patrolmen, and she started to move away when a tap on the shoulder stopped her. She turned to confront a thin, angry-looking girl with long blond hair and reddened eyes who thrust a clipboard toward her.

"What is it?" Anneke asked.

"It's a petition to the FBI, asking for federal intervention under the Civil Rights Act. It's the only way we'll ever get justice for James; we certainly won't get it from the Ann Arbor police." Her voice was harsh with bitterness. "We're asking everyone here who cared about James to sign it."

"I'm sorry." Anneke felt torn between pity and irritation. "I really can't." She saw the contempt on the girl's face and the pointed look at the shearling coat. She stifled an urge to defend her appearance, to defend the police investigators, to defend her safe, ordinary, straight life against the girl's glare. There was no point.

The girl shrugged finally and departed, to join another young woman in a long black 1940s coat thrown open to the mild weather. Underneath the coat, Anneke could see a black sweater and a long necklace of pottery beads on a leather thong. How different they looked from the older group—Dave Seligson, the Ropers, she herself—in their formal clothes and authentic jewels. She saw Cass and Gail falling into position as the marchers formed a ragged line, and the girl with the petition hurrying to catch up to them.

And suddenly Anneke knew who had murdered James Kenneally.

Or at least . . . No, it was too ridiculous. All she had was a single notion, and she couldn't even be sure it was correct. Besides, it didn't make sense. Or did it?

The number of police seemed to have grown; she looked around quickly, wondering for an instant if Karl might be there, but she didn't see him. And he's far too big to miss, she thought, choking back inappropriate laughter. She still hadn't told him Michael's revelation about the cottages, either. She'd better call him right away—well, soon. She needed to think it all through first.

TWENTY-ONE

* * * * *

She found herself standing next to the Firebird in a state of thorough mental confusion. Without thinking, she slid behind the wheel, maneuvered the big car out of its parking spot, and headed east out Washtenaw. She turned left onto Huron Parkway, rammed hard on the accelerator, and shot northward, dodging carnivorous chuckholes as she hurled the car around slower-moving traffic.

As usual when she drove, instinct more than intellect took over; the major portion of her mind was engaged in going over and over the revelation she'd had outside the chapel. She didn't turn her full attention to the road until she heard the siren behind her.

She pulled over, fingers crossed, but her heart sank when the uniformed figure climbed from the police car behind her. No one she recognized; she'd have trouble talking her way out of this one. She ran down the window and placed both hands in plain sight on the steering wheel.

"License please, ma'am?" The young patrolman was scrupulously polite after a single startled look inside the car. Well, how many middle-aged women drive metal-flake Firebirds at excessive speeds on local highways?

"Are you aware that I clocked you at seventy-two miles an hour?" he asked after checking her license. There was, Anneke thought with amusement, a certain amount of respect mixed with the severity in his voice.

"*How* fast?" She poured incredulity into her voice. "Are you sure?"

"Yes, ma'am."

"God, I'm sorry." She contrived to look anxious and guilty. "I just got this car a couple of days ago, and I'm not used to it yet. It just seems to take off if I even *touch* the accelerator. It really is much too much car for me, but most cars are so small these days, and I just don't feel *safe* in one of those tiny things, you know? And they told me when I looked at this that it has one of the highest trade-in values, so . . ." She spread her hands in girlish appeal. "It's silly, really, I know. I think I'm going to have to take it back and get something more sensible. Are those minivans that everyone's driving really safe?"

"If you drive them within the speed limit, they are," the patrolman said sternly. "These muscle cars are very hard to handle; the salesman should have warned you about that." He put his pad back in his pocket. "Look, I'm just going to issue you a warning this time, but you be much more careful from now on, okay?"

"I certainly will, Officer." She watched in her rearview mirror as he climbed back into the patrol car, then continued to watch as she started the Firebird and pulled away at a demure thirty-five. He drove behind her for a short distance and then turned off onto Glacier Way; when the police car was finally out of sight, Anneke brought her foot down on the accelerator with a shout of laughter and roared away up the parkway.

Prof was right, she thought gleefully; there was a lot you could get away with if you fell into one of those groups the culture refused to take seriously. The patrolman hadn't even—thank God—run a check on her license; he might not have been so forgiving if he'd known about the two other speeding tickets she'd collected in the last three years.

The thought of Prof set her mind back to the murder. If she

was right about her preposterous supposition, then . . . She slowed for the Plymouth Road intersection, started to move into the left-turn lane, then slewed abruptly across three lanes to the right, eliciting an angry honk from an outraged matron in a gray Ford Taurus. That's the kind of car I'm supposed to be driving. Anneke grinned to herself, feeling a sudden fondness for the great Firebird. She swung the car into a fast right turn, enjoying the smooth cornering, and sped east toward the hospital.

Prof was awake and looking more grumpy than ever.

"I don't suppose you came to break me out of this place," he grumbled at her.

"Next time I'll bring a cake with a file in it," she told him acidly. "How much longer do they want to keep you?"

"What people want isn't necessarily what they get," he muttered darkly. "You came back to pump me again, didn't you?"

"In fact, yes." She sat down on the chair by his bed. "Prof, I really need to know why you were in the barn."

"You know, don't you." It was a statement rather than a question.

"Know what?" she hedged.

"Pfah. Don't pretend stupidity; you're no good at it and it doesn't become you." He leaned back and closed his eyes, and Anneke thought at first that he was ending the conversation. But after a moment he opened his eyes and surprised her by asking, "How old are you?"

"Forty-eight. Why?"

"Hmph. Old enough, I guess. Nowadays I never trust anyone under thirty—in fact, under forty's more like it." He peered at her. "You're not going to let me alone until I convince you that I'm just an extraneous detail, are you? Well, what the hell, there's no cops around, and even if you blew the whistle on me they couldn't prove anything."

"Cops?" Anneke felt a twinge of misgiving.

"Yeah. See, there's a space in the wall there, behind one of the beams. That's where I keep my stash."

"Your what?"

"My stash. Come on, you're not that old."

"Oh, for God's sake." Anneke started to laugh, and Prof looked offended.

"Think good weed's only for kids?"

"No, I suppose not." She choked back more laughter. "But why the hell don't you just keep it in your house like everyone else?"

"And get busted for possession? With my background they'd throw away the key. Never have more than one ounce in the house; that way all they can do is hit me with a twenty-five-dollar fine. If they find the main stash in the barn, they can't prove it's mine, see?"

"Isn't that carrying sixties paranoia a bit far?" she asked sardonically.

"Yeah, well, even paranoids have enemies." He glared at her. "If you tell your pet cop about this I'll deny it, you know."

"Believe me, there's more at stake here than a random joint." She returned his glare.

"I know." Prof suddenly looked old and tired. "Look, don't let Barbara find out, okay? She'd have my hide for a doormat."

"I promise. And now I'd better get out of here and let you get some rest." Anneke leaned over and kissed Prof on the cheek, ignoring his snarl of protest. "I'll try to come visit again soon, and in the meantime, call me if you want anything, okay?" His grunt of assent, she knew, was all the response she was going to get.

When she got back to the office, it was almost five o'clock. There were two message slips telling her Karl had called, but when she dialed the police department she found she'd just missed him. Swearing to herself, she left word that she'd be at home, went over current work with Ken, and headed back to Mackinac Court.

When she pulled the Firebird into the parking area, Ross scampered over to greet her.

"Wow, is that yours?" he asked, wide-eyed.

"Yes. Like it?"

"It's awesome." Ross patted the black eagle decal spread across the hood, his expression awestruck. "How fast can it go?"

"Flat out, I don't know," Anneke said thoughtfully. "Maybe one forty?" She'd have to find a stretch of road somewhere and crank it up. "I do know it'll do zero to sixty in under seven seconds." She gazed at the Firebird with growing affection before turning to Ross. "Now, how about some computer time?"

Inside her cottage, they shed their mud-clotted boots, and Anneke set Ross to work before trying Karl again. Still out. With a sigh, she turned her mind back to computer lessons, and for the next while managed to put murder and arson—and Karl—out of her mind. They were in the midst of a tricky subroutine when the doorbell rang.

"Finally!" she said with relief, throwing open the door. She'd been impatiently storing up a dozen different things to tell him, but now for a moment she simply looked at his face, feeling a great wash of emotion roll over her.

"Sorry, I didn't realize you wanted me that urgently." The corners of his mouth quirked upward slightly, imparting an uncomfortable ambiguity to his words. Or was she reading double entendres where none existed? she wondered, feeling her face grow warm.

"I've been trying to get hold of you all day," she said severely, and this time there was no mistaking the grin on his face. "Stop it." She laughed helplessly.

"Anything you say." He took a step toward her and then stopped as he saw Ross staring at him. With a mock scowl he dropped his hands and gave her a chaste peck on the cheek which nonetheless sent a small electric flicker through her.

"Time to go, Ross," she said to the boy.

"Okay, Miss Haagen." He saved his work to disc, with occasional glances at Karl. He'll always associate Karl with his terror, Anneke thought sadly.

"How are things going?" Karl asked the boy.

"Okay." Ross ducked his head shyly. "I wore the jersey to school today."

"I hope everyone was suitably impressed." Karl grinned and ruffled the child's hair.

"Yeah. Ronnie Evans didn't believe it was real," Ross said scornfully, "but I showed him the rip from when you tackled Earl Campbell in the play-off game." He looked at Karl wide-eyed. That isn't anxiety, Anneke realized suddenly, it's pure hero worship.

"I just gave him one of my old jerseys," Karl said almost defensively when Ross had left.

"And you didn't even get a Coke in return." Anneke laughed. "Would you like one now, or something stronger?"

"Definitely something stronger." He pulled her to him and kissed her, thoroughly and for a long time.

"Much more of that," she said breathlessly when he finally released her, "and I'm going to forget everything I've been storing up to tell you. Karl, I've found out some things about the murders."

"Hmm. I had a feeling all those messages weren't from motives of pure passion."

"There's nothing pure about it," she retorted. "Anyway, you're right. Karl, I found out why James went to Chicago."

"Oh?" he said quickly.

She reported her conversation with Michael Rappoport, pouring drinks as she spoke and setting them on the coffee table. When she was finished, she sat down on the sofa and watched as Karl examined the cottage intently.

"What are the odds that Rappoport is right?" he asked finally.

"Ninety percent or better, I'd say," Anneke asserted. "Michael has the touch, or the sight, or whatever you want to call it. He hardly ever makes mistakes about antiques. Besides"—she gestured around the room—"once you know, it seems so obvious I can't believe I didn't recognize it myself."

"Yes, it is your period, isn't it?" he commented. "Like that lamp."

"Oh! I almost forgot—that's why Michael was here in the first place. Karl, that lamp is a Wright."

"Is it really?" He looked at the lamp without appreciation. "Extremely valuable, I assume?"

"Too valuable to keep." She realized suddenly that, regardless of its pedigree, she had no intention of living with that metal monstrosity. "I think I'll ask Michael to sell it for me; he knows a Wright collector who's paying ridiculous prices for anything he can get."

"Good." Karl dismissed the lamp with what sounded like relief. "Well, we can check that Wright Foundation tomorrow about Kenneally."

"They should be able to confirm the provenance of the cottages, too."

"Yes. It doesn't really get us much further forward, you know," he warned her.

"Well, but at least we know for sure now what the motive was."

"Not beyond a doubt, we don't. There's still the possibility of a pure coincidence of timing. I know, I know"—he held up a hand to still her protest—"it's not likely."

"Besides, it provides a tie-in with Rosa Barlow's murder," she insisted. "They were both killed to make sure the Division Square project would go ahead."

"Probably. All right, even almost certainly. But that still doesn't eliminate any of the suspects we've been considering all along."

"Yes, but . . ." Her own earlier suspicion flooded back, but she didn't want to go into it yet; her chain of logic was still too fragile. "I think I can eliminate one of them at least," she went on.

"And that is . . . ?"

"Prof. I got him to tell me why he was breaking into the barn—but you've got to promise not to do anything about it."

"You know I can't make a promise like that," he said mildly.

"But it has nothing to do with the murder. Oh hell, all right." She recounted Prof's admission, and was relieved to see Karl's expression of irritated amusement.

"What an idiot." He grimaced. "No, of course I won't do anything about it. Still," he added, "that only explains his presence in the barn. You do realize it doesn't eliminate him as a murder suspect."

"I know." She shook her head irritably. "Actually, nothing I found out today really helps."

"Oh, yes it does," he replied. "For one thing, if we can confirm this Frank Lloyd Wright connection, I think we'll release it to the press and get the gay activists off our tails."

"How did the march go?" she asked.

"Noisy. Ridiculous." He scowled. "Well, reasonably peaceful at least. But a little reality testing would do them all good." He sighed and sipped his drink. "Well, I was probably the wrong person to have talked to them, even if I am the one heading the investigation."

"The prosecutor should have been the one to meet with them, shouldn't he?" Anneke asked, angry for him. She knew what he meant—had seen it happen before. There were people for whom Karl's sheer size seemed to be a personal affront, a kind of macho symbol they couldn't get beyond, especially when they found out he'd been a professional football player. It didn't matter that he wasn't responsible for his physical appearance.

"The prosecutor is a successful politician because he knows when to delegate," Karl said dryly.

"Yes, and to whom." Anneke tried to visualize the scene—Karl surrounded by a mob of angry gay activists—and suddenly the comical aspect of it overwhelmed her. "My God," she giggled, "I'll bet you were a sensation."

"Very funny," he growled, struggling against amusement. He said finally, grinning: "I admit I got one or two interesting offers, but I decided to see if you'd like to better them."

There was a long interval, during which Anneke was too involved to think much about anything extraneous.

"Damn," he said at last, "there isn't time to make love to you properly—I've got a dinner meeting with the prosecutor in half an hour."

"We could probably manage," she murmured.

"Now, now, show some patience." He grinned at her. "Besides," he went on, abruptly more serious, "I'm probably going to have a late night. If you don't mind, I'd like to get you out of here and safely stashed at my apartment before I go back to City Hall."

"Yes, all right. No, wait." It struck her all at once. "Karl, that's not the point anymore."

"What do you mean?"

"Don't you see? I was right the first time. I *wasn't* the arsonist's target. The cottages themselves were, and now we know why."

"Maybe." He sounded unconvinced. "But there's no doubt that your cottage was the more immediate target than the one next door. And in any case," he said reasonably, "that hardly lessens your danger."

"No, but simply moving me out isn't a good enough response anymore. For one thing, you can't just leave Cleve unprotected; for another, until this is over, you don't dare leave the *cottages* unprotected."

"Oh shit," he said savagely, and for a moment Anneke wondered what she'd done to produce such anger. "You're really not good for my thought processes." He shook his head. "I should have worked that out myself, but I was too busy worrying about you."

"I suppose that . . . comes with the territory," she said awkwardly, feeling emotion begin to spiral around them.

"Yes, it does, I'm afraid. If that's a problem for you," he said roughly, "you'll just have to learn to cope with it. Now," he stood and strode to the phone, "I'd better set up another stakeout."

"Could you please," Anneke asked plaintively, "make it someone else this time?"

"I think that can be arranged." The twitch of his mouth told her he understood her request rather too well.

"Karl, look," she said when he finished telephoning instructions, "if there's going to be a police car out front all night, and someone here inside, and if you're going to be tied up until very late, anyway . . ."

". . . you figure you may as well spend the night here," he finished the sentence for her. "Well, I have to admit," he said in a noncommittal tone, "I can't think of any objections on the grounds of logic."

"It's just that all my things are here," she said hastily. "The computer, and all my clothes, and books . . . and you won't be there, anyway."

"All right, I can see your point." To her relief, he nodded. "We'll talk it all over later." He kissed her once, started toward the door, then turned back and kissed her again, long and hard, before finally disappearing through the door.

TWENTY-TWO

* * * * *

Left to her own devices, she wandered through the cottage for a while, then microwaved a frozen dinner and ate absently in front of the television. As she got up to dispose of her plate, she saw a police car pull into the court and roll to a stop nearly on her doorstep.

"Hi, Jim." She opened the door to Jim Zelisco with relief; at least it was someone she knew and liked.

"Hi, Anneke." He stepped inside and removed his heavy jacket, making a face as water dripped off its collar. "Starting to rain," he said unnecessarily. "So this is a Frank Lloyd Wright house." The sharp eyes that peered out of his dark face flicked around the room taking in details.

"Come on in and look around," she invited. "Would you like some coffee?"

"No thanks. Can I dump these in your refrigerator?" He indicated two six-packs of Coke.

"Sure." She gestured toward the kitchen. "Where would you like to set up?"

He settled for a chair and a small table by the front window, sank into it, and popped a can of Coke.

"Are you just going to leave the car out front like that?" she asked.

"Lieutenant's orders." He nodded. "This is what you might call a preventive stakeout. Well"—he saluted her with the upraised can—"here's to a nice, boring evening. You just go ahead and ignore me. I'll let myself out in the morning." He took a paperback book out of his pocket and leaned back in the chair.

He's a nice guy, she thought, friendly and unobtrusive; still, it felt odd to have him sitting there protecting her against her neighbors. She stood for a moment looking out the window at the dark and silent courtyard, the lights from the circle of houses diffused by the increasing rain. For a while this afternoon, she'd thought she had a solution, but now, the longer she pondered it, the more she felt her certainty leaking away. The scene outside looked almost aggressively normal.

Still, there had been two murders in this ordinary little neighborhood. And her original flash of insight remained fixed in her mind. It fit, damn it, however absurd it seemed. She tried to shake her thoughts into logical order, organize the events in Mackinac Court into some kind of pattern, but no pattern emerged. Too bad there are no algorithms for murder, she thought with aggravation.

She regarded the keyboard for a minute, then sat down in front of it, loaded Word for Windows, and set it in outline mode. She stared at the blank form for a while, trying to decide how to proceed.

Well, when in doubt, remember the old axiom KISS: Keep It Simple, Stupid. She set up nine main heads, in order, from "Wednesday, December 29" through "Thursday, January 6." Under the first of these she entered "Rosa Barlow murdered" as subhead one, then moved down and entered "James Kenneally murdered" under January 1 and "cottage fire" under January 5.

That left a lot of empty space, she mused, looking at the mostly bare screen. She started to move the cursor to a new line, then paused. The trouble was, how much detail should she include? In the mass of events and occurrences over the last ten days, what was relevant and what wasn't?

All right, damn it, just start filling space, even if the entries seem totally meaningless. She typed "blizzard," and "Prof breaks into barn," and "Ross sees vampire on computer," added "store antique chest in barn" and even "University classes begin," setting them under their appropriate dates, searching for any starting point to the tangle. But none of it jogged her muddled brain; what she had was another computer axiom, the one called GIGO: Garbage In, Garbage Out.

And anyway, even with all her irrelevant detail, there was still too much empty space. The blank areas on the screen nagged at her, and it took her a while to realize why. It was one particular area—there was too much empty space between "James Kenneally murdered" and "cottage fire."

She leaned back and stared at the screen. *Why* were there four days between the two events? Whoever had murdered James and ripped those pages out of his notebook had known at once the secret of the cottages. Yet the fire had not been set for four more days. Why the wait? Or alternatively, what had happened in the intervening time to make the arson necessary, where it had not been before?

And then, simply and finally, she knew. Not all the details, but the why, and especially the who, unraveled itself in her mind all at once.

The realization made her almost physically ill. For once in her life, the intellectual joy of analytic breakthrough was absent; this was no academic exercise, but a real-world tragedy that would destroy lives.

Should she call Karl at once? No; she wasn't ready, she decided, hoping she was being honest with herself. But what she had so far was still a fragile web of conjecture; she needed to think it through, work out details. She powered down the computer and turned toward the window, where Jim Zelisco sat reading. Nothing more would happen tonight, she told herself, and there were still too many questions she couldn't answer. Tomorrow would be time enough.

When she woke Saturday morning, bright sunlight was jabbing the room through the crack in the drapes. She sat up in bed, her eyes squinted against the glare, and leaned over to peer out the window. What she saw made her eyes widen with awe.

It was a world of crystalline brilliance. Last night's rain had given way to sunlight that glittered and coruscated off a world entirely encrusted in ice. Every branch, every evergreen frond, every twig was individually encased in a thick, perfectly transparent, perfectly gorgeous coating. She scrambled into a robe and raced to the front window. Jim Zelisco was gone; she spared only a brief thought for him as she stared outside.

The courtyard was even more spectacular than the side had been; the big oak tree was a shimmering centerpiece through which sunlight leapt and sparkled. A small holly bush outside her door was a perfectly sculpted masterpiece, each individual leaf and branch and berry standing out in sharp relief. Dazzled and enchanted, she shaded her eyes and looked across the court. What she saw brought her back to reality with a thump.

The ice had laid its gorgeous hand on more than trees and leaves. Every car in the parking area glittered from antenna to hubcap with its own thick integument. Outside the protective confines of Mackinac Court, the rest of the world would look the same—including buildings, and streets, and sidewalks. It was going to be one unholy bitch of a day.

Well, it would have been anyway, she thought, recalling what she had before her. The last of her ice-induced euphoria shattered; still barefoot, she padded shivering into the kitchen, ran water into a mug and set it in the microwave. But when she pushed the starter button, nothing happened. She was really freezing, too; the room was far more frigid than mere early-morning chill would account for. With a wave of foreboding she flicked the kitchen light switch, and was unsurprised when no bulb lit in response. Power lines didn't take well to inch-thick coatings of ice.

She returned to the bedroom, donned a pair of jeans, and layered on two shirts and a thick sweater. She glanced at the clock, but the digital display was dark. She picked up the Vacheron, which informed her it was nearly nine. No wonder it was so bright outside.

Back in the living room, she took stock of the situation. No power meant no coffee. The sheeting ice outside meant no driving—or walking, for that matter; the sidewalks would be, if anything, worse than the roads. She looked at the telephone with hesitation, lifted the receiver, and heard the dial tone with a gust of relief. She dialed the police number and asked for Karl.

"I need to talk to you as soon as possible," she told him without preamble, hearing the tightness in her own voice.

"Did something happen?" He sounded instantly alert and tense.

"No, nothing like that," she reassured him quickly. "But I think I can tell you where you can find dental tape here in Mackinac Court."

"I'll be there in ten minutes."

"Oh, wait." She caught him just as he was about to hang up. "Please, would you bring me some coffee?" she asked plaintively.

He arrived carrying a large grocery bag which he set on the counter. Anneke reached in without ceremony, grabbed the large Styrofoam cup, and sank her face gratefully into the steaming liquid.

"I was getting desperate enough to make dorm coffee," she said after her first sip.

"Dorm coffee?"

"Hot water from the tap." She wrinkled her nose. "It's awful, but it's caffeine."

"Well, this should keep you going until they get your power back on." He reached into the bag and withdrew a second Styrofoam cup, a large aluminum thermos bottle, and a white bakery box. "Last I heard, they figured to have the lines repaired by noon, at least in the downtown area."

"How bad are the roads?"

"Fierce. We've had over thirty accident reports already this morning, and that doesn't even count the fender benders. And if anything, the sidewalks are even worse." He grinned. "I saw one guy lose his footing walking up the State Street hill, fall on his rear end, and slide all the way back down the block to Packard. For a minute I was afraid he'd slide right off the curb into the intersection."

"God, what a winter," Anneke said when she stopped laughing. "We've had just about everything this year but an earthquake." She opened the bakery box. "Muffins! God bless you, Lieutenant, you've saved my life."

"Glad to hear it." He smiled. "I have plans for it. Now, what's this about dental tape?"

Anneke took a bite of muffin and began to talk, starting with the memorial service. She talked without interruption for nearly half an hour, while Karl listened silently, occasionally scribbling a brief line in his notebook.

When she was done he continued to say nothing for a time, staring out the window at the sun-bright morning. Anneke watched him anxiously, aware of how painfully frail her web of reasoning was. It was pure theory, unencumbered by evidence.

"There won't be much evidence," he said finally, mirroring her thoughts.

"The dental tape . . ." Anneke's voice trailed off.

"Not enough. It's too common. Anyone else could have had the stuff, too, and thrown it or flushed it."

"Could Ross make an identification . . . no. So I've just been clutching at straws."

"Not at all." He shook his head firmly. "I don't think there's any question that you've hit it straight on. I just don't know if we'll ever get enough to convict." He stood up. "One way or another, this is going to be nasty. I'd better get back to the station and start the ball rolling."

"I think I'd better get out of here myself," Anneke said, shivering. "Before I freeze to death. I guess I'll go to the office and see if I can get some work done."

"Your office won't have any power either," he reminded her.

"Oh, damn, that's right. A computer isn't much good without power." She looked around the cottage. "I wish this place had a fireplace."

"Well, the power isn't out in the Briarwood area."

"Hmm. Then maybe I'll spend a sybaritic morning at the mall." The murders belonged to the police now; she wanted to shake it all off, pretend it was all over. "I assume the main roads have been salted by now?"

"The main ones, but not much else. Division's okay, and so is South State, anyway."

"Good." She took her coat from the hook, and he held it for her to put on. "I'll call you this afternoon, if that's all right?" She felt obscurely guilty for leaving him to clean up the mess, even though it was his job.

"Of course. By then, with luck the higher-ups will have decided what they want to do."

Outside, Anneke was somehow surprised to see activity in the courtyard. Ross and Cashin were skating gleefully across the courtyard, the younger boy on double-bladed runners. And there were people in the parking area. She could make out T.G. and Joe bending over their respective cars, hacking at thick coatings of ice.

"Oh hell, I didn't think. Karl, I'll never get the car cleared off."

"I'll give you a hand," he offered.

"I don't know," Anneke accepted dubiously, "but we may as well try." They crossed the court in silence with careful, flat-footed steps, eyes on the ground, all their concentration fixed on remaining upright. When they reached the parking area, Anneke stamped her feet into a pile of snow, breaking through the ice coating and getting a firm purchase on the ground at last. Only then did she look up.

T.G., muttering and swearing under his breath, was hacking viciously at the windshield of the big Lincoln, digging the plastic scraper into the ice with short, angry strokes. Next to him, Joe Roper patiently chipped away at the Buick, chopping small holes and working back and forth from edge to edge. The ice, Anneke saw, was well over a quarter of an inch thick.

The Buick's engine was running, and a series of thin grooves in the ice on the rear windshield indicated the defroster was making minute headway against the ice. Through the crystalline coating over the side window, Brenda was visible in the driver's seat, her beautiful face fixed in an anxious pout.

On the other side of the Buick, the big Firebird looked like a malevolent mammoth peering from its iceberg grave. The sides were frozen solid, too; they'd have to scrape it clear merely to get the door open.

Brenda cracked open the door of the Buick and leaned out. "Joe, can't you hurry? We'll miss our plane. And where on earth is Victoria?"

"She's right over there, on the porch with Marcella," Joe answered gently. "Take it easy, love, you still have plenty of time."

"Going somewhere, Mrs. Roper?" Karl asked.

"I'm flying Victoria back to school, and then I have an appointment with my banker in New York," Brenda said fretfully. She was wrapped in the wonderful long-haired fur coat, beneath which the gleam of the great pearls was just visible. Anneke looked at Karl, but all his attention was on the beautiful woman inside the car. His face was impassive as he pointed to the pearls.

"May I see your necklace, please, ma'am?"

"Yes, of course." Brenda looked startled, but pulled back her coat to display the heavy triple strand.

"No, ma'am. Would you take it off, please?"

"What? Of course not. Joe, please hurry!" Brenda slammed the car door shut and turned back to the steering wheel, gunning the engine.

"Mrs. Roper, I have to insist on seeing those pearls," Karl repeated, rapping on the window.

"No!" Brenda reached for a button on the console, and Anneke could hear the click of doors locking. Karl, swearing under his breath, jumped forward and reached for the door handle.

"Mrs. Roper, there's no point to this. If you don't give me the pearls, I'll have to place you under arrest."

Joe looked up curiously; he had been at the far side of the car, and the noise of his ice chipping and the racing engine had covered the exchange between Karl and Brenda. Now he paused in his labors.

"What's the matter?"

"Mr. Roper, I urge you to advise your wife to let me examine her pearl necklace."

"Brenda . . ." Joe croaked out the name, his voice cracking. His face seemed to crumple, to fall in on itself; for an instant he looked a hundred years old. He knows, Anneke thought; he's probably known all along, but God help him, he still loves her.

"Mrs. Roper, please open this door," Karl said, standing firm next to the car.

And then it all happened in a second, like a series of flash frames. Brenda gunned the engine, and the Buick leapt backward out of the parking area, sluing wildly on the ice of the courtyard. Anneke saw children scatter, screaming; heard Karl swear violently as he ran, with agonizingly careful steps over the ice, toward his own car; and, beyond everything, saw the look on Joe Roper's face before he buried it in his gloved hands.

How Brenda got the Buick under control Anneke never afterward understood, but the car finally accelerated in something approaching a straight line, and when it reached the drive it roared out into Division and disappeared. Karl had only just reached the door of the Land Rover, and he didn't try to follow her at once. Anneke could see him through the windshield, speaking urgently into the radio.

When he was done, he started the engine and backed carefully into the court. Once he had it aimed toward the driveway, he looked at Anneke through the windshield and shook his head grimly; when she waved him on, shakily, he gave her an abrupt nod and disappeared.

TWENTY-THREE

• • • • • •

"She was dead when they pulled her car out of the river?" Cleve asked.

"Yes." Anneke poured them both more wine. "It's awful, and yet I can't help thinking it was just as well. The publicity of a trial would have been absolute hell for Joe and Victoria."

They sat on Anneke's sofa, exhausted and drained, after a day of horrors.

"I don't understand any of it. Did she really kill James?"

"James, and Rosa as well."

"It still doesn't make sense. Brenda?"

"It does if you assume one basic fact: Brenda was nearly broke."

"Broke?" Cleve said incredulously. "But she inherited millions. It's almost impossible to go through a fortune like that."

"I don't know what went wrong, but according to Joe, there's very little left." Anneke tried not to think about Joe Roper, alone with his daughter in the ancestral mansion. "I imagine when they contact her New York banker they'll find out how it happened, but it doesn't matter, really. The point is, by her terms she was pretty close to broke."

"I wonder," Cleve said thoughtfully. "I'm willing to bet she still had more assets than either you or I have right now."

"Probably so. It's all in the frame of reference, isn't it?"

"So all the time, she needed Division Square as badly as T.G. did. But why did she pretend she *didn't* want to sell? Why the convoluted secrecy, for God's sake?"

"And have anyone suspect she wasn't still wealthy? That lady-of-the-manor persona was more important to her than anything else in her life." More important to her, in fact, than life.

"My God. I admit I wondered about Rosa's death, but only . . . you know. And at that, I focused on Harvey. It never occurred to me. . . ." He shook his head. "How did she kill Rosa? And why couldn't anyone tell the death wasn't from natural causes?"

"She probably just put a pillow over Rosa's head and smothered her. It would have shown up in an autopsy, of course, but why would anyone bother to do an autopsy on a seventy-eight-year-old woman found dead on her own sofa? Apparently, the doctor just took a quick look at her, shook his head, and wrote out the certificate."

"And all the time she seemed to be such a friend of Rosa's. In fact, I think she'd been in and out of there a lot lately."

"The museum exhibit."

"The what?"

"Brenda's been working on a costume exhibit for the art museum," Anneke explained. "Apparently Rosa was donating some of her old theatrical costumes; Harvey remembers her mentioning it. And there are some old pieces in the barn; she and Brenda probably went through all Rosa's old things together." She paused. "That's what Ross saw."

"What is? You mean the vampire? That was Brenda?" Cleve said in disbelief.

"Yes. At least . . . Here, let me show you something." The section of newspaper was still on the coffee table, left there after she'd shown it to Karl. "This is the outfit she was supposed to model at the exhibit opening." Anneke handed Cleve the picture of Brenda in the evening cape and hat. "I think she was trying it on that night. She must have stopped to see Rosa on her way home, to collect the costumes, and I'd guess to pump her about her intentions. When Rosa made it clear she was absolutely refusing to sell out, well . . ."

"It makes sense." Cleve squinted at the grainy newspaper photograph. "Between the cape, and those feathers sticking up on the hat . . ."

"In silhouette, they'd look something like bat's ears, wouldn't they?"

"To the imagination of a half-asleep kid, anyway. God, poor Ross."

"I know." Anneke pursed her lips. She felt angrier, somehow, about Ross than about Rosa. Even though, she reminded herself, Ross's fright had to be the last thing Brenda would have wanted.

"And then, just when she thought she was all set," Cleve mused, "James threw another monkey wrench into her plans. So she killed him, too?"

"Yes. Joe admitted that the night of the murder she'd been sitting up late in the kitchen restringing those pearls when he went to bed." She paused. "You know, we should have thought that through from the very first. James gets back at midnight, bursting with the news that he's going to save Mackinac Court, that Brenda won't be thrown out of her home. After all, who *would* he have gone to first with the news?"

"Brenda. Of course. Especially if there were a light on in her house." He shook his head. "So he told her his news, and she knocked him unconscious and then strangled him. But why with dental floss, for God's sake?"

"It just happened to be what she had right at hand. I think she wanted to get those pearls restrung fast, so no one would examine them too closely."

"Why?"

"Because they were fakes."

"Fakes!" Cleve looked nonplussed. "Are you sure? They certainly looked real enough."

"Positive. Remember the night they broke, when we were all

scrambling around on the floor for them? I ran one of them over my teeth. Real pearls always feel rough to the teeth; these were perfectly smooth. At the time, I just assumed she wore imitations for safety, and kept the real ones in a safe-deposit box. But it turns out that nearly all her jewels are fakes. She'd been selling pieces off for a couple of years."

"It still seems so . . . unlikely. Dental floss, for God's sake."

"It was the floss that finally gave it to me. I was watching one of the kids in my office hanging a mobile with the damned stuff, and somewhere in the back of my mind the thought registered that dental floss isn't just used for cleaning teeth. People use it for all sorts of things. And then, at James's funeral, I saw a girl there with beads strung on a leather thong, and it reminded me of beads— one of the things dental floss is most useful for is stringing beads; I've used it myself.

"There was another thing, too. After the pearls broke, New Year's Eve, she said she was going to have them strung with knots between them—and in fact, I can't imagine a jeweler who'd string them any other way. But when I saw her at James's funeral, she was wearing the pearls again and there were no knots. So somewhere in the back of my mind I knew she'd restrung them herself. It just took me a while to put together all the pieces."

"Isn't it *too* thick?" he asked. "I wouldn't think pearls would have holes big enough."

"Actually, it works very well—you get a nice snug fit, so that even if there's some give, the pearls don't slide around. And remember, these were *big* pearls."

"Yes." Cleve drained his wineglass and reached for the bottle, pouring more for each of them before continuing. "And afterward, she just hauled the body outside to the parking area? How did she manage it? James was no lightweight."

"We'll never know for sure, but I'd guess she dumped the body onto one of the sleds; they were all over the place, remember? That was the only risky part, but we were all pretty tired after all that exercise. I imagine she waited until quite late, to be sure everyone was asleep."

"So she was home free," Cleve said gloomily. "Wait a minute —what about the fire?"

"She did that too—rather badly, thank God."

"But why?" Cleve spread his hands. "Once James was dead, no one else knew about the cottages, did they? And anyway, why wait so long?"

"That was the question that threw me, too. No, nobody else knew about the cottages, but somebody should have," she said grimly. "Me."

"Why you?"

"Because I'm supposed to be an expert on the Art Deco period, that's why," she responded acidly, still smarting at her own blindness.

"Are you really?" he asked, diverted. "I didn't know that."

"Nobody else in Mackinac Court knew it, either. My entire collection went up in flames with my house, so there was nothing for anyone to see. And the subject never came up in conversation. Except once."

"Brenda?"

"Yes. Wednesday morning." She recalled again her stupid exercise in one-upmanship the day she'd brought home the antique chest. That moment of ego had very nearly cost her her life.

"Was she trying to kill you, or just destroy the evidence?"

"I don't think she really cared much one way or the other." Anneke shuddered. "I think by that time she was very nearly beside herself—every time she thought it was all over, some other threat turned up. I guess I was just the last straw."

"It's still hard to believe."

"I know. It seems so impossible. I think they'd have had a hell of a time convicting her if she hadn't tried to run."

"That's another thing. Where on earth was she going?"

"Presumably to the river. My guess is she was going to throw the pearls off the bridge. She had to get rid of them, once she was suspected, in order to get rid of the evidence of the dental tape." She paused. "I think, if she'd managed it, she'd have gotten off.

The tape those pearls were strung on was the only physical evidence there was."

She stood up and wandered over to the computer, started to flick the switch, then turned away, moving toward the window. The ice had melted; the courtyard was now a morass of mixed snow and mud.

"What's going to happen to them all now?" she wondered aloud.

"Well, I imagine Prof and Harvey will just go on as before," Cleve said, thinking about it. "I don't think Prof really wanted to move anyway—if he had, he'd have sold the house a long time ago. And I doubt that Harvey will ever manage to *decide* to sell."

"I hope Joe does," she said, and he nodded agreement.

"T.G.'ll probably have to bail out too," he said. "Without Division Square, I think the TGS empire is pretty much bankrupt." There was satisfaction in his voice.

"Would you like some more wine?" Anneke asked after a few moments.

"Yes, I think so. Let me get it," he forestalled her, moving to the cabinet. When they were seated on the sofa, he sipped at the wine somberly for a moment, staring into space. "How is Joe? And Victoria?" he asked finally.

"Not good. Barbara's with them now. The doctor gave them both something to help them sleep."

She thought of Joe's face watching the Buick hurtle out of the courtyard. She had stayed with him while he waited, had been with him in the huge, empty house when they came to him with the news of Brenda's death. He had broken down utterly then, answering Karl's questions in a flat, blank voice while tears streamed down his face unheeded.

"He knew about it, didn't he?"

"Pretty much. He loved her." The word covered such a multitude of sins. Anneke stared into the wineglass, contemplating the sort of love that would accept murder as a kind of personality flaw.

"Did you get anything to eat today?" He looked at her care-

fully. "You didn't, did you? And I could use something myself."
He strode to the kitchen, ignoring Anneke's protest, and opened
the refrigerator. After a moment he began pulling things out and
setting them on the counter—eggs, half a green pepper, a chunk
of cheese, and finally the butter dish. "Just sit still; I make the best
omelettes in San Francisco."

She didn't think she was hungry, but when he set two omelettes
on the coffee table, the smell made her mouth water. Gratefully
she sank her fork into the creamy mass, and for a while they both
concentrated on eating. The day's horrors receded a little into the
recesses of her mind.

Afterward, they sat for a while sipping wine, buried in their own
thoughts.

"I'm leaving next week," Cleve said finally.

"Leaving?" Anneke asked, startled.

"Yes. I'm going back to San Francisco. I'm pretty well through
with my research here; I can finish the rest at Berkeley." He
sounded oddly defensive, and finally he added defiantly, "I want
to get home to Andy."

"I can understand that. You're one of the lucky ones too, I
think." She looked at him and thought of Joe, and of Karl,
thought about the different faces of love. "Look," she said
abruptly, "will you give me a hand with something tomorrow afternoon?"

"Sure, with what?"

"I need to move that chest out of the barn."

Karl called late in the evening, full of unnecessary apologies.

"Closing a case can be more trouble than investigating one."
He groaned.

"I know," Anneke said sympathetically. "Especially this one, I
imagine. Look, why don't I meet you at your apartment tomorrow night and cook you dinner?"

There was a long moment of total silence.

"Would you mind repeating that?" he said finally.

"Yes, I would." She laughed at him. "It's an absolutely single, one-time-only offer. Never to be repeated."

"This," he said solemnly, "I have got to see."

Early Sunday afternoon, having confirmed that Karl would indeed be busy at his office throughout the day, she and Cleve wrestled the semainier into the Firebird, wrapping it in blankets and wedging it into the tiny trunk.

"It looks good in here," Cleve said when they had finally maneuvered it into Karl's apartment. He looked around appreciatively. "So do you, oddly enough. He's a lucky man," he added seriously.

"We're both lucky," Anneke agreed. "I nearly blew it."

"Well, don't," he admonished her. "Visit me in California, will you? Both of you."

"I promise," she agreed, meaning it.

She drove him back to Mackinac Court, then went to Kerrytown, where she bought shrimp and ham and hot Spanish sausages, along with saffron and okra and sweet red peppers. For the rest of the afternoon, she cooked, discovering all over again that competence and enjoyment are not necessarily the same thing.

By the time she heard Karl's key in the door the meal was ready, the table was decked out in full regalia, and she had showered and changed into a flowing black-and-white silk outfit that she'd bought with misgivings, afraid it was too revealing. One look at his face informed her that she'd been both right and wrong.

"I hope you're hungry," she said at last, when he continued to stand and stare at her.

"Hungry? Yes, you could say that." He reached for her.

"That's not what I meant." She laughed, disengaging herself with an effort. "I've just spent all afternoon cooking dinner, and you're damned well going to eat it."

"I hope you're not suddenly turning all domestic on me." Behind his mocking tone Anneke could have sworn she heard a note of real apprehension.

"God forbid." She made a face. "Today has forcibly reminded me why I quit cooking in the first place, as soon as I didn't have to anymore."

"Good. You were definitely made for better things." He kissed her again.

"After dinner," she chided him.

"If you insist. Just let me clean up first."

They ate jambalaya with rice, buttered biscuits studded with jalapeno peppers, and chocolate mousse for dessert—blender-made in three minutes, a fact Anneke kept to herself. When they were done, they piled the dishes into the dishwasher and sat together on the sofa with coffee and brandy.

"If you can cook that well," he commented, "I'm surprised you don't want to do it more often."

"I can change the oil in my car, too," she retorted, "but I'm still passionately grateful for the existence of service stations."

"Hmm, yes, point taken." He put down his coffee cup. "There are better things to be passionate about."

"Wait," she said as he ran his hands over the black-and-white silk. "There's one more thing."

He leaned back and raised an eyebrow at her.

"Is this some sort of test?"

"Well, it wasn't meant to be." She sputtered with laughter. "But now that you mention it . . . Come over here. There's something I want you to see."

She had tucked the chest into a corner of the living room half-hidden by a large breakfront, leaving the lights low. Now she switched on a nearby floor lamp and turned it so its beam fell on the richly patined wood.

Karl looked from the chest to her and back to the chest, then knelt down in front of it, pulling open drawers and running his hands over the smooth finish. When he stood up he looked oddly disturbed.

"This is an authentic Georgian semainier," he said accusingly.

"Regency, actually. At least according to Michael. Don't you like it?"

"Like it? Of course I like it."

"It's not perfect," she said anxiously. "Two of the handles are reproductions, and there've been some repairs."

"Even so, it must have cost the earth. I can't let you spend that much on—" He stopped when she laughed aloud.

"It's not so easy, is it?" She grinned.

"Yes, but . . . Look, I know how much you make; Anneke, you can't afford this," he protested. "And you just laid out God knows how much for that damned Firebird. . . . Oh hell," he swore, seeing the look on her face.

"Just say thank you," she said evenly.

"Thank you," he capitulated finally with a grave nod and the smallest twitch of a smile. "And now, if you are finally out of surprises . . ."

It wasn't until a long time later, when they lay curled together in the big bed, that he returned, obliquely, to the earlier subject.

"You know, money is one of the things we're going to have to discuss."

"Oh? Why is that?" she asked sleepily.

"Because it's one of the things that causes the most trouble when two people combine their lives."

The words seemed to hang in the air between them. Anneke took a deep breath.

"Is that," she asked, "a proposal or a proposition?"

"Whichever one you'll say yes to."

"Well, I've always wanted to live in sin, Lieutenant."